Harriet Grote

Collected Papers (Original and Reprinted)

In Prose and Verse, 1842-1862

Harriet Grote

Collected Papers (Original and Reprinted)
In Prose and Verse, 1842-1862

ISBN/EAN: 9783337252809

Printed in Europe, USA, Canada, Australia, Japan

Cover: Foto ©Andreas Hilbeck / pixelio.de

More available books at **www.hansebooks.com**

COLLECTED PAPERS,

(ORIGINAL AND REPRINTED,)

In Prose and Verse.

1842—1862.

By MRS. GROTE.

———

LONDON:

JOHN MURRAY, ALBEMARLE STREET.

1862.

INTRODUCTION.

THE desire of preserving from oblivion some literary productions, which may possibly interest, if not instruct, a certain class of thoughtful readers, has supplied the motive for the present publication. Among the number, some few relate to political events of which the public have ceased to take account. Nevertheless, it is no unprofitable task to recal attention to a bygone condition of things, wherein the germ of actual results may be discerned. To compare the past with the present, and to trace the inexorable connexion of cause and effect, is always an occupation becoming a reflecting mind. And I will venture to observe that, vain as may be the attempt to foreshadow the course of political events in these days of surprises, I am confirmed in my views of the probable prospective changes in the position of the " Eastern question," by all that is now going forward in countries more or less subject to Ottoman rule.

As to the opinions, political, economic, and social,

comprised in these *my* "Essays and Reviews," I can
only say that they are the product of many years of
attentive study, pursued with an honest desire to
arrive at sound and solid convictions on various
subjects of vital interest to my country.

H. G.

LONDON, *October*, 1862.

CONTENTS.

RURAL ŒCONOMY OF ENGLAND.

---

1. *Essai sur l'Économie rurale de l'Angleterre.* Par M. Léonce de Lavergne, de l'Institut. 1854.
2. *Gisborne's Essays on Agriculture.* 1843.
3. *Coleman's Visit to England.* 1850.
4. *Un Voyage à Londres.* 1851.

FOREIGN travellers, in shoals, have printed and published their impressions of the British Isles; we have had our portraits painted in all conceivable styles, whilst our national vanity has certainly been ministered to by admiring strangers in a way to satisfy the most exigent John Bull amongst us. At the same time, it is as well to admit that some of the Continental ramblers who have visited our shores, pretend to have discovered many imperfections in the social arrangements of England which justly displeased them and offended their taste: with one or two of these dissentients we intend one day to have a passing word, but our chief purpose in approaching the subject of foreign criticism upon the British people and their domestic economy, is to present, in somewhat of a prominent manner, the remarkable work which stands at the head of this article, by M. Léonce de Lavergne, Ex-Prof. at Coll. Agron. of Versailles. The book would seem to have been written, in great part, with a design to convey information and instruction to his own countrymen, especially those engaged

B

in agriculture. Long inclined to a belief in the superior science and advancing progress of English husbandry, the author resolved to examine into it personally, and having devoted some time to the work of inquiry and observation—constantly taking notes of what he saw and learned—he has digested his views at leisure into a comprehensive form ; drawing parallels or contrasts, according as the case suggested, between the rural economy of France and that of England. It is hardly necessary to add that the comparisons run a good deal in our favour ; their backward science, and the incomplete methods pursued by a large proportion of French cultivators, being repeatedly adverted to, with obvious regret, not to say humiliation. To incite our neighbours to improved efforts being, as has been stated, one of the leading aims of the author, he never hesitates to place in the broad light of contrast, sometimes of ridicule, the shortcomings of those amidst whom it is his fortune to dwell. And if lucid exposition, practical appeals to their interest, and counsels inspired by a thorough comprehension of the subject, could awaken the emulation or quicken the apprehension of the French " paysan," this book ought to make a sensible impression upon that numerous body. Indeed, we have reason to believe that it has already done so, and that it is obtaining considerable circulation. Meanwhile, our own people will do well to study in the pages before us, the history as well as the theory and practice of modern improvements in husbandry. In a picture traced by the hand of a stranger, curiosity blends itself with the simple appetite for knowledge, and we become as interested in his account of "short-horns," "new Leicesters," and "improved South Downs," as though it were untrodden ground.

In setting forth the principal features which distinguish the agriculture of England from that of his own nation, M. Lavergne naturally attaches the highest importance to the introduction of the Norfolk husbandry, with its wide-spread system of root culture, and its green crops : enabling the cultivator to dispense in a great measure with fallows, to rear a much larger number of animals, and to hasten their arrival at maturity.

The author estimates the number of sheep maintained in the British islands and in France as double in amount to what it was a century since. In 1750, the number in each kingdom respectively was about seventeen to eighteen million head; whilst the total now existing he sets at thirty-five millions. But here the equality stops ; the extent of ground devoted to the maintenance of our flocks being, he says, equivalent to thirty-one millions of hectares, whilst in France it must be set at not less than fifty-three millions! And this striking fact becomes yet more instructive when we learn that "England proper" feeds about thirty out of the thirty-five millions of sheep on fifteen millions of hectares;* Ireland and Scotland furnishing between them the remainder, in the proportion of two and four, speaking in round numbers.

From this one element of agricultural progress is deducible a whole series of results, of which M.

---

* A hectare is nearly equal to two and a-half English acres.

Lavergne exhibits the advantages accruing to the general community; impressing upon his countrymen the necessity of adopting, as far as circumstances enable them to do so, the cycle of operations pursued by their energetic neighbours. "It is said of us," remarks M. Lavergne, "that we do not *care* to feed on animal food, *preferring* vegetables and farinaceous substances; that we eat rye rather than wheat, for the same reason. The fact is, that we eat what our farmers can manage to grow for our subsistence. They cannot rear oxen, sheep, or swine in such numbers as to bring meat within the reach of the lower class, because they have nothing to give them during winter; and we eat rye simply because we cannot grow enough wheat, or even oats, of which to make bread of a more nourishing quality."

In truth, rye is treated by M. Lavergne as the most profitless and contemptible of all products. "It would be most desirable," he says, "to abandon it, but this is not always possible.* It is one thing to renounce rye, and another to raise better corn successfully, for it is not every one who is capable of forcing nature. The English, in order to achieve what they have done in the way of wheat culture, have been obliged to fight against the qualities of their soil as well as of their climate" (p. 70); and he goes on to insist further upon the policy of raising wheat *only* in situations and on land favourable to its growth and its ripening,—one of the principles now steadily adhered to by our best agriculturalists, in pur-

---

* See also a passage (page 187) in the chapter on "Les Débouchés" (markets), full of sensible and acute observations on this head.

suance of which, in combination with improved methods of cultivation, a smaller surface seems to suffice for its growth with us, than would formerly have been supposed possible. M. Lavergne states that whereas, in France, one-fourth of the ground under cultivation is required for the growth of cereals destined for human food, in these islands one-sixteenth of the soil under plough suffices to yield such an amount of wheat as it consists with good husbandry to raise. The annual produce of cereals in France is thus stated by our author: wheat, seventy millions of hectolitres; rye, thirty millions; maize, seven millions; buck-wheat, eight millions. The yield of wheat, upon the 1,800,000 hectares devoted to that grain in the British Isles, is given as forty-five millions of hectolitres, of which thirty-eight millions are grown in England at a rate of produce per acre fully double that of France.

Passing from the all-important feature of root crops, on which the whole circle of scientific farming now revolves, M. Lavergne explains in his chapters on sheep and cattle the circumstances which have led to the wondrous amelioration of our domestic animals. In that section which treats of cattle, many instructive observations abound, mingled with a minute exposition of the merits of our various breeds. Indeed, the manner in which the author, up to a recent period wholly occupied with the highest functions of a political career, deals with the subject of cattle management, attests a singular aptitude for mastering new and dissimilar subjects. He seizes, and expatiates upon what may be termed the philosophy of " Grazing," with a perspicacity worthy of one whose life has been absorbed in the calling.

He, like most modern agriculturists, is an advocate of "stall feeding" for cattle; or, as we have heard a friend humorously style it, "the subjecting cattle to a fixed position, upon bare boards, in a current of cold air." The fact is that ideas of profit, when once they have obtained possession of a farming mind, carry all before them; thus a French traveller, naturally smitten with the desire of emulating our practice, and appreciating the merit of skilful adaptation of "means to ends," readily falls in with this universally recognised aim—viz., the making of money by the shortest process. On other grounds, we confess ourselves inclined to look with complacency upon the old system of warm and clean litter, coupled with the liberty of turning about. But we must not give way to kindly, antiquated prejudices, in the face of tabular demonstrations of profitable results, such as are supplied by the apostles of a later school.

The names of Bakewell, Ellman, and Collins, have here derived an additional chance of enduring fame and honour, by the mention of what they have effected for the improvement of English domestic animals. Of the former of these, M. Lavergne speaks as "a man of genius in his way, who has done as much to augment the wealth of his country as either Arkwright or Watt." (p. 22.)

The value of Bakewell and his disciples' system, consisted, he tells us, in persevering "selection." Individuals combining the properties of rapid growth, disposition to acquire flesh and to assume rounded, handsome forms, were alone permitted to reproduce their kind; and by attentive, unwearied noting of their experiments for a series of years, these eminent breeders of stock succeeded in arriving at the desired combination of qualities—the "Dishley," or New Leicester sheep, the "Short-horned," or Teeswater bull and cow, and the improved South Down sheep, being at the present time regarded as realizing the utmost perfection of which each class of animal is susceptible.

M. Lavergne seems not to have been aware of an opinion entertained by the late Mr. Thos. Gisborne, which is stated in that gentleman's "Essays," recently collected and published under the supervision of his friend, Mr. Joseph Parkes. He believes that "breeds" are destined to pass away, but that "races" are eternal. In other words, that a given type of animal will reproduce itself, in strict conformity with its original character, through ages; whilst that "breeds," formed by artificially crossing, and selecting the re-producers, will revert to the pristine type so soon as they are left to themselves. This is a physiological question which, though chiefly interesting to the curious inquirer, is not without value to the stock-farmer, and we should like to see it taken up by our scientific class. Another theory, very lately started respecting the disease called "fingers and toes," pre-valent among turnips chiefly, happens to proceed upon a somewhat analogous hypothesis. Assuming our actual edible bulbous roots to be nothing but improved forms of an originally wild and far inferior plant, this theory supposes "fingers and toes" to be neither more nor less than a struggle on the part of the genteel modern turnip to get back to his homely origin; diving down in a tapering, and often bifur-cate root, as its remote and indigenous progenitors had always done before him. There is a certain cor-

respondence between this plausible suggestion and
the convictions of Mr. Gisborne, and both the one
and the other possess that species of attraction for
speculative thinkers which always attends a reference
to universal tendencies in nature.

The high condition of our corn cultivation, our
live stock and teams, our buildings, implements, and
effective methods of enriching and renewing the latent
powers of the soil, call forth in turn the cordial
admiration of the French visitor. Supporting his
general statements by careful computations, his picture presents a body of information on which the
imitators of English systems might safely rely. But
whilst M. Lavergne contemplates, with something
akin to wonder, the astonishing march of our
modern agricultural movement, he is too wise and
reflecting a teacher not to take account of the inhe-
rent difficulties which stand in the way of its adoption by his own people. It is in this mood that he
writes as follows:—

" The causes which have led to the agricultural
superiority of the English, originate in the history
and organization of our two nations. The rural
economy of a people is not an isolated fact; it forms
one element of a great whole. It is not upon our
cultivators that the accountability for our backward
condition should be chiefly cast, neither ought we to
rely on them altogether for future progress. And it
is not so much the concentration of their attention
upon the soil itself which will secure progress, as a
careful study of the general laws which govern the
economic development of a community.

" Up to this time," he goes on to say, "these

studies have not been attractive to them; it has been
held that such inquiries are fraught with danger to
the cultivator. I believe this to be an error, and I
trust to show that it is such." (p. 105.)

Beginning with a quotation from Arthur Young
(p. 13), the author of the " Essai" lays down the fact
of the infinite superiority of the soil of France over
that of England; not content with a general assertion, we have a comparison of the most elaborate kind
set before us, proving that, tract for tract, zone for
zone, the French possess the advantage of a better
fundamental element of production. Then their
climate is confessedly preferable; and in descanting
upon this happy difference in their favour, M.
Lavergne obviously finds a secret " dédommagement"
for our superiority on some other points. But although
the French sun can ripen the ear of corn, can mature
all kinds of fruit, and bring to perfection many other
precious products—wine, olives, silk, oil, hemp, flax,
and the like—nevertheless, as has been remarked
already, the one thing needful to "high farming" is
wanting. The French eat but little meat, for want
of more cattle and flocks and swine; and they lack
manure wherewith to grow thirty and even forty tons
of food to the acre, as we manage to do, in favourable
years, with our swedes and mangolds. This matter
of meat and manure is, in truth, a revolving circle,
wherein the great difficulty consists in seizing the
departing point. M. Lavergne maintains that if the
farmers occupying cold, moist mountainous tracts in
France (of which he indicates no small number)
would grow artificial grasses, turnips, carrots, mangolds, and such sort of crops, instead of slaving, as

they do, to extract miserably scanty crops of rye and
oats, they could very soon rear animals for food.
Animals would yield "engrais," or "dressing," bring
capital to the farm, invigorate the labourer, and
cause the land to revive under generous treatment.
How to begin is the problem, and of course M.
Lavergne is at no loss to prescribe the means.
Capital must be invited to co-operate more liberally
with labour. He would persuade the owners of
capital to embark in scientific farming, commencing
by degrees, and would engage to justify the enter-
prise by its results if properly conducted. But here
we come upon the discussion concerning "large and
small cultivation," for no change can be thought of
in the rural economy of France without fully exploring
that thorny question. M. Lavergne has, we think,
set it very fairly before his readers, and in a vein of
investigation which strikes us as somewhat original.
And in the first place our author disputes the fact, or at
least denies the extent, of the extravagant subdivision
of land in France. We will give his own words:—

"All the world is familiar with the celebrated
calculation, giving eleven millions and a half as the
number of 'cotes' (taxable properties in houses and
lands); but so they are, likewise, with the delusive
nature of this calculation, as demonstrated by the
researches of M. Passy. Not only does it happen
that an individual contributor often pays several
'cotes,' which in itself suffices to invalidate the
general proposition itself; but, furthermore, town
habitations equally count as 'cotes,' thus diminishing
the actual total of *rural* proprietors to five, or at most
to six millions." (p. 109.)

" Now," says M. Lavergne, "of the whole eleven
millions and a-half alluded to as representing the
numerical amount of properties, town and country
inclusive, half a million, only, possess parcels of the
value of one hundred francs, or four pounds; five
millions and a-half own parcels of the value of five
francs each, two millions at from five to ten francs,
three millions at from ten to fifty francs, six hundred
thousand from fifty to a hundred francs. But the
sum of the land possessed by these eleven millions,
consisting of lots all ranging under the value of one
hundred francs, reaches only one-third of the entire
surface under cultivation." [Pasture and woods
being included, we presume.] " Remains, then, two-
thirds of it in the hands of four hundred thousand
proprietors; deducting one hundred thousand for
such owners as possess town lots, this gives an
average extent of eighty hectares to each, or two
hundred English acres."

M. Lavergne next endeavours to establish a correspondence between this section of the French
people and our middle-class and second-class gentry
taken together. Granting that the annual value of
land is greater in England, acre for acre, still, he con-
tends, the disproportion is less than is usually supposed. He sets the share of the soil possessed by
our largest proprietors against that of the eleven
millions who own a third of all France; and maintains that two-thirds in each country are possessed
by a class of owners differing from each other far
less widely than it has been the habit to represent
them. In France, he says—

" Estates comprising an extent of 500, 1000, and

2000 hectares are far from rare, whilst properties even of 25,000 francs to 100,000 francs a year value, and beyond it, are not unknown. A thousand landlords in each of our departments might be found, on a level, as to landed property, with the secondary class of English country landlords, which is the one most diffused among them. It is true, we have, proportionably speaking, fewer, and they are planted amidst small neighbours; whilst the English gentry live under the shadow of huge aristocratic fiefs. It is only under this aspect—*i. e.*, the proportional amount —that it can fairly be affirmed that property is more concentrated in England than in France." (p. 111.)

After exhibiting this view of the actual distribution of the surface, M. Lavergne examines the evidence in favour of large farms, the advantages of which it has recently become so much the fashion to extol ; we regret that we must restrict our extracts in reference to this most vital question, as between " large and little culture" (to translate it literally). The author has treated it with a rare impartiality, and our readers will find many valuable facts arranged in a manner to leave the solution easier than has yet seemed to be attainable. Solution, in the sense of decided preference, however, it is not easy to arrive at. But we can, more distinctly than before we perused this chapter, appreciate the bearings of particular circumstances in determining when large cultivation should prevail, and the converse. M. Lavergne is clearly a *partizan* of neither. His accurate acquaintance with the whole condition of French husbandry, together with his practical familiarity with various other forms of industrial life, enable him to steer clear of dogmatic generalization, and even inspire him with a certain dislike of such as indulge in it. We subjoin a few of his comments on this head.

" In the same degree as people exaggerate the amount of concentration in England, do they overrate the effect of large estates upon the progress of agriculture. Large properties do not necessarily imply large culture. The most considerable of them are not unfrequently split up into small holdings;* what matters it, indeed, though one man do possess 10,000 hectares, if they be broken down into 200 farms of 50 hectares each? .... We have seen that, in the United Kingdom, two categories prevail; large, and moderate estates. The first class of properties occupying, then, a third of the soil, and part of this being distributed into small lots, or tenantcies, it is obvious that large culture obtains upon no more than one quarter of the whole land. Now is it true that this one quarter is farmed in the highest and most skilful style? I suspect not. .... The richest districts of England are those of Lancashire, Lincolnshire, Leicester, Worcester, and Warwickshire; and here a mixed proportion as to culture subsists. In one of the most fertile of these, viz., Lancashire, it is the mean, or possibly even the small, culture which preponderates. Taken as a general fact, it may fairly be affirmed that the best farmed land in the kingdom, Ireland included, is *not* that belonging to the largest occupants." (p. 114.)

" In France, again," continues M. Lavergne, " two

---

* See the account of the Marquis of Lansdowne's estates in Kerry, of about 100,000 acres, full of sheep walks and bare rock. There were, till lately, 3000 farms upon this ! (p. 449).

categories likewise appear—middling sized, and great
estates. In the former, small cultivation predomi-
nates, and these generally exhibit the greatest advance
in agricultural aptitude and knowledge. Such is the
case in the ' Département du Nord,' and of the ' Bas
Rhin,' and indeed in the richest cantons of other
departments. With us, division of the land is a
means of developing improvement. This results from
the national habit of thought. Similar causes produce
the like results in other countries; in Belgium,
Rhenish Prussia, in Upper Italy, and even in Nor-
way." (p. 115.)

"In all countries, with the single exception of
Great Britain, overgrown estates have done more
mischief than good to agriculture." After assigning
the reasons of this, the author adds, " Still, for all
that has been advanced, I am ready to admit that
the state of landed property in England is more
favourable to agricultural prosperity than that of
France. It is simply the exaggeration employed on
this topic that I have striven to dispel." (p. 116.)

We must now take leave of this important chapter,
with the remark that, after all, there can be no
practical utility in proving to the French people the
disadvantages of " la petite culture;" since the subdivision and possession of land is among the most
unassailable of their national predilections, and is,
moreover, linked with that passion for "equality"
which, naturally enough, grew out of the intolerable
abuse of its opposite down to 1789. We are indeed
not disinclined to believe, with M. Lavergne, that
where small cultivation is accompanied by capital
adequate to keep the land, whatever be its extent,

" in heart," *there* will be found, if not the maximum of profit, the highest average of comfort, content, and independence among the inhabitants. (See page 114, where the condition of things in the island of Jersey is described.) In districts where the above-named condition is wanting, of course the cultivators must be poor, degraded, and embarrassed. Such as these must either learn to exchange their labour for money wages, or remain at the bottom of the scale. M. Lavergne should begin by preaching to them the expediency of such an industrial revolution, and perhaps capital might presently be induced to unite in its achievement. Englishmen have lived so long under an unchanged constitution of things, in connexion with land, that they commonly go through life with very little inquiry into the practical operation of their laws and customs, or the rights of privileged classes. A foreigner, on the contrary, takes note of every cluster of causes and effects which comes before him, and if he happen to have a philosophic turn of mind (such as M. Lavergne possesses), he endeavours to " map out," as it were, the ramifications of this or that principle throughout the political constitution of the nation which he is studying. He does not hesitate boldly to handle and dissect laws and customs which, to English minds, are consecrated by antiquity, and regarded as inseparable from national prosperity. Sometimes they obtain from the author of the " Essai" unqualified approval—often disapproval; but in every instance the opinions are sustained by reasons, delivered with the unmistakeable accents of a love of truth and a genuine attachment to the social interests of mankind. We cannot resist making one extract (from the chapter on the Tenure of Property) terminating a brief notice respecting the law of inheritance, and the liberty of bequest, so different in our respective countries.

" Should the period ever arrive in France when it might be granted to the head of a family to exercise more freely the right of bequeathing his property— or should we think fit to restrict by laws the unlimited distribution of personal property now practised in cases of intestacy—let us hope that considerations tending to favour the formation of large properties will not be suffered to enter into the question. Large estates have not been cut up or absorbed by *law* in France, but by the revolution; and not only is their reconstruction by artificial methods impracticable, but, the course things have taken considered, it is extremely doubtful whether it could serve any useful end." (p. 123.)

The chapter " On the Constitution of Cultivation" (a clumsy phrase enough in English, but still one not easy to render less so) is short, treating in great part of the same subject as the one on " La Proprieté." And the same oscillation is here observable in the author's mind as is apparent during his comparison of the two modes of culture (great and small) in the previous chapter. The prodigious results of our skilled farming on a great scale naturally excite his professional sympathies; yet anon the deep-seated feeling which belongs to a Frenchman inclines him to regard small occupations with partiality.

" Small cultivation (he remarks), as well as small properties, are more congenial to our habits. Fortunes being more divided among us than amongst the

English, it is expedient to keep the quantity of land occupied, on a suitable level with the amount of capital available for its culture. . . . ." (p. 133.)

" There are districts of my country with which I am familiar, where small culture is a curse; others which I could name flourish under it, and would not prosper if farmed on the contrary system." (p. 134.)

It is, to say the truth, a hard matter to discover how much of change, or of imitation of England, M. Lavergne would wish to bring about in the agricultural system of his own country, seeing that he so thoughtfully and impartially scans the actual merits of the latter, taking into account national circumstances, together with the inveterate attachment of the French to certain social principles. His work reminds us of nothing so much, in fact, as of a person playing three-handed whist with a "dummy" as partner. The author plays, of course, both " hands," and, as a professor of agronomic science is bound to do, tries to "win the trick" with bold, enterprizing play. " Dummy," on the other hand, holds a " strong suit" in " social equality," as well as some other good cards; for example, "individual independence," " models of honest industry," " perfection of small cultivation" (admitted by the author, as we have seen), as exhibited in Flanders, amongst French vine dressers, and the like. Thus, although M. Lavergne is strongly impelled by the predominant passion of the day to recommend the pursuit of agricultural wealth—destined, in its turn, to engender the multiplication of the comforts and advantages of civilization—he nevertheless makes "dummy" play his game with so much effect as to preserve

c

himself from one-sided advocacy; and accordingly, we find him disposed to prescribe none but moderate and practicable improvements in the rural economy of his own nation.

These prescriptions, if we comprehend the author's leanings justly, would consist of the following leading ingredients, mixed and employed with discrimination. 1. The cultivation of green and root crops wherever possible. 2. He would have more care bestowed upon the breeding of sheep and cattle, and would discontinue the employment of oxen and cows in tillage, as a mistaken economy. 3. He would adapt the choice of the products to the nature of the soil and local character of the district (see pp. 134, 135). 4. He would persuade the owners of land whose capital is insufficient, to hand it over to the cultivation of those who have more, taking rent for the use of it; changing the relations between capital and labour most advantageously, on such parcels of land as represent the mean ratio between large and small occupations. The French cultivator being forced, under the actual condition of things, to provide the *whole* apparatus of farming, he is under the *necessity* of borrowing capital. If an English tenant farmer were thus situated, it would be equally necessary for *him* also to borrow. But in England the "Squire" furnishes so large a portion of the matter of farm capital, in the form of buildings, repairs, fencing, draining, and the like, that the farmer can apply all his own money to positive cultivation. As a precedent for the transfusion of cultivating proprietors into tenant farmers, M. Lavergne recounts, in a brief but most pertinent manner, the gradual change which the present century has witnessed of our yeoman and "statesman" into renters of farms (page 131, and again page 188). He regards the combination of capital with labour as most desirably exhibited in the union of landlord and tenant, as in England, where each party has an interest in the land tilled. In other countries the cultivator, who either has not the means of doing justice to the land, or who is saddled with an obligation to pay interest on the shares possessed in it by his co-heirs (a frequent cause of embarrassment in France), must borrow to carry him through; and thence his chance of bettering his condition becomes next to hopeless.

The general propensity of French cultivators to get into debt is admitted by our author. But if possessors of capital are willing to lend upon the security of land, there is every reason why they should be encouraged to do so. Check borrowing by the straitened farmer, and you check production. And if you ask why the farmer does not sell, and why the capitalist does not buy, this same land, the answer is obvious—such is the mode, clumsy, if you please to call it so, in which capital and labour are in the habit of co-operating in France. The capitalist prefers to lend rather than cultivate, and the owner clings to possession on any terms. But, as M. Lavergne remarks, land in England is also enormously indebted, only that it is the landlord, and not the cultivator, who borrows. Every one conversant with English provincial affairs, is aware of the vast extent to which estates are mortgaged. But, he adds, "this is less matter of regret in a rich country, such as England, where the debtors have commonly other sources of

income on which to eke out their living." Still, the
fact ought to be borne in mind when we talk so
compassionately of the landed property of France
being "crippled with debts." We earnestly commend
to our reader's attention the whole chapter " Sur les
Débouchés," where ample and instructive explanations abound of the various differences in the economic condition of the two countries.

As a relief to the foregoing somewhat dry though
instructive speculations, concerning the best modes of
holding property in land, and the various conditions
under which it may be cultivated, we enter upon
what we may describe as the picturesque portion of
M. Lavergne's " Essai," entitled " Country Life."
But under this general and familiar head there is
unpacked and rolled out before us, to our no small
surprise, a whole shipload of literary merchandize.
And in the face of such a mass of facts and erudite
researches, so extensive a knowledge of the works of
our poets, such intimate acquaintance with the springs
of national life, and the sources of English social
peculiarities,—how, we should like to know, is a
reviewer to approach the task of furnishing even an
outline of this truly comprehensive chapter? We
feel that it is beyond our capabilities, yet we *must*
attack it.

It is, first of all, our duty to apprise the reader
that he will be carried as far back as the " Saxons
and Normans" for the origin of that peculiar characteristic for which the English are famed—viz., a
passion for country life; he will therefore be prepared
for a pretty extensive journey over the field of illustrative historical gleanings. And he will do wisely to *be*

prepared; for we ourselves, not having been so, were nearly run out of breath in toiling after the author through this maze of black-letter lore. Only think, too, of coming unexpectedly upon a passage so grandiose as this, when we imagined ourselves to be dealing with a quiet treatise upon the " hum-drum topic of farming!"—

" When the barbarian multitudes came swarming down upon the Roman Empire, from every quarter, they spread themselves over the face of the country," &c. &c.

Then we have William the Conqueror and Doomsday Book, Henry VIII., Charlemagne, Queen Elizabeth, Cambrian Bards, Magna Charta, and the like imposing persons and things. They file off, however, after having opened the piece with a certain amount of solemn parade, and leave us to the company of English gentlemen, and we may add English ladies, for they naturally form one of the features of " country life," as agreeably depicted in this chapter.

The bearing of the rural habits of our gentry upon the political machine is skilfully sketched, and compared with the opposite tastes of the modern French noblesse, who usually prefer spending the winter in towns. We say prefer, although we do not think that they would like towns better, having the same inducements set before them as are present with English country gentlemen; but their political world is and has been so organized for the last hundred and fifty years, that rural existence has long been, in great part, stripped of its charm and interest for French gentlemen of independent fortune.

M. Lavergne has penetrated the crust of English

society, thereby acquiring an insight into our provincial mind, such as is exceedingly rare with
foreigners. He of course notes, and indeed goes so
far as to admire, the complicated but unseen network
of powers which forms the internal administration
of this unique country. He quotes the anecdote
of Queen Elizabeth sending back to their "demesnes"
her nobles who came thronging to court, with a
metaphor signifying that they would be of more use
and importance there than in the capital; and he
remarks that neither Henri Quatre nor his grandson
would have done as much. The rulers of France,
with their narrow, selfish aims, took the most effective course to disgust the territorial aristocracy with
provincial life, when they deprived them, step by
step, of all local authority and influence, and laid the
foundation of the system of carrying on internal
government by an army of officials : a system of which
we have lived to see the many disastrous consequences.

But we must return to M. Lavergne's description
of English life, and the contrast it presents to that of
the Continental " classes aisées." "Such as the Palace
of Chatsworth is, on the grand scale of residences,
such is the abode of each private gentleman, only on
a lesser footing. The smallest squire must have his
' park,' or park-like enclosure. The number of these
sort of residences is enormous, beginning with such
as contain some few acres only, and mounting up to
others of more than a thousand in extent. . . . It
is easy to perceive how much this habit—so universal
with the English—of passing their lives in the country,
affects the prosperity of the land itself. Whereas in
France it is the produce of the fields which serves to

maintain the opulence of our cities, in England it is
the industrial towns which sustain the progress of
husbandry. They enrich the farmer by the demand
they furnish, and farming flourishes accordingly.
Again, the self-love of the occupier of a country seat
will not permit him to neglect the appearance of his
farming establishment. Ostentation, in rural England,
finds a vent in fine teams, substantial farm buildings,
handsome cattle, and the like. A 'crack home farm'
may, in fact, stand as the equivalent of a splendid
'hotel,' luxuriously furnished, in Paris." (page 155.)

We pass over the comparison between the burthens
borne by the land in both countries, although it is set
forth with candour, and will be found instructive; our
limits force us to *select* among the topics treated in
the " Essai," and we prefer touching upon the chapter
headed " Political Institutions."

Though short, it is perhaps the one which, by the
extent of its range of information, its historical illustrations, and intelligent commentary, offers the liveliest
interest to the student of *social* economy, of any in the
book. How one is led to reflect upon the waves which
advance and recede in the course of human affairs;
and what striking differences may we not discern in
the groups of facts which command the approval of
the actual generation of the day, to be contemned and
avoided by that of another!

Like all foreign interpreters of the causes of our
advance in material wealth, M. Lavergne naturally
ascribes the largest share in its development to our
exemption from internal discord and ruinous revolu-
tionary wars. " The eighteenth century, so disastrous
throughout for us, exhibits England in a state of con-

tinuous progression; so that when we at length did
make an effort onwards, she had got the start of us by
three-quarters of a century." (p. 158.)

The author affirms that, two hundred years since,
France was, in every respect, in a better state than
England, not even excepting what regarded agriculture. Sully, to be sure, formed, in his time, the very
antithesis of our modern statesman. He would, we
verily think, have hung up the " Bagman," if he had
caught him jogging along the highway, instead of
crowning him with civic garlands as we now do. On
the other hand, Sully was a warm patron of the plough,
promoting agricultural industry with all his power,
and that with the happiest success.

"A writer of that period, Olivier de Serres, has
bequeathed to us an admirable work, attesting the
universal *élan* (or movement forward); the author, a
Protestant nobleman, Seigneur of Pradel in the Viva-
rais, had lived retired on his country estates during
the religious and political troubles of those times."
His book was dedicated to Henri Quatre, and M.
Lavergne pronounces it not only the most ancient,
but the best treatise extant in modern language!
(p. 159.)

" All recognised maxims of good farming were
already known to the contemporaries of Olivier, and
his precepts might well serve to guide our own
cultivators of to-day." (p. 160.)

Why France did not persevere in the path of
scientific cultivation, and what calamitous hindrances
arose on that path, M. Lavergne briefly but impres-
sively explains. We would advise our readers to study
this portion of his work carefully. A whole book

could not more clearly trace the course of national decline, and its incontestable causes, than this truly mournful chapter of only a few pages.

About the period at which Olivier produced his valuable book on Agriculture, French gentlemen of rank and condition habitually spent their lives on their " Terres;" forming, with the labouring classes, a social whole, now remembered only by faint traditions, but the disappearance of which M. Lavergne regards as a national misfortune.* We happen to have also heard an eminent French writer (M. Alexis de Tocqueville) state this fact as incontestable, adding that the " débris" of hundreds of country "chateaux," as well as of lesser residences (termed in the provinces " Gentilhommeries"), still exist in all parts of France. So that the taste for country life was, at a period not farther removed from us than a hundred and fifty years, probably as widely diffused among our neighbours as amongst our own people. We have already said that agriculture, according to M. Lavergne's opinion, was decidedly better understood by the French than by the English during the seventeenth century, the former even supplying us with corn out of their abundance (p. 162). Subsequently, however, the picture becomes reversed. Having achieved our great change, from enslavement to constitutional government, in 1688, English productive industry " draws ahead," whilst the exhausting effect of Louis XIV.'s prodigality, with his reckless extortion of the means of expenditure from his too patient people, becomes painfully manifest. During

---

* Note on Madame de Sévigné.

the latter half of the eighteenth century it is England which supplies France, and that to a considerable extent.

A contrast is thus drawn between the then condition of the two nations:—" The English people, happy, and proud of their government, confiding in its protection, and labouring with activity; our people, ruined, humiliated, oppressed; turning aside from industrial occupations of which they are not permitted to enjoy the fruits, and feeling towards their rulers nothing but hatred and contempt." (p. 162.)

It is pleasing to observe with what admiration this intelligent writer regards the course of our past domestic history; but we are sadly afraid that a closer acquaintance with the internal economy of England— still more that of Scotland and Ireland—during the eighteenth century, would dispel much of the envy with which our institutions are viewed. For the conduct of the Government during that century, especially during the whole reign of George II. and the earlier portion of the reign of George III., was in every way disentitled to the respect and affection of the English people. Indeed, the interesting contributions to our domestic history which have made their appearance, in the shape of personal memoirs, during the last twenty years, supply ample evidence of how little we owe to the paternal care of our monarchs, or the purity and wise administration of our ministers, until the period when the reins of power were grasped by the younger Pitt.

The distinguishing, and in fact the most valuable attribute of the English Government, is its non-interference with individual action : that is to say, it suffers its subjects to produce at their discretion; protecting the results of such industry by law, taking for State purposes but a fraction of them, and this only through and with the consent of the Commons House of Parliament. The check thus exercised over the expenditure of the State absolutely regulates the amount of our military force; and it was to this vital element of security, more than to anything else, that we formerly owed the preservation of our political liberties. No one but a native Englishman comprehends how infinitely small is the direct action of the executive government in this kingdom. Four-fifths of the prodigious progress made in the arts of life, and in the scientific application of the capacities of nature to production, have been effected by private citizens. The incessant working of the British mind in a practical direction leads to a gigantic total of results, such as could never be reached by any but a free community, it is true; but it is the character of the people and not their government which has achieved the social greatness of England. Whether our mercurial neighbours would ever devote themselves, body and soul, to the work of enriching themselves, at the price of sacrificing the taste for present enjoyment, as well as of stifling the development of the imaginative faculty, it is very difficult to conjecture. Our impression is that they would not, under any system of government, become the slaves of that passion for acquiring wealth by which most Englishmen are subjugated.

For example, here is a man, himself lately a professor of agronomic science, who, although his studies lead him to feel the liveliest interest in the march of productive cultivation, nevertheless finds, in the actual position of England, no small ground for healthy regret at beholding the changes which are creeping over her rural features.

Although a master of "Tabular demonstration," and a skilful hand at statistical computations, his French turn of thought revolts at the eternal apparition of "the shop." Poetical sentiment is never wholly smothered by the balance sheet, whilst the growing necessity of drugging mother earth, and of dosing her with nasty compounds, turns his heart chilly. M. Lavergne not being an Englishman, he can see that which no native sees, or rather that which no native chooses to see—*i.e.*, the inconvenience resulting from a superabundant population. It is this ever-present fact which lies at the bottom of half the difficulties of our internal administration; including that of the countless larvæ of infant felonry with which no vigilance, no legislative apparatus ever can effectually cope, at least in free England. And it is not less the parent of those ingenious devices which science is now invoked to apply to the latent capacity of the earth. After adverting to the stupendous laboratory of Mr. Lawes, near St. Albans, for compounding medicaments wherewith to whip up nature, exhausted by the ordinary methods of production, M. Lavergne goes on to say:—

"That which sufficed yesterday will not satisfy the wants of to-day. The produce of to-day will fall short of the morrow's demand. Fresh calls must be made upon the earth, our common parent, for additional treasures, and unless she can be forced to yield them, famine, depopulation, and death await us."

And a little further on he remarks that, "such is the growing conviction in England of the necessity of calling in the aid of chemistry to quicken the powers of nature, that you will hear a common farmer of the present day talking about ammonia and phosphates, as though he were acquainted with their composition;" so persuaded is this class of the imperious need of extorting more and more from natural agents.*

The efforts made in agricultural progress some fifty years ago, proceeded from members of the aristocratic class. Those now at work result in great part from the enterprize and emulation of a class somewhat lower in the social scale, of which the spirited owner of " Tiptree Hall" is one of the most instructive specimens.

" It is said that M. Mechi buries money in his farming experiments, and I can readily believe it; but I like this vein of expenditure better than most others. A Paris cockney would perhaps lay out his money in a smart villa, with Gothic portico, and a Swiss hermitage, and other silly whims. Which is the preferable mode?" (p. 256.)

The system of distributing, by tubes or otherwise, fluid stercoraceous matter over the surface of our soil, mainly due to the example set by the Rev. Mr. Huxtable and Mr. Mechi, now ranks among the most effective of the stimuli, to the employment of which

---

* " The agricultural mind is now becoming alive to the fact that, task the powers of cultivation and of the soil as we may, we are likely to be wholly unable to keep up with the demands made upon them by our rapidly increasing population ; a population, too, whose powers of consumption are increasing even in a greater ratio than its numbers, so that it exhibits day by day an increasing desire to revel in beef and mutton," &c. &c.—*Agricultural Gazette for the week ending December* 2, 1854, No. 48.

we are in course of being driven. M. Lavergne seizes the value of this provocative, describing the system with care and exactness in the chapter " High Farming."

As to the stall-feeding practice, the author again expresses himself thus :—" One cannot suppress a dis- agreeable emotion on beholding these poor creatures, whose relations still stray over the immense pasture grounds of Britain, here deprived of liberty and exercise, and on thinking that possibly a day may come when the numerous herds which yet roam at large amid green fields, frisking with gaiety, shall all be clapped up within these dismal walls, which they will quit only to be driven to the slaughter-house. These workhouses for the production of meat, milk, and manure, where the animal figures as a mere machine, offer something which is unpleasant to the imagina- tion; after a peep into one of these, one's stomach has little relish for meat for days after. But the loud clamours of necessity impel you to produce food, at all cost, and no matter by what means : with never slackening pace your population strides onward, whilst its wants even outstrip its numbers. Fare- well, then, to the pastoral scenes and features of which England has ever boasted the charm, and which poets and painters have striven with emulous rivalry to depict and illustrate." (p. 215.)

He suggests indeed two chances—viz., that the quality of the meat thus managed may at last grow too bad to be endured, or, that the unnatural regimen itself may give rise to diseases unknown in our flocks and herds under the old healthy plan of grazing. All of us, at least all persons above forty years of age, re-

cognise the difference between the old down-fed mutton
of former times, and the present pallid, tallowy article
supplied by butchers, and deplore the impossibility of
obtaining for money any better meat. The decline of
flavour and quality in our mutton, nobody indeed disputes, but we are told that the farmer can send the
sheep to market cheaper at 20 months old, than at five
years. So conclusive to all English minds is this argu-
ment, that the counteracting contingencies contem-
plated by M. Lavergne, of, firstly, an universal
murrain, or, secondly, a wide-spread distaste for oil
cake as a bottom dish, however disguised by the out-
ward semblance of fibrine and caseine, as checks to
the cheap production of meat, do not re-assure us.
But our limits warn us to terminate this vein of pro-
phecy, which we will do by one more quotation from
our economist's more sentimental pages.

"Black clouds of smoke now curl over the verdant
landscapes so delightfully chanted by Thomson: the
charm peculiar to English rural scenery is disappear-
ing with its pastures and hedgerows. The ancient
feudal character of country life is changing under
the disappearance of its game. Even its parks are
regarded with a sort of jealousy, as occupying a
surface capable of being more profitably cultivated. . . . . .

"In all this we may perceive much more than an
agricultural question; nay, it concerns perhaps the
whole structure of English society. No one ought
to affirm that revolutions find no field in England;
on the contrary, revolutions go forward there as else-
where, only that they proceed silently and in a
leisurely way." And he adds that he believes in the

possibility of adapting the new to the old forms of society, in such a manner as that we shall all come out gainers; though this seems to us a persuasion requiring vast faith in the agents of the compromise.

After a brief glance over the English counties, their most striking external features, soil, productions, and varying relations between owner and cultivator, we come to the chapter on Scotland.

Here, as indeed is the case with the author's description of England, much more than an agricultural "coup-d'œil" is presented to the reader. One of the characteristics on which M. Lavergne dwells with obvious pleasure, is the approximation, in that country, to the negation of government.

"Viewed in a political light," says he, "Scotland may be pronounced to be England perfected. Nowhere in Europe is there less of administrative machinery: one must go to America to find an equal measure of simplicity in this respect. A centralized administration, so much lauded, which both vexes and taxes three-fourths of the French nation for the advantage of the remaining fourth, stifling throughout the land all local or individual initiatory action, is here unknown." (p. 345.)

Again:—

"In this little nation, of less than three millions of souls, a sense of common interests (that fundamental truth so hard to inculcate through the lessons of science) is recognised by, and is present to all. Scotland, in short, is a family." (p. 347.)

As with most travellers, Scottish scenery, coupled as it is with traditions of a picturesque age, disposes M. Lavergne to poetical musings. He appears to be perfectly familiar with the creations of Sir Walter Scott, and delights to find a locality for his favourite fictions as he wanders over ground hallowed by those marvellous romances. Shaking off this seductive mood, however, he conducts us through the " Lowlands," lecturing as he goes along upon the culture pursued, and the races of domestic animals prevalent, in that section of North Britain; touching, by way of conclusion, upon the superior prudence and self-control displayed by the Lowlanders in regard to marriage; their numbers never exceeding the limits of comfortable subsistence. Whilst in England, he says, the population has tripled its numbers, and that of Ireland quadrupled, Scotland has, during an equal interval, only doubled hers; in the Lowlands, that is to say, for in the Northern counties a vastly different state of society has always subsisted.

" The Highlands" forms a chapter apart, and will be found to contain much that is not generally known to Southern readers.

The author " commences with the Deluge," it must be premised, but, having started, runs so rapidly over the historical antecedents of " Bonnie Scotland" that the reader is safely landed, at the end of about four-and-twenty pages, enriched with so much information respecting the extraordinary mutation that Scottish industry, social institutions, and manners have undergone, as will surprise him, when he can take breath and reflect upon the space he has travelled over.

To sketch an outline even of the domestic revolution effected in the sister kingdom, is what few foreigners would have had the hardihood to attempt.

Still fewer would have attempted it with success. Taking up Scottish internal history at the point of pure and complete Feudalism—of which he presents a striking, and we need scarcely add an attractive, picture—the author traces the slow but inevitable causes through which this semi-barbaric form of society came to be at length fused into civilization. The most marked epoch of change may be referred to the final expulsion of the Stuarts, in 1746, after which period the powerful Scottish nobles began to think of framing their lives somewhat more in accordance with certain new ideas which then broke in upon their minds: ideas chiefly inspired by their occasional intercourse with France and other countries; nevertheless, M. Lavergne is of opinion that the feudal character and sentiment lingered amongst the Highland clans longer than in any other portion of Europe.

Not until the introduction of more regular habits and agriculture,—accompanied by the repression, by vigorous efforts, of the old system of living on plunder—had altered the condition of Highland life, did the Lairds become aware how difficult a matter it was to maintain honestly, in those poverty-stricken, barren tracts, the multitudes which, under a more ancient form of society, had proved a source of power to the "chiefs of clans." Accordingly, measures were set on foot for the purpose of "thinning" their estates of the now superabundant natives.

" It was in the Highlands that depopulation on a regular system was carried forward, which depopulation made much noise in Europe some thirty years since. M. Sismondi, among others, doubtless with the best intentions, but certainly not with the most clearsighted views, helped in his day to stimulate the public disapprobation of this proceeding; nevertheless, although it may perhaps have been somewhat roughly executed, the measure itself has been productive of excellent results." (p. 367.)

It so happened that the disposition to sweep off the redundant mouths from large landed properties, was displaying itself actively at the commencement of the present century, just at which period the great bard of feudalism, Sir Walter Scott, first rose upon the horizon of literature. His captivating chivalric poems had the effect of swelling the storm of opposition to the schemes already in progress for bringing the mountaineers within the dreaded pale of prosaic institutions. But in spite of this, and although earnest appeals were made to traditional rights against the justice of the expulsions (appeals in themselves far from ill-founded), the great landlords, backed by the far-sighted co-operation of the Imperial Government, carried their purpose through. Expedients were employed to mitigate the hardship of the proceeding, and to facilitate the removal of the exiles to other lands. A part were regimented and blended with our regular army, of which they have proved themselves gallant and loyal members, whilst those who remained on their native hills were induced gradually to adopt more settled habits, and to pursue more honest means of living.

Whoever will be at the trouble of following M. Lavergne's lucid account of one of these memorable transactions, exhibiting the effects of "clearing," on the largest scale, will, we are persuaded, be inclined to yield a cordial assent to the judgment he delivers,

whether as "economist," or as friend to civil order
and progress.

The passage we allude to relates the prodigious
detrusion carried out under the orders—we might
almost say under the reign—of the late Duchess
Countess of Sutherland, in the decade ending with
the year 1820.

Rarely has the exercise of power been attended with
results more beneficial. We regret to be unable to
reproduce the details of operations of which the fruits
have been prosperity, content, and moral improvement;
insomuch that already in 1825—" From the towers
of their feudal castle of Dunrobin, the heirs of Mhoir-
Fhear-Chattaibh looked down upon a spectacle of
thriving industry such as it never could have entered
the mind of their ancestors to conceive of." (p. 378.)

Many suggestive observations accompany the history
of the transition we have been contemplating; among
them is one alluding to a somewhat analogous change in
England after the wars of the Roses (see p. 384). We
will terminate this episode with a passage quoted by the
author, in which sober reason is permitted to guide the
pen of a poet. "In contemplating a landscape bounded
by mountains," writes Sir Walter Scott,* "rocks,
precipices, and forests assume, in a summer's evening,
the most delightful forms and colouring. It requires
an effort to recal to one's mind their actual sterility
and desolation. So it is with the mountaineers themselves. Seen from a distance and through the medium
of the fancy, how they affect the heart and imagination! Yet it must not be forgotten how incompatible

---

* In his *History of Scotland*.

was Highland clanship with all progress, moral or religious, or with genuine freedom." (p. 385.)

If we have dwelt somewhat at length upon the foregoing topic, it is because so vast a cluster of facts and deductions is involved in the consideration of the change from the romantic to the prosaic state of society—the substitution of flocks of sheep for tribes of brave and devoted, but lawless warriors.

" Should some stray descendant of the Highlander of yore be yet discerned here and there, perched on a crag, his traditional plaid flung over his shoulder, and droning out on his bagpipe some dolorous old ditty, it is not a fighting man whom you behold, but a shepherd; one no longer subsisting on plunder and war, but on the wages of the neighbouring farmer. Little can *he* tell you of the valiant deeds of his sires; but, to compensate for this ignorance, he will inform you how the lambing season has sped, and whether wools are 'up.' This is all which remains of a lost race." (p. 379.)

This verbal paraphrase of Sir Edwin Landseer's picture of " Peace and War," is not exhaustive, however. A handful of men still survive, whose peculiar organization, physical and moral, entitles them to be regarded as true Gaels. They are chiefly engaged, in connexion with richer sportsmen, in occupations germane to their former condition, such as hunting, and shooting, fishing, and exterminating the brute competitors of man, in the pursuit of " Feræ naturæ." And it is to be hoped that these few representatives of a race which will ever live in the picturesque traditions of distant periods, may never become really extinct.

The chapter on Ireland we must forbear to touch upon; partly because the mere sound of that name has generally had the effect of dispersing the stoutest-hearted audience, and also because we cannot venture to devote more space to M. Lavergne's book. It will suffice to state that he has imparted to that hitherto hopeless subject as much interest as it is possible to connect with it; bringing into cheerful prominence the improved prospects of Irish industry, together with the benefits arising from the operation of Sir John Romilly's Act for disposing of encumbered estates.

POSTSCRIPT IN 1862.

SIX years have gone over since the foregoing review of M. Lavergne's work upon England was penned, yet on reflection, there appears in it but little to modify. On one point, perhaps, it may be well to note a change ; I mean in what regards the interference of the English Government in the domestic affairs of the people.

It is remarked in the review, how small the amount of Government interference has ever been in this nation ; but I regret to say the case is altered of late. For instance, the expenditure, by the Executive Government, of a sum of money reaching the enormous amount of 800,000l. in the year, for the purpose of educating the children of parents, unable or unwilling to bear the expense of school teaching for them, has led to a system of widespread centralized influence and control over the rural population throughout the land. In nearly every part of the country, the village school is now brought under the management of a Government official. The condition of granting to any school a portion of the money voted by Parliament for education is, that the school must be presided over by a "certificated teacher." After this comes a stipulation that a Government officer or inspector shall periodically visit and examine into the mode of managing the school. And in the third place, a class of persons is created, dependent on Government employment and favour, called "pupil teachers;" maintained at the public cost, and lodged in capacious and expensive public buildings, and all this, forsooth, in order to train young people to teach reading, writing, and summing, or the "A, B, C," of learning.

Without entering into statistical details concerning the
results, beneficial or otherwise, of this vast, and I may add,
unwieldy machinery, I must be permitted to observe that, the
introduction of it into the social economy of this country tends
to destroy one of the recognised features of English character,
viz., the ability and disposition to manage our own affairs
without being interfered with by Government. Many benevolent country residents assuredly feel the presence of official
rule as unpleasant. Proprietors of land, who would naturally
interest themselves in the schooling of their districts, find
their suggestions overridden, and the superintending function
wholly exercised by the Parson and the Government. The
numerous candidates for places under the Committee of
Education of the Privy Council, form a body of humble
dependents, and the idea of pleasing the dominant authorities
takes entire possession of their mind.

This state of things is a novelty amongst us, and I must
add that its establishment is likely to weaken, if not to efface,
the habit of local activity and spontaneous organization for
purposes of useful expenditure. It has something of the effect
of a poor law, in so far as it renders people in humble circumstances careless of the obligation contracted by the parental
relation ; disposing them to claim the aid of the State for
the schooling of their offspring, in like manner as they claim,
in right of the poor law, food and shelter, when unable or
reluctant to procure these by their own industry.

It is beside my purpose to go into the arguments by which
the necessity for bringing village or rural schooling under
Government superintendence is generally sustained. Perhaps
we have reached that stage in our social history, wherein the
imperfect performance of the duties required of rural
parishioners comes to be felt as a species of disgrace, and
wherein the ideas of the community, as to the skilful employment of means to ends, have outrun ancient modes and habits.
We may see daily instances of the impatience manifested by
the English public, of the smallest shortcomings on the part
of individuals entrusted with the management of any machi-

nery bearing on the general convenience—post-office, railway companies, innkeeping, packet companies, telegraph workers —no matter what the inaccuracy or incompleteness, John Bull is become so exigent since he has grown so wealthy, that he will not endure the old dilatory methods of carrying on the business of administrative life by voluntary or quasi-voluntary agencies.

When a nation has come to be pampered by extraordinary facilities of locomotion and intercommunication, and indeed by the adequate organization of most of the departments connected with material comfort, the few examples which remain of old systems strike us as intolerably clumsy, and inappropriate to the circumstances of the period. And, at this point of public sentiment, a lively conception of the comparative advantages of centralization lays hold of the imagination, and so gradually allows this principle to take root in our institutions.

The spread of this principle in Great Britain I take to be fraught with injurious consequences to the national character; we are entering upon a changed state of things, wherein for the sake of escaping the tiresome obligations involved in citizenship, the indolent man accepts the direction of the Executive Government. Commissioners, lay and ecclesiastical, inspectors, and "Boards," now control the action of a great portion of our domestic economy, whilst the ramifying fibres of the "Committee of the Privy Council," appear to pervade the entire surface of society.

Of course the feeling of a rich man is first to enjoy, and next to avoid trouble. And when this last desire reaches the amount now apparently present in the English mind, centralization offers an easy relief, and the surrender of individual shares in the conduct of the national concerns is made without compunction.

Thus I have briefly sketched the course which a community follows when influenced by two puissant causes. 1. A condition of great wealth, raising as it does the standard of "performance" throughout the functional scale; and 2, this same wealth engendering an inordinate appetite for enjoyment, which is incompatible with the discharge of gratuitous, obscure, and laborious services to society, or " civic functions." Centralization, in short, to my view, is a symptom of social decline in a free, active, and healthful community; but whether it be destined to enlarge its operations over the English people, or whether they will offer timely resistance to its progress, must chiefly depend upon the conduct of our political teachers in and out of Parliament. In comparison with an able " platform" speaker, even good writers exercise but a secondary influence.

I shall be told that the step taken by Government, in assuming the direction of the enormous expenditure voted for purposes of education, was prompted by the annually augmenting evil of its maladministration by the parochial and other resident managers. But I demur to the expenditure itself. It is out of all proportion with its objects. And I am persuaded that less than one half of the sum voted by Parliament out of the taxes, in aid of the teaching of poor children, would suffice to impart so much elementary education as the State ought to be called upon to assist in supplying to the working classes. However, these speculations have extended to a length which obliges me to conclude, after remarking that an undue portion of the wealth of this country seems to be, at the present time, employed in teaching the poor to rely on the rich for obtaining many things which they ought properly to aim at obtaining by their own labour and their own virtues.

THE CASE

OF

THE POOR AGAINST THE RICH

FAIRLY CONSIDERED

BY

A MUTUAL FRIEND.

THE AUTHOR TO THE READER.

THESE pages have cost me too much thought and too much labour to be consigned to oblivion without an attempt to render them of some use. They were designed for publication in one or other of the quarterly periodicals, but could obtain admission into neither, for various reasons, not necessary to assign here.

The hope of obtaining the attention, and, possibly, the concurrence in my opinions, of even a small number of readers, induces me to print my "rejected article" in an independent form; and it will compensate me for the pains bestowed upon its composition, if I should succeed in rectifying, even in a slight measure, certain errors (all the more formidable for being conscientious) which prevail on the subject of the inequality of conditions between Rich and Poor.

London, Feb. 1850.

THE RICH AND THE POOR.

Though the work we are about to notice* is by no means a recent production, it has been selected from a mass of similar labours on account of the rare qualifications brought to it by the author, and the ability with which he has embodied certain views which, in our opinion, require to be controverted and corrected.

At the time when M. Léon Faucher made his tour through the manufacturing districts in England, the question of ' Le droit de travail' had not acquired that formidable pre-eminence which we have lived to see it arrive at in the minds of his countrymen.

The question of poverty and its painful derivatives has, however, long engaged the attention of some of the clearest-headed and most benevolent individuals among the political men of France, and especially of M. Léon Faucher,† a writer formerly known to the public as the able "rédacteur-en-chef" of the "Courrier Français;" an instructed political economist and financier, and wielding, perhaps, one of the finest controversial pens of the time.

---

* Études sur l'Angleterre. Par Léon Faucher. Paris. 1845. 2 vols.

† Lately Minister of the Interior under Louis Napoleon.

This gentleman, profiting by a period of leisure which his secession from the "Courrier Français" afforded, undertook a journey through several of the British provinces, with a view to obtain an insight into the comparative condition of the people in Great Britain, as well as to examine the working of our manufacturing system; to portray its material and industrial features, and to acquire, if possible, the means of communicating to his countrymen the secret of our prodigious prosperity. M. Faucher was, indeed, already in some sort familiar with the subject, having previously travelled in England (of which he possessed the language sufficiently well), and made notes of much that appeared to deserve attention. Moreover, his connexion with many leading public men here, and the facilities with which they furnished him for penetrating into the very heart of our manufacturing hives, gave M. Faucher advantages which rarely attend a foreigner on a tour of curiosity in a rival country. His work, therefore, of which we have given the title at the head of this article, is entitled to respectful attention, as containing, first, a thoroughly veracious account of what the author saw with his own eyes (and which, by the way, very few of us, we suspect, have seen, or would even wish to see with ours); and secondly, a tolerably comprehensive summary of the views, opinions, and aims of a class who may not unaptly be described as "operative philanthropists."

To give any adequate notion of the quantity of facts and speculations comprised in these two interesting volumes would require long extracts, as well from M. Faucher's descriptive chapters, as from those in which he seeks to unravel the incoherent mass of

phenomena composing our motley, and probably
unique, form of society. But the leading impressions
he seems to have carried away with him are, that
England offers the most forcible contrasts which human
life can furnish. Splendour and comfort are everywhere to be found side by side with misery; benevolence, piety, love of order, in company with squalid
indigence, and debauched and vicious habits; whilst
industry, talents, and the domestic virtues are to be
found flourishing in the centre of depraved multitudes.
The manufacturing "hives" present equally marked
contrasts—vast masses of workpeople shall be comfort-
ably cared for and their morals watched over, in one
district; whilst in others, the human species shall be
found degraded to the level of swine. Beholding these
monstrous inequalities of lot amongst the members of
one community, M. Faucher is prompted to express a
sentiment which, indeed, seems but too just and
natural, in regard to the sacrifice of human life and
powers by which the prodigious wealth and power of
England have been acquired. M. Faucher deems the
price paid for our superiority too great—he considers
the manufacturing system to have been reared upon
an *inhuman* basis, and thinks that a severe *retribution*
must overtake the capitalists sooner or later. Furthermore, whilst he accords to the over-worked factory
labourer a measure of deep commiseration, he reserves
a scarcely inferior feeling of pity and sympathy for the
agricultural or out-door labourer. No class, in short,
earning their subsistence by labour in this country,
but is an object of profound compassion, excepting,
perhaps, those individual factories whose proprietors,
like Messrs. Greg, Strutt, Ashworth, and Ashton,

E

consent to dedicate a portion of their time and attention to the well-being of their people.

"Lorsque les premières atteintes du mal industriel se firent sentir
en Angleterre, on essaya d'abord d'en détourner les yeux; l'on en
contesta la réalité. .... Plus tard, le recensement de la population
ayant fait connaître l'effroyable mortalité des districts manufacturiers,
et la publication des tables criminelles ayant montré l'accroissement
des délits, il ne fut plus possible de prolonger ces illusions. Alors
la discussion reporta sur les causes du désordre nouveau qui venait
de se révéler. Pendant que l'aristocratie foncière en accusait
l'industrie elle-même, et ne voyait dans l'activité des ateliers que des
germes de mort, l'aristocratie industrielle s'en prenait aux lois et à
l'état de la société. Bientôt les avocats des manufactures, quittant
la défensive, ont cherché à établir que la condition des populations
rurales était encore inférieure à celle des ouvriers fileurs ou tisseurs ;
mais tout ce qu'ils ont prouvé en jetant sur les faits cette cruelle lumière,
c'est que le mal existait des deux côtés."—Tome i. p. 381.

Without concurring in the loose declamatory accusations against the wealthy, which are now so commonly
vented by the "friends of the poor" *par excellence*,
M. Faucher is nevertheless impelled, by the strong
feelings of humanity he cherishes, to address them in
the following language—in reference to the foregoing
statements :—

"Il y a là un scandale qui pèse à la conscience publique ; chacun
sent bien que, dans un pays où de pareilles maladies se déclarent, les
hommes qui président à la direction de l'ordre social ne sauraient
échapper à toute responsabilité. ....

"Il est triste, quand on aspire à une renommée de richesse, de force,
et de moralité, de se voir montré au doigt en Europe, et de devenir pour
les uns un sujet de reproche, pour les autres un objet de pitié. ....

"Enfin, l'Angleterre comprend que son avenir même est menacé.
Un peuple aussi profondément attaché au culte de la matière doit
mettre la force physique au premier rang des élémens sur lesquels
repose la puissance d'un état, et il doit s'alarmer plus qu'un autre
dès qu'il voit décliner, sous l'influence des privations combinées avec
l'intempérance et avec l'excès du travail, la constitution des ouvriers.
..... Il s'est organisé (*i. e.*, le peuple) pour une sorte de lutte
universelle avec le monde civilisé, qu'il défie tout ensemble dans les
conquêtes aussi peu pacifiques de l'industrie. Comment ne trem-
blerait-il pas, à la seule idée d'une diminution probable dans l'effi-

cacité des instrumens avec lesquels il combat et il produit."—Tome i.
pp. 377—380.

These appeals to the conscience as well as to the
fears of the educated classes, dictated as they are by
the sincerest benevolence, have their use in keeping
alive that sense of duty towards inferiors which is
indispensable to the existence of civilized society. But
we must be allowed to observe that, to English ears,
they savour of that entire ignorance of what we are
doing, and what has been doing, in regard to our
domestic organization, which is so universal in the
French mind when treating of England. It is,
perhaps, on this account, superfluous to wonder that
M. Faucher should not be aware that no subject,
bearing on our internal condition, has occupied anything like the same degree of laborious attention and
earnest solicitude, both on the part of the legislature
and the influential classes, lay and clerical, for the last
twenty years, as this very problem of the increase of
indigence. And if we are no nearer to the discovery
of a means of extinguishing it than before, it is well
to have laboured heartily to that end, as we have done,
and to have accomplished the most effectual mitigation
of the evil which the actual condition of society
admitted of,—viz., the New Poor Law of 1835.

But in order to appreciate the efforts made by
England towards a healthier state of morals and
comfort among her working population, it ought to be
carefully ascertained how much of human suffering is
curable by human agency, and how much incurable.
The Turk or Egyptian fatalist quietly resigns himself
to misfortune and suffering, in the belief that no part
of it is curable by man. This is one end of the scale

E 2

of faith. At the opposite end may be found sanguine
and self-sufficient social doctors, who affirm " that it
savours of impiety to say that *any* form of evil is
beyond the power of society to remedy." Such a
declaration was actually published by a "club" formed
a short time since at Paris, calling itself " Le Cercle
Constitutionnel," in which many respected names were
enrolled; among others, that of M. Gustave de
Beaumont, late Ambassador of the French Republic
in England. These persons, we repeat, are at the
opposite end of the scale. We should ourselves be
glad to hit the precise "juste milieu," but not having
that pretension, we think it a righteous employment
of our faculties to sift the efficacy of current projects,
by tracing their indubitable effects beforehand.

To begin with the most generally approved specific,
increased charity. " If the rich would only open their
purses wider," cry the *plate-holders*, "we should hear no
more complaints about want and suffering." " It is the
indolent neglect of the poor by the wealthy," say the
Puritans, "which causes the dreadful spread of poverty
and crime." These, and a hundred forms of the same
proposition, are as familiar to our readers as the song
of birds, no doubt, and leave a certain indefinable but
disagreeable trace behind them. We will look into
the value of this nostrum first in order, beginning with
its practical side, apart from its sentimental character.

There can be no doubt that every shilling bestowed
in alms is a shilling the less in that fund destined to
remunerate labour withal. For nothing is more fabulous than the thing called " superfluity." People in
easy circumstances either spend, or give away, or save
the money they have to dispose of. What is given away

to the poor is, of course, also spent, by the party receiving it, unproductively. What is saved might be likewise given; but if no savings are made, all provision against casual reverses, as well as all accumulation of capital, destined to reproduce wealth, is annihilated—a consequence which cannot be too emphatically deprecated. But whilst we estimate the agency of charitable donations as a very inadequate counterpoise to the pressure of the general mass of poverty in a community, it is fitting that the wide extent to which the habit of benevolence is practised in Great Britain should be placed in a strong light, by way of proving that the experiment has at least been extensively tried.

When, indeed, we come to look into the amount of what is given, without a shadow of return, by rich to poor in this country—not counting various services in person rendered by rich men—its magnitude is astonishing. Setting aside the enormous standing provision for sick and infirm (the result of endowments), and for educational objects, an Englishman of fortune seldom has his purse out of his hand. He pays all sorts of legal demands for the subsistence of the poor in the first place; next, he subscribes to various public charities, also to ploughing-matches, &c.; he assists poor dependents; supports decayed relations; he gives alms on the highways; he drops money into the charity-plate at dinners and after sermons; he encloses five-pound notes to the police magistrates, as from "A. X."; he distributes coals, clothes, meat at Christmas; he gives land to build a school upon; he pays for the doctors of the poor; he lends to inferiors, and never gets paid; finally, he dies and leaves bequests to half-a-dozen eleemosynary institutions, and to humble servitors, and not unfrequently founds a provision for an annual gift.

The female members of the gentry class are, all this time, toiling at the work of benevolence in its domestic forms—overlooking schools, stitching sedulously at nightgowns and baby-linen, or at " fancy-fair" articles; teaching girls straw-plaiting, lace-making; hearing catechisms on Sundays, tormenting their acquaintance to purchase the useless productions of surabundant hands; distributing soup-tickets;—in fine, co-operating, with their gentle, kind efforts, in the grand and commendable purpose of mitigating the evils of poverty in the lower ranks of life.   Go into what neighbourhoods you will, the standing feature in every country residence is " the charity" business.   Where, indeed, is the rural abode, we would ask, where the visitor is safe from " the plate," or the subscription-book?   Is there a provincial dinner-table at which the topic of poor-law, board of guardians, or the like, does not take precedence of all others?   It is hardly prudent to attend your host's parish church, even; for it is ten to one but that you are " let in" for a " collection" at the door, after sermon; and all this on the back of a tax amounting to something like seven millions of pounds per annum!

Such is but an imperfect outline of the " charitable" habits of an English family of average benevolence and means, for we do not believe that any one except a native of Great Britain has any conception of the extent to which an Englishman's fortune and time are dedicated to the work of doing good.   It is, perhaps, unmatched in the world.   After this, one would suppose that the gentleman (or gentlewoman), who gives

and labours in all these forms, would be allowed to
spend and enjoy the rest of his or her income, and
attend to their six children in peace and quiet. Not
a bit of it. "Is it in human nature," said the late
Sydney Smith, in one of his Essays, "that A should
see B in distress, and not order C to assist him?" The
whole squad of humanity-foragers are upon him with
their appeals on behalf of some species of misery which
they have undertaken to assuage; and in fact, if we
would listen to these eternal emissaries, nobody would
have a moment's respite so long as any poor folks
could be found lacking something or another, or a
disease unprovided with a special asylum. Under this
sort of persecution, the possession of wealth almost
ceases to be a blessing. If we were not to resist such
attacks, the world of England might, in due time,
become one vast field for the labours of the Dorcas
tribe, whilst the more wholesome sources of good-will
and sympathy would be vulgarized and transmuted
into the most commonplace of all ties—the connexion
between rich and poor through the medium of the
purse.

It would be doing injustice to the sound understanding of M. Faucher to imply that he is a believer in the
efficacy of charity as a *cure* for our social evils, although,
as a wholesome exercise of the beneficent principle, he
is, naturally, anxious to see it practised. As might
be expected of so sensible a man, he has other suggestions to offer, and does not, after the manner of
" Boz," leave his readers with nothing but a vague sentiment of pity for the oppressed, and an equally vague
detestation of the oppressors—by which is understood,
in modern parlance, the comfortable classes. We are,

however, unable to concur in the merits of M. Faucher's principal scheme as a counterpoise to the moral and physical degradation of the poor; we confess that we see in it little else than another form of charity, and feel therefore that its impracticability is scarcely a matter of regret. He, like most Frenchmen, considers the occupancy of land, in never so small a parcel, by the poor man, to be the proper remedy against indigence, as well as a pledge of his disposition to maintain the laws and ordinances of society. " The larger the number interested in agricultural occupations on their own account," says M. Faucher, " the safer are your national institutions." Now, there can be no doubt that the possession of property of any kind binds the party by so much to the protection of the institution of property ; but does it not occur to the advocates of this doctrine that, in order to multiply proprietors of land, you must first find possessors of land willing to part with it, and next, poor men able to purchase? If the working man have money, he can purchase, not else. *In France, land is sold, not given;* the same would happen here at the present time if the poor man were able to buy land. " But let him have land on hire, then," say the friends of the system of " petite culture." Here we not only meet the obstacle we alluded to above, viz., the reluctance of owners to give up land for this purpose; but we are compelled to justify it by adducing the example of landowners in a neighbouring island, who, having once granted their land on hire, are absolutely cut off from all control over it in time to come. In the county of Donegal, not many years since, a gentleman, wishing to re-enter into the occupation of his own domain at the expiration of the term for which it had been let to

a number of small cultivators, was met by a threat of
assassination; and on his causing his agent to enforce
his orders, the agent was doomed to death, and would
have been shot without scruple, had not one of the
party, suspecting the fidelity of his confederates, anti-
cipated their treachery by informing against them, and
thus saved the steward's life.   Experience shows that
few things are more difficult than to recover possession of land once yielded up to persons of very small
means; for that which is granted on a revocable tenure
passes sooner or later into something like fixity of
tenure, so incomplete is the process by which the real
owner endeavours to regain it.   It was remarked, in a
recent number of the *Edinburgh Review* ("Claims of
Labour"),that the holding land on hire did not, after all,
impart a sense of independence to the labourer, whilst
it had the disadvantage of impeding his removal to
other districts as occasion might serve.   It would not,
at all events, meet the case of the town workman, for
the mill-hands could not cultivate the soil if they had
it; nor, even assuming that they knew how to do so,
would they have energy and strength left sufficient to
walk out (after dark, for the most part, too) to the
plots granted them in the vicinity of densely-inhabited
towns, necessarily distant from their abodes.   And
indeed, whilst overwork is the real curse of their condition, who would recommend night walks and spade
culture in addition?   As to farm-labourers, few of our
cottages are without a bit of garden-ground adequate
to their wants, which furnishes employment for them
at spare times; and we are far from believing that the
major portion desire to rent more, unless upon terms
implying a sacrifice by the owner in their favour.

When Lord Radnor, for example, kindly consented to let portions of ground to labourers at a rent equal, or nearly equal, to the market value, a perfect outcry was set up against him, both by labourers and by " friends of the labourer," because he did not offer it at half its worth, giving the labourer the difference! This incident plainly shows the *animus* with which the "friends of the poor" ask the rich to " encourage" them.

M. Faucher's proposal for granting allotments we must, then, respectfully dismiss as impracticable, except in detached districts; as well on account of the difficulty of getting the land yielded up for it, near to large towns, in sufficient quantity, as on the ground of the factory workpeople having no spare power of toil left, after working all day in the mill.

We have now to consider another of M. Faucher's expedients. It is, that the capitalist, or master of a mill or factory, or establishment for industrial operations of any sort, should be induced to forego that character, or to blend with it that of associate, or partner, with the workmen whom he employs; and this, in the view of engaging a " moral support" on the part of the co-operative workpeople.

"Quant aux bénéfices, après avoir mis àpart un cinquième pour le fonds de réserve, on les partagerait, par égales moitiés, entre le maître et les corps des ouvriers. Il va sans dire que j'entends ce partage comme une concession volontaire, à laquelle chaque manufacturier apporterait les conditions," &c. &c.—Tome i. p. 432, *et seq.*

It may be an error; but, for the life of us, we cannot discern, in this ingenious contrivance, anything beyond a tendency to raise the wages of the workman at the expense of the master. But this could be easily done without the contrivance, sup-

posing the capitalist to be brought into the humour
required.* View it on which side you will, however,
it involves an interference with the laws that regulate
the proportion which profits and wages shall bear to
each other, where industry is free. And be it added,
that, its adoption being confessedly optional, it would
occasion endless variety in the rates of profit, tending
to dislocate the scale of prices—introducing a confusion into the economy of manufacturing life which
might prove eminently disastrous to the whole community. The further effect of forcing up wages (and
the plan is nothing else) would simply be to discourage
capital from being set to work. On the ratio in which
profits can be extracted from mill labour hinges our
chance of holding our own in the markets of the
world. Raise our rate of wages (the population
continuing to increase, and to press upon profits as
paupers), and you paralyse the power of competing
with other nations. The dire necessity we labour
under of keeping the increase of capital a-head of the
increase of population, closes the door upon purely
present humane considerations. This is a sad truth,
but it had best be told. Your capital will flow out of
the country if you increase the cost of production by
raising wages. Of course, if bread be cheapened,
wages will virtually rise a trifle without deranging the
rate of profit. Yet this alleviation cannot endure
long. Fresh discoveries annually supersede human
arms in mill machinery, and the excess in the supply

* The incapacity of the workpeople to meet the reverses incident to
commercial existence, would form an insuperable obstacle to such a co-
partnery. It is only a capitalist who can await the return of a profitable
season; the workman must subsist himself in the meantime, since there
are no profits on the concern. But subsist on what?

of live labour will have to be provided for by a tax (or poor-rate), which tax, of course, falls upon profits and rent, and by so much lessens the return upon the capital of the country. A clever French writer expresses himself on this contingency as follows :—

"Ce serait pour la nation Anglaise un immense malheur, si cet intérêt, au lieu d'augmenter, diminuait, et elle en est véritablement menacée. Mais ce qui doit, plus que toute autre chose, exciter la sollicitude du gouvernement Anglais, c'est la situation de la classe industrielle, qui forme une partie si forte et si énergique de la nation. Il n'est pas de grande ville en Angleterre où cette classe si laborieuse et si pauvre n'inspire une pitié profonde," &c. &c.—*Rev. des Deux Mondes, pour Février*, 1842, p. 675.

No conclusion, it would seem, can rest upon sounder premises than this to which the writer in "La Revue des Deux Mondes" has arrived. The main instrument through which the deplorable evils attending the spread of pauperism may be staved off, consists in the steady increase of the capital of the nation. By means of a continual accumulation of capital, the sore may, perhaps, be kept at its present level. The same proportions which now pervade the shares of the respective classes, may be preserved. We shall continue to have a layer of want, disease, and vice at the bottom (and that a pretty thick one, alas !), a larger stratum above, of thriving industry; with, lastly, a thin top vein of wealthy capitalists, including the enjoyers of "rent." This appears to be the best condition we can hope to realize, supposing population to proceed at its present pace. That charity, however extended, hardly makes any impression upon the evil it is engaged upon alleviating, we have, in this generous land at least, ample proof. By a

compulsory interference with the laws of distribution
—in other words, taxing the rich for the enjoyment
of the poor, or forcing up wages and lowering profits
of trade, by way of diminishing the inequality of
conditions; or by compelling capitalists to employ
their fortune in augmenting the production of food
(whether profitably or unprofitably, no matter), or
by forcing persons having capital to employ more
labour than is conveniently needed, or, by the fusion
of "master" and "man," to stimulate an increased
production—by none of these violent experiments and
expedients should we advance nearer to the desired
object, whilst we should be storing up still more
intractable difficulties for our successors. All the
remedial suggestions we have heard (with the exception of emigration), may be resolved, ultimately, into
an interference with the law of property, more or less
plausibly veiled; and the modern phrase of "*le droit
de travail*" would appear to have been invented to
disguise, for a season, what must presently come to be
recognised as an attack upon that principle. Such,
therefore, as desire to uphold and defend that principle,
our "ark of the covenant," as it were, will do well to
study the insidious artifices by which it is, in these
days, imperilled. "*Le droit de travail*" is among the
most formidable of them, and one which, if not grappled
with in time, may possibly come to serve, as the wooden
horse of the Greeks served at Troy, to introduce the
besiegers into the very citadel of the economic and
social structure of Europe.

Anything which sounds like a remedy will always
be caught at by the mass of mankind, if it but relieve
them from the task of probing the evil to the core.

The dread we entertain of being forced to confess
that mankind multiply inconveniently fast, drives
us to employ the most untenable arguments and the
shallowest devices. One of these is to affirm, " that
the land of Great Britain ought to be made to produce
a vast deal more food than it does." " If the soil were
adequately cultivated," say they, "we should see all the
labouring people employed, and every one would have
enough to eat out of the abundance." This is so
attractive a nostrum, that it is worth while to communicate a mode of dealing with it which we have
employed with tolerable success. We simply put the
question—" Do you mean, that the increased food
should be produced at a profit, or at a loss ?" In every
case, the projector has seized the drift of our interro-
gatory reply, and been dumb. The same man would
hardly sanction the Government in taking *money*
from " Farmer Drill," sending it to New York, and
exchanging it for meal, to be distributed gratis, in
due season, to the English poor; yet it comes to much
the same thing as compelling him to produce corn at
home at a loss. If produced at a profit, he will need
no compulsion.

The institution of the Poor Law, providing as
it does against the necessity of any one individual
starving for want of food and shelter, is, we think,
sufficient to exculpate the English nation from the
imputation of indifference to the claims of a sound
humanity. M. Faucher lays it down that the State
has no business to interdict the practice of mendicancy,
unless it provide legal means of relief to the needy.
Differing from him as we do upon the principle, we
would nevertheless observe that this is precisely what

the English government does. No one need die of hunger in England. But he who would eat the bread of others must eat it in the workhouse; and the State does well to reduce the cost of furnishing food and shelter to its lowest form. The sensitive but short-sighted advocates of a more generous provision ought to reserve a portion of sympathy for those who are taxed to furnish the subsistence of the indigent, among whom are the industrious and frugal peasants of the cottage class, as well as every possessor of a mansion.

But there are agencies at work, having a contrary tendency, and of which we would say a passing word. The phases of misery in which the effects of over-population reveal themselves in the present day, are so various as to have actually engendered a literature of their own! A class of writers have betaken themselves to the composition of heart-rending fictions, bearing a resemblance with certain forms of life among our lower classes, and they have succeeded, to a certain extent, in inspiring every eater of daily dinners with something like a sentiment of shame and self-reproach. Where this feeling fructifies into almsgiving, all that ensues is a diminution of the operation of the " positive check" for the moment; a fraction of privation is absorbed, and the consequences of a great natural law interrupted for a brief season. But the law resumes its march, and the weeping reader of Mrs. Norton's, " Boz's," Hood's, and other tragical works, must either sacrifice more of his own substance, or let it march. We cannot too strenuously insist on the fact that every complaint uttered on behalf of the poor and needy, against the possessors of property, as such, is at variance with the recognised fundamental principles

of civilized society, which rule that the lawful possessor of property shall enjoy it, as far as that enjoyment does not interfere with the interests of others.
It is time, indeed, that we understood what this
modern cry of reproach means. If we are never to
be unmolested in the use of our own property (great
or small, as the case may be) so long as poverty is
prevalent in the land, let the humanity-preachers say
so, and we shall know how to deal with the demand.
We have always presumed that one of the privileges
belonging to the rich and elevated classes is that of
delegating to others the function of dispensing their
alms, and that, when a liberal contribution to the
solace and relief of the poor had been made, the
donor might be permitted to frame his own life after
his own tastes. But the charity-crusaders would
have it otherwise. They positively erect it into an
accusation against a nation, that any one man should
be reclining on a soft chair, digesting his mutton and
claret in a placid state of mind, whilst " thousands of
shivering wretches are starving in cellars and garrets."
This sort of appeal to the vulgarest of all fallacies
succeeds in alarming many kind and timid persons;
and they accordingly, when attacked by the alms-
levier (who puts this phrase to their heads with as
much effect as if it were a pistol), " stand and deliver"
their money.

The fundamental error on which this weakness
rests, lies in believing that all this poverty is the
result of blameable conduct in the existing generation of rich men. It is, on the contrary, the consequence of a natural and universal law—viz., the
predominance of present over distant motives in man,

—and is no more the fault of the rich of this period
than of foregone generations of rich. Poverty, in all its
disastrous aspects, is, and has always been, exhibited
in every country on the face of the earth; and the
pen of the pauper's novelist would find ample subject-
matter for harrowing descriptions even in the most
thriving cities, such as Hamburg and Berne; or even
in Boston, in the least pauperized country in the
world. It is one among many inevitable consequences
of human imperfection and human necessities, and can
only be eradicated, if at all, by a new course of pro-
vident and self-denying conduct on the part of our
working people. For to pretend that one class of
society could, and ought, by unceasing devotion to
the task of making the rest of the community prudent,
careful, self-controlling, and virtuous-minded, to
achieve the extinction of the faulty and vicious tendencies of our common nature, were to outrun the
visions of Plato by many degrees. Man, individually,
follows his instincts towards pleasure of various kinds,
with more or less regard to distant consequences.
Classes of men do the same, and pay, like individuals,
the penalty of their improvidence. Governments have
aimed at interposition; witness Bavaria and Prussia,
and, we believe, Austria, where it is rendered difficult
for persons in indigent circumstances to get married,
and where, consequently, paupers are less numerous
than with us. But the notions of English liberty
which are rooted in the national mind forbid our
having recourse to such precautionary regulations,
and we are thus forced to leave the evil to the
operation of natural laws, of which the "positive
check," or death from poverty, is one.

F

The conclusions to which a sober contemplation of the subject leads us are, first, that the evils of wide-spread poverty, privation, and physical deterioration, are not to be annulled by either compulsory govern-ment action or private benevolence; and next, that the remedy, if any such may be hoped for, must be sought by enlightening the lower classes themselves upon the real principles which affect the condition of individuals in civilized communities. A respect for property is a strong and admirable element in the English character, and nothing but rampant hunger can overcome it with the large majority of our people. It is the especial duty of the higher classes to cultivate this sentiment in their poor dependents; whilst, on the other hand, policy, no less than humane consi-derations, dictates large sacrifices at critical periods of scarcity or want of employment, in the shape of gifts, by the rich, in order to avoid the risk of the law being violated. But the fewer of these efforts that are made, the longer will capital keep ahead of the pressure of population.

How far a national conscience ought to be at rest under a state of things such as M. Faucher exhibits, must, after all, depend upon the degree in which the evil is susceptible of cure, and on the amount of efforts made by society to apply the cure. That prodigious exertions are made by the humane of all ranks in this country—by alms, by legal provision for the destitute, and by protective laws—to redeem their suffering brethren, is matter of familiar notoriety; yet the sore does not disappear; nay, it even seems to extend its baleful ravages.

We have already said that, as a feature of social

intercourse, charity possesses a claim to respect; serving, as it does, to animate and expand the love of doing good in the rich; the value of which sentiment it were folly to dispute. But, taking a long-sighted view of the certain tendencies of actual causes in operation, we must earnestly and emphatically insist upon the unpalatable proposition, that alms-giving does not act as a remedy either against pauperism or against the degradation of our manufacturing population; nor, on the other hand, in a free country, can a Legislature step in between a starving man and his bread, be it gained by never so large a sacrifice of toil, comfort, and self-respect, provided he offend no law in so doing.*   It is for M. Faucher† and

* A lesson on a small scale has been afforded us—in the attempts of the British Parliament to protect the young against undue toil—of the futility of opposing the exchange of human labour for bread, if offered.

The State, aiming at the mitigation of the evil of over labour, bearing upon the young, or those under eighteen years of age, framed enactments with this view long since, which have for some years been in operation. But the instincts of self-preservation are stronger than the statutes of the realm, and we need go no farther than the pages of M. Faucher to find ample details concerning the way in which the benevolent intentions of the Legislature are frustrated, by collusion between greedy masters and needy workpeople.† Their effect is accordingly but partial and incomplete, though not wholly nugatory.

Remain yet, moral teaching, emigration, limitation of births. With regard to the first, it has always struck us that to attempt to raise the moral tone of the poor factory helots, without furnishing the physical means of adjusting their habits to it, was perfectly fruitless. To inspire the wretched inhabitant of a Manchester cellar with a craving for decency of apparel, for a cleanly abode, or for the use of books, is to augment by so much his sense of privation and helplessness. We have in vain listened for some one to tell the working classes that the secret of ameliorating their condition is to limit their numbers. Nobody will " bell the cat."

† See tome ii. p. 102. et seq.

his disciples to point out a method by which bread shall be earned and eaten, without such conditions, by the mass of the labouring manufacturers; the inviolability of property always remaining sacred and unquestioned, notwithstanding. Failing in this, M. Faucher will do well to temper his animadversions on the English "social plague-spot" by a juster appreciation of our benevolent struggles to bring about its amendment, in time past, time present, and to come.

We venture to add, in conclusion, a few words upon the much canvassed subject of emigration. It can hardly be called in question, we think, that the sending away of half-a-million of our people must relieve the pressure upon our social system; and therefore, as long as we are rich enough to buy out a portion of our population, annual depletion may prove a sensible benefit. But let no one persuade himself that those *left behind* are the gainers. They lose the best young blood of the country, and with it large masses of capital; they lose the effective labourer, and the capital that might set him to work. The emigrant profits, no doubt, but he alone. Those who remain will probably discover that the void is speedily filled up, and that the State must continue to expend large sums in order to keep the home population at its altered level. The secondary advantage, of setting up distant markets for our home produce, sounds plausibly enough; but in the actual state of the commercial world, it is hardly possible to calculate upon any permanent demand from the dweller at the Antipodes. So many casual changes in the laws of production and conveyance now hang over the relations of different countries, that the wisest

prophets may easily be proved short-sighted by a
few years' experience. Still, we are not among the
number of those who deprecate experiments in
emigration; we would have them tried in earnest, and
on a vast scale. It is as good an employment of the
surplus revenue of the nations as many others, and
must benefit those who leave the mother-country,
whatever disappointment may result to those who
remain behind.

SUPPLEMENTAL REMARKS, 1862.

THE course which public opinion has followed since this essay was printed, can scarcely be said to have changed its character during the interval—now twelve years. To expect, therefore, that my views will meet with any more favour—I ought to say with any less disfavour—at the present day, would be vain. It seems to me, on the contrary, that the English people become more and more determined to disregard the operation of general laws, and to assume that, so long as the wealth of the country goes on augmenting, it matters little how rapidly the demands of indigence and the necessities of the afflicted multiply upon us.* The young men of the rural districts are, at the present time, being gradually drawn away from farm work, by the temptation afforded by higher-paid employments, such as the railways, the police force, the Government works, the arsenals, the army, domestic service, the constabulary, the "navvy" line, and the like. All these modes of employing working hands, being more remunerative, absorb a considerable amount of able-bodied men. The farmers, accordingly, complain of an insufficient supply of husbandry labourers, and of being compelled to pay higher wages to those whose services they do obtain.

If such increased "wage" led to permanent benefit, by raising the standard of comfort in this class, and improving their way of living, it would be a welcome sign. But the

---

* The proportion in which the amount of Pauperism now stands to the population in England, according to returns quoted in the *Times* newspaper of July 18th, 1862, is "one in 21 of the population, or 4·8 per cent., showing an increase of 6 per cent. over that of 1861."

fact is, that the price of every one of the articles required for
the family of a poor working man has risen to a level above
his means. Bread, it is true, continues at a moderate price,
because it is easy to obtain breadstuffs for our market from
foreign countries. But go one step farther: ask the village
shopkeeper what is now the value of bacon, cheese, butter,
candles, cocoa. He will tell you that they have each risen
30 per cent. within the last seven or eight years. Ask the
butcher, and he will reply that mutton has advanced from
6d. and 7d. to 9d. and 10d. per pound.

Thus it is evident that the slight rise which has taken
place in agricultural wages is insufficient to balance the increase in the value of commodities. Again, the excessive
anxiety of benevolent persons to keep village boys at school
beyond the age at which their labour becomes available, tends
to the disadvantage of their parents. Complaints are made,
by education commissioners and others, that parents are
unwilling to keep their boys at school beyond the age of ten
and eleven years (just when, as they affirm, their education is
taking a higher character), seeing that "Billy" or "Jemmy"
ought to begin to earn his own living. Yet what can be more
unreasonable than to expect a labouring man, who has, by
the sweat of his brow, won the bread for the infant during
eight or nine long years, to forego the relief which his
boy's labour might bring to the cottage purse! Moreover, a
lad of eleven to thirteen, who has never been "put to work,"
but who has filled up his playhours with nothing harder than
a game of cricket, is indisposed to become a farm servant.
He is unused to bear hardships, to sit shivering under a
hedge "crow-keeping," to walk to work through the snow,
to travel home alone after dark, to get wet through, and, in
short, shrinks from the rough apprenticeship inseparable from
husbandry life.

Many kind-hearted people, when they come to know what
the life of a farm boy is, rather rejoice than not that "poor
little Bobby" should avoid its hardships, and should, instead,
get a snug berth in the "Eagle Brewery Company's" employ,

or get work in making cartridges, for the manufacturer of those articles. One gentle, fair philanthropist of my acquaintance, commiserating the *ennui* of a cow-keeping boy in my parish, kindly took him "a story-book" to relieve the weight of it. Of course the "Nanny Cow" broke through the neighbour's hedge into the clover, for want of being watched. But to be serious. This interposition of the rich in behalf of the youthful members of the population is, to call it by its right name, an attempt to prevent the play of a general social principle : and *that*, by applying their money and their personal influence towards the unsettling of the natural relations between demand and supply. In other words, educating the children in such fashion as shall render them unfitted for those employments in which their fathers and mothers before them earned their living; causing humble labour to be regarded with aversion, and diminishing the supply of such labour to what I believe to be an inconvenient extent.

The excuse for all this interference with the distribution of employment, is, ever, that it leads to a desire on the part of the boy or girl, as it may be, to better their condition. Now, it may be questioned whether this ardour, to be shown in the struggle to rise in the scale, be altogether a wholesome feeling to inculcate. Beneficial to certain well-endowed individuals it certainly has been, and always will be ; but whether it be a desirable thing to cultivate, in every humble breast, a dissatisfaction with their actual condition : to inspire an ordinary rustic with a restless longing for change, for the excitement of town life, for gain, and for the means of indulging his appetites, does, in my view, admit of grave doubts. Indeed, whilst the lessons imparted by the Scripture readings and the catechisms of the Church, enjoin humility and contentment under the dispensations of Providence, the education enthusiasts would fain teach that, not to exert the faculties we possess to "get on in the world," is to be foolish and contemptible.

To return to the point where I note the causes which seem to be conducing to the increased burthen of pauperism.

The extreme dearness of provisions weighs down the cottager. The boys eat, and earn nothing. The girls do the same. The young men marry early to obtain a fireside (no longer afforded, as heretofore, under their employer's roof), and have numerous families. For the summer *semestre* all goes well enough ; but winter brings slackened employment, savings are rarely forthcoming, nay, are almost impossible. The rich step in with charitable aid, but cannot wholly mitigate the pressure of want, and the parish does the rest. Thus the rich, in the first place, intercept the action of the natural law, by which I mean the efforts of the children to assist in maintaining the family, by insisting on their staying at school. Next, the boys, for the reasons given above, quit the district, thinning the parish of local " bread-winners ;" sick and infirm women press upon their adult male kindred at home. Need outstrips the means of relief, and hunger gradually assumes the tone of importunity. The parish finally supports those who cannot support themselves, and " the union" becomes crowded with recipients of public bounty. This is the circle in which English rural affairs commonly revolve. That it is far from a healthy circle will not be contested. The point to be considered is, how far the evil of pauperism is referable to the faults of the poor, and how far to the mischievous action of the rich.

In a country so advanced in artificial modes of living as England is, nothing is more difficult than to specify and follow out the effects of any one cause in bringing about social changes. Nevertheless I must select a feature in our domestic history, to which it seems to me fair to attribute a sensible influence over the well-being of our rural population. I mean the enormous increase in the consumption of meat in England, consequent upon the introduction of the " Norfolk system." Formerly perhaps even within the memory of man—fresh meat in winter was a luxury confined to the wealthy classes. In the north of England, assuredly, salted legs of mutton were as common as salted pork. There being no food to give animals in winter except hay and corn, horses and cows could alone be supported during this season. The culture of root crops, however, speedily led to the multiplication of sheep and oxen for food, and the prodigious prosperity of our manufacturing class furnishing an almost boundless demand for meat, flocks and herds were extensively reared, to the corresponding profit of the landowners. Labour, during the period of this transition, being in demand, wages rose, and with them the desire for more succulent aliments, and not only the factory operative, but the English rustic, came to regard animal food as a necessary of life all the year round. To meet the increased cost of human labour, machinery was invented. An augmented rate of production followed, to be balanced by an augmented rate of consumption. Presently the demand came to be so excessive that we were forced to import meat; that is to say, live cattle, calves, and sheep, from the Dutch and the Danes. The average amount of which, I believe, was in 1861, during the navigable season, somewhere about 3000 head per week by the river Thames alone.

That we could no longer produce meat sufficient for own own consumption, became apparent. But the habit, acquired at a period when the population had not reached the amount we now possess, of living on meat, remained in force; and since the expense of rearing animals for food naturally rose with the demand (because inferior land had to be cultivated in order to keep pace with it), the price of meat, together with that of cheese and butter, which must equally be counted as animal product, has reached a point which, as I have observed, all but forbids its purchase by the cottager. And as to bacon, it is positively at a fabulous figure. The vast amount of milk, too, consumed by the populous towns now-a-days, by so much lessens the quantity available for cheese-making, whilst the buttermilk is lost to the " swill-tub," and so renders pig-feeding less and less general.

I have shown that the habit of living upon animal food, for some years past widely diffused, is now checked, by the growing difficulty of procuring it at a reasonable price. Butter and cheese also are well nigh out of reach for the cottager, and he is obliged to depend upon his own pig, when lucky enough to possess one, for his " modicum" of bacon. But this is scanty measure for the ploughman or reaper. His beer, too, is wretched stuff. The beer-shops and inns are mostly owned by brewers, who force the tenants to vend their respective mixtures. The labourer must drink this, or go without, unless his wife is a " capable woman," and will brew a cask at home, now and then, of wholesome liquor.

Failing to obtain adequate sustenance in the articles of meat, cheese, and beer, the labouring man buys "dripping," to season his bread and potatoes withal, or the offal bits at the butchers ; and, to soothe his unsatisfied cravings, indulges in tobacco, even in fine weather. The women of this class commonly drink tea at their meals, and I fear, occasionally, gin. But they struggle on with persevering courage, often in a way to excite cordial admiration and sympathy from a humane observer.

Now, it may be asked, how it comes to pass that the poor man can get so little meat to eat, seeing that the nation is prosperous and wealthy, the capacity of the land to produce food strained to an unprecedented limit, and the generosity of the rich incontestable ?

The answer is not far to seek. The working man is outbid by the classes above him.

The pay given to the higher descriptions of labourers, including that of the factory operatives, is larger than his, and whilst these classes compete for the necessaries of life with the peasantry, the latter are distanced in the race. The immense consumption of meat by all English families, by the army and navy, and public establishments—eleemosynary, and of other kinds—causes the price to range above what the farm-labourers can afford to pay.*

The share, then, which the rich have borne in causing

---

* At one time butter was largely imported, as was also cheese, from the United States. But I have been informed that, for several years past, our Australian colonies have proved more lucrative markets, and a less amount of such commodities is sent to England.

certain privations to the labourer, is this : they have caused such a rapid increase of population, by the skilful application of existing capital to purposes of industrial life, and they so largely remunerate that population whose aid enables the capitalist to enrich himself, that the number of buyers at last outruns the powers of the producers, and, of course, he who has the smallest purchasing power must give way before the possessor of the greater. This is the explanation of the extravagant price of meat, the quantity of this particular product being limited.

The rich have also had a direct share in causing the deterioration of the beer sold to the poor, which, coupled with the diminished quality of their food, is, I fear, bringing about a decline in the physical strength of the working people. Owners of alehouses have been but too ready to accept brewers as tenants, or, whenever tempted by price, as purchasers The results are obvious.

So far forth as this active pursuit of wealth has affected, indirectly, the social position of the labourer, I conceive the upper classes to have lessened the amount of comfort enjoyed by the peasantry, compared with that possessed by them in times anterior to the present, and this in spite of the reduction in price of coffee, tea, sugar, and spirits, all of which are but secondary objects of desire.

But no working man does live, or support a family, on his wages. I wish he did. He would be a better member of society, and would respect himself more. The real fact is that he subsists partly upon his earnings and partly upon alms. The rich make up in charity the shortcomings of the farmer, who, as a general rule, will never pay his men a farthing more than what he can persuade them to work for, whilst the exigencies of the labourer's condition force him to accept whatever the farmer will give.

When the boys have been prevented from helping out the parental earnings, as I have set forth, and the girls, taught to aim at " something better" than farm service, remain on his hands, the poor man finds himself scarcely able to " rub along."

Then, to be sure, the rich neighbours bestow charitable assistance upon him, and, in one form or another, his scanty means are eked out. So that our farm labourers subsist, as I have said, upon the twofold source of wages and charity. It would tend to raise the character of the cottager if the aggregate amount were received in the shape of wages, and if he were taught to rely on his own conduct for keeping clear of debt. However, the rich amongst us prefer dispensing their bounty in the shape of alms, rather than in the mode calculated to engender a feeling of independence among their humble neighbours. And this I count as another of the ways in which the poor have been disadvantageously used by the rich, although the rich have not *designedly* done them injury ; to do which is altogether contrary to their disposition. Whatever wrong they inflict, I believe that it is unintentionally done. Their worst fault, after all, is the neglecting to improve the knowledge of their peasantry on the subject which most concerns their permanent interests, viz., the true relations between capital and labour, demand and supply.

Those relations lie at the bottom of all civilized societies ; and although they are frequently disturbed, by the agency of various artificial causes, nothing can permanently destroy or supersede their influence.

In my history of the hamlet of East Burnham, I have set forth the mischief of doing too little for the improvement of the poor by the lord of the soil. In other parts of England, perhaps too much is being done. The true way to assist humble labouring folk is to help them to help themselves. After attending to the due provision of weather-tight dwellings, a bit of garden, and a schoolhouse, to which their children may be sent (if possible, at their own expense), the care of the rich should be directed to the inculcation of sound principles of social economy, including the habit of saving, and depositing those " savings" at interest.

But, before all, the rich should emphatically point out the advantages of restricting the numbers of the poor. Too much encouragement is given, in England, to improvident marriages

among the working people, whereby a large increase of the
population is induced, to the sensible injury of the class at
large. Hence the efforts to relieve itself by extensive emigration, a remedy of which it is impossible to deny the expediency,
although it is well to remark that each individual emigrant
must occasion an expenditure varying from twenty to fifty
pounds sterling, for freight, and subsistence during the passage.
So that, whilst we get rid of the surplus people, we also get
rid of money, not in surplus.

Whilst touching on this feature of our present condition, I
must be permitted to refer to an opinion, published in another
country, wherein the writer pretends to discover, in the imprudence of English men and women, a source of wealth and
power to the nation.

M. Maurice Block, writing in *Le Temps*, French newspaper, in January, 1862, gives a statement, compiled from
statistical documents, showing the *annual* increase of population in various countries, at periods comprised between 1818
and 1861, as follows:—

40 years.	In England,	from	1821 to 1861	...... 1625.
36 years.	In Prussia,	„	1822 to 1858	...... 1440.
36 years.	In Russia,	„	1822 to 1858	...... 1410.
39 years.	In Austria,	„	1818 to 1857	...... 692.
35 years.	In France,	„	1826 to 1861	...... 340.

Now, after exhibiting this striking comparison between the
rate of increase in France and the rate of increase in England,
M. Block proceeds to lament over the small number of births
in his own country:—

"It is matter of notoriety (he says) that among town
artizans, young men are accustomed to defer their marriage
until the day arrives when they have acquired a certain position in their trade. Once married, many of them are careful
to have no more offspring than can be competently provided
for, and can be fairly endowed at the death of the parents.

"This habit is likewise adopted in a great number of rural
districts. It is affirmed, indeed, that in several of our departments, the peasantry habitually limit their families to two

children ; and since all of these, even, do not reach a marriage-
able age, an absolute diminution of our numbers would take
place, if it were not that some couples are to be found, who,
relying on Providence, and on their own industrious efforts,
bring into the world a larger number than the generality.

"It is this excessive forethought (continues M. Block) which
retards our numerical progress." . . . .

Again. "If France does not possess more numerous
colonies, it is because children do not swarm with us, as they
do in England (*ne pullulent pas*), and that, consequently, we
possess not the amount of over population requisite to set up
fresh communities !" &c. &c.

Few persons can, I think, fail to perceive, in the almost
ludicrous lamentations of M. Block, the source of the difference
between the condition of the French people, taken as a whole,
and that of the English people.   Those to whose imaginations
the ideas of boundless wealth carry unmixed delight and
pride, will deem the English form of existence the preferable
one.   But persons of a really philanthropic turn of mind will
probably regard the prudent, independent habits of the French
peasant with approving sympathy.   Nay, they may even come
to regard the advantage of setting up distant colonies as
dearly purchased, by the painful sacrifices involved in a system
of inconsiderate, improvident multiplication of families,
necessitating, as a last resource against want, an expatriation
from country, coupled with, possibly, a life-long separation
from home and friends.

NOTICE

OF THE

LIFE OF THOMAS MOORE.

Being the substance of an Article in No. CII. of the
" EDINBURGH REVIEW."

G

PREFACE.

THE author of the following pages has deemed it but fair to herself to reproduce, for private circulation, the "article" such as *she intended* to offer it to the readers of the *Edinburgh Review*.

The author thought (and still thinks) that the character of the late Thomas Moore had received somewhat hard measure at the hands of contemporary critics. Whether, in the review here taken, she has or has not succeeded in presenting a fair account of Moore's merits and failings, it must be for the reader to judge. But one thing is certain, viz., that such as he was, the best and highest in the land coveted the possession of his society and friendship with eagerness; so that, if Moore really was what some have striven to make it appear that he was, then the gentlemen and ladies of England must lie open to the reproach of a signal want of taste and discernment.

There is no escaping from this conclusion, except by admitting the substantial claims of their Idol to the admiration and affection of which he was the object. And it may be observed, in behalf of this much censured favourite of all ranks, that he enjoyed his popularity to the last; only ceasing to receive the cordial attentions of his friends when the sad visitation of physical and mental infirmity rendered it imperative on him to renounce all commerce with society.

H. G.

London, *October*, 1854.

MEMOIRS OF MOORE.

Memoirs, Journal, and Correspondence of Thomas Moore. Edited by the Right Honourable Lord John Russell, M.P. Vols. I. to VI. 8vo. London: 1853.

To those who, like ourselves, are verging upon their "grand climacteric" (all the world knows we were born in 1802), these volumes cannot fail to afford many an hour of delightful and interesting reading. We confess to having been absorbed in the retrospective details of a period which, in a social and literary point of view, had so much to distinguish it; details sketched by one who floated on the tide of pleasurable existence in both these forms, and whose capacity for enjoyment seems to have kept pace with his opportunities.

Like many men of ardent sensibility, Thomas Moore had a vivid conception of the value of posthumous celebrity. To be able to interest his fellow men and women in his personal feelings, in his pleasures and pains, his triumphs and successes, was with Moore an object of undisguised solicitude; and to this we are indebted, in great part, though not entirely, for a minute record of his almost daily life, his innermost thoughts, and his relations with society during the meridian of his existence. If it be objected—as, indeed, we have already heard it objected—to this publication, that it is little else than "a tissue of egoistical, vain, and trivial passages in the life of an improvident, selfish adventurer," the answer would be, that all autobiography, to be worth reading at all, must be egoistical and vain; because nobody would take so much trouble except for the sake of being allowed to talk of themselves all through the work, and to dwell, *ad libitum*, upon their own merits and achievements. The use of the personal pronoun has long been, by a very natural instinct of self-protection, restricted within narrow limits by the higher classes of society; hence poor Moore could not *talk* of his own glory and successes whilst alive, and it was a hard case, considering how much he had to be vain of. To fly to his closet, and record the flattering incidents of the day, was his best and most obvious resource. By thus "entering up" the tributes as they poured in, little and great, Moore indemnified himself, by anticipation, for the suppression of all signs of present pride and satisfaction. And since we have discovered incontrovertible evidence in these volumes of the prodigious amount of praise and flattery heaped upon his head, our wonder—recollecting how unaffectedly he bore his honours—becomes greater and greater as we read.

Until the appearance of this publication, it had not, indeed, been fully present to us how extensively Moore was read and relished, nor how widely his reputation, whether as a poet, as a wit, a lyric composer, or, God save the mark! a sound political writer, had circulated, in Europe as well as in the British Isles. Yet it cannot be denied, with the proofs before us, that in each of these walks of composition, Thomas Moore was regarded with enthusiastic admiration by contemporaries, throughout the social scale, from the "man of letters" proper, "down to the Miss in her teens." And as to personal successes, no one, surely, ever surpassed him. By his touching sentimental singing, he enchanted all who were susceptible to the charms of music; by his vivacity; sparkling conversation, and literary accomplishments, he captivated those of his own sex who prized convivial talents, whilst his more solid merits secured for him a place in the esteem and friendly regard of some of our most celebrated countrymen. Add to these sources of honourable gratification, the remarkable fact that Moore enjoyed, and deserved to enjoy, his own self-respect, and cherished his mental independence throughout all vicissitudes of life, and we have before us perhaps the amplest justification of human vanity which purely personal qualities can well furnish.

A general outline of Thomas Moore's life will, we apprehend, be acceptable to most of our readers. Born in 1779, of decent, but obscure Irish parentage, in Dublin, he had the advantage of being the son of a clever, active-minded woman, who seems to have steadily kept in view the main purpose of forcing education upon the boy, as far as her slender means could serve. Moore disliked study, and would much rather have sought his fortune as an actor, or (what he would have liked still better) as a harlequin! But Mrs. Moore compelled him, with her firm, yet affectionate authority, to acquire such an amount of learning as should qualify him to make his way in some one of the walks of educated labour. This purpose accomplished, by his having graduated at

Trinity College, Dublin, young Moore quitted the
parental roof, and at the age of nineteen dropped
down into a humble lodging near Portman Square,
with but a small sum of money in his pocket, and
without the slightest plan for earning his present
subsistence. He possessed scarcely any friends, and
knew nobody of any mark in the world, but after a
while contrived, by means of some letters of introduction he had brought from Dublin, to gain admission
into a few families (chiefly Irish, however) where he
could pass his evenings and occasionally dine. After
getting himself admitted of the Middle Temple, he
went back to Dublin for a space, but shortly returned
to London (in 1799), with the double object of pro-
secuting his legal studies and of procuring subscriptions to his translation of the *Odes of Anacreon;*
the latter endeavour was, by the fortunate accident of
Dr. Lawrence pronouncing a very favourable judgment upon the work, attended with unlooked-for
success. At this period Moore makes the acquaintance of Lord Moira (also by letters of recommenda-
tion from Irish friends), who takes kind notice of
him, and asks him to his country seat, Donington
Park. With the Marquis of Lansdowne, too (father
of the present peer), he becomes acquainted, by soliciting his subscription to the *Anacreon,* which Lord
Lansdowne consents to give, and adds an invitation
to young Moore to call upon him in London. The
Anacreon comes out at length, with a brilliant
list of patrons' names attached to it, and makes a
decided "hit." Moore becomes a "Lion," is *fêté* in
fashionable circles, gets introduced to the Prince of
Wales (to whom, by the way, the *Anacreon* was

dedicated, by "permission"), pays a visit at Donington Park, is so much liked there that it is with
difficulty he can get away; and, in short, finds himself
completely launched upon the great world. Here are
extracts from letters addressed to his mother early in
1801, at the age of two-and-twenty:—

" MY DEAREST MOTHER,—You may imagine I do not want society
here, when I tell you that last night I had *six* invitations. Everything goes on swimmingly with me. I dined with the Bishop of Meath
on Friday last, and went to a party at Mrs. Crewe's in the evening.
My songs have taken *such* a rage : even surpassing what they did in
Dublin. . . . .
    " There is not a night that I have not three parties on my string,
but I take Hammersley's advice and send showers of apologies. The
night before last, Lady Harrington sent her servant after me to two
or three places, with a ticket for the 'Ancient Music,' which is the
king's concert, and which is so select, that those who go to it ought to
have been at court before. Lady H. got the ticket from one of the
princesses, and the servant at last found me where I dined," &c. &c.
    . . . . " Never was there any wight so idly busy as I am. Nothing
but racketting; it is, indeed, too much, and I intend stealing at least a
fortnight's seclusion, by leaving word at my door that I am gone into
the country. I last night went to a little supper after the Opera,
where the Prince and Mrs. Fitzherbert were; I was introduced to
her. . . . .
    " I dine with Lord Moira to-morrow, and go in the evening with
Lady Charlotte to an assembly at the Countess of Cork's. . . . .
    " I assure you I am six feet high to-day, after discharging my debt
of 70*l.* yesterday, and I have still some copies on my hand to dispose
of for myself. The new edition will soon be out," &c. . . . .
    " I was last night at a ball—everybody was there—two or three of
the princes, the stadtholder, &c. &c. You may imagine the affability of
the Prince of Wales, when his address to me was, ' How do you do,
Moore? I am glad to see you.' . . . .
    " I go on as usual; I am happy, careless, comical,—everything I
could wish: not very rich, nor yet quite poor; all I desire is that
my dear ones at home may be as contented and easy in mind as I
am." . . . .

Such an extraordinary start into popularity and
favour with the London world afforded the young
poet of two-and-twenty a hopeful glance into a lite-

rary career, and he seems accordingly to have
neglected the pursuit of "Grim Gribber"* for the
flowery paths of imaginative composition. In this
mood he gladly avails himself of Lord Moira's kind
hospitality, and spends three or four weeks alone at
Donington, storing his mind by assiduous reading,
for which a fine library supplied ample resources.
Strange to say, during this studious seclusion, Moore
appears to have had but slender longings after the
excitement of the London *salons:* and evidences are
thickly strewn throughout the pages of his Diary
that a taste for rational and even simple occupations
was not wanting when his friends would permit him
its exercise.

Lord Moira was not long in procuring for his
countryman, what was hailed by the latter as a piece
of most gratifying good fortune, the appointment of
Registrar of the Admiralty Court of Bermuda. In
spite of the sneers with which this piece of prefer-
ment has been mentioned, as having been productive
of more injury than benefit to the recipient, Moore
himself never regarded it but with becoming grati-
tude towards his noble patron. He thus writes to
his mother on learning the news of his appointment :—

"September 12, 1803.
"MY DEAREST MOTHER,—I enclose you a note I received from
Merry yesterday, by which you will perceive that everything is in
train for my departure. Nothing could be more lucky. . . . .
"Heaven smiles upon my project, and I see nothing in it now but
hope and happiness. . . . .
"If I did not make a shilling by it, the new character it gives to my
pursuits, the claim it affords me upon Government, the absence I shall

---

* So Jeremy Bentham called the study of Law.

have from all the frippery follies that would hang on my career for ever
in this country,—all these are objects invaluable in themselves, ab-
stracted from the pecuniary. . . . .
   " My dear father should write to Carpenter, and thank him for the
very friendly assistance he has given me; without that assistance the
breeze would be fair in vain for *me*," &c. &c.

After a year's absence, chiefly at his post in the
confessedly delicious island of Bermuda, but making
besides an agreeable tour in the United States and
in Canada, in his way to embark for England, Moore
returned, to the undisguised joy of all his friends.
He was allowed to appoint a deputy in his place at
Bermuda, and began to turn his mind to bookmaking
as a means of earning money.   On Mr. Pitt's death
a new political combination seemed to promise some
advantage to Moore, and in fact, Lord Moira did
obtain the comfortable berth of barrack-master in
Dublin for the father, pending some suitable promo-
tion in favour of the son.   The latter, on the *qui vive*
of expectation, writes to his friend Miss Godfrey
(July, 1806), " Lord Moira has told me that the
commissionership intended for me is to be in Ireland,
and that if there are any such appointments, I am
to have one of them.   Such are my plans, and such
are my hopes.   I wait but for the arrival of the
Edinburgh Review, and then 'a long farewell to all
my greatness.'   London shall never see me act the
farce of gentlemanship in it any more," &c. &c.
   The *Edinburgh Review* arrives, and contains, to
Moore's infinite mortification, a somewhat contemp-
tuous notice of his new production (*Odes and
Epistles*).
   Hence the well-known duel with Jeffrey; or,
rather, the prelude to one, for the belligerent parties

were interrupted by peace officers. And at this point of Moore's history there enters upon the scene one whose constant kindness, whose undeviating attachment, friendly counsel and assistance, must be counted among the most precious possessions of the poet throughout his life. We allude to Mr. Rogers, who stepped in to offer bail for Moore's appearance if called upon. However, the less that is added about this silly affair the better. The would-be combatants became firm friends within a year or two, and when Moore's unfortunate affair of the Bermuda defalcation fell out (in 1818), Jeffrey was among the first to tender his contribution in aid.

We gather from the *Letters* that Moore spent great part of the years 1807-8 at Donington Park, by permission of its usually absent lord, amusing himself, and working at the same time, on Lord-knows-what literary projects. " I read" (he says to Miss Godfrey in a letter dated March, 1807) " much more than I write, and think much more than either." Again, to his mother (April in this year):— " The time flies over me as swift as if I was in the midst of dissipation, which is a tolerable proof that I am armed for either field, for folly or for thought. The family do not talk of coming till June, and if that be the case, I shall not budge."

But few letters are to be found relating to the period from 1807 to 1811 inclusive, which Moore seems to have distributed between Donington Park, Dublin, and lodgings in London. We learn, however, by looking into his *Notices of the Life of Lord Byron*, that it was in the autumn of the year 1811 that he formed the acquaintance of that distinguished

genius. It arose out of a little epistolary skirmish
between them about a supposed imputation upon
Moore's veracity, which ended by an offer from the
noble poet (having meanwhile " explained" it to the
satisfaction of his correspondent) to meet him on
amicable terms. It was at the dinner-table of Mr.
Rogers that Byron and Moore first came together;
the fourth member of the party being Thomas
Campbell, who (as was, indeed, the case with Mr.
Rogers himself) also enjoyed Lord Byron's company
on that day for the first time.

This memorable introduction between Moore and
Byron resulted in an intimacy and an attachment on
both sides, which never lost its charm to the latest
moment of Byron's existence. The rapidity with
which their mutual friendship grew up was somewhat
extraordinary, as Moore himself admits. But it is
not so surprising when we recall the captivations of
Moore's society on the one side, and the admiration
which Byron excited in the breast of " Anacreon"
on the other; opportunities of meeting, too, were
furnished in abundance, since they frequented the
same circles, and were at this period both plunged in
dissipation and folly; that is to say, in 1812, and
again in the London season of 1813, wherein Lord
Byron's fame first rose to its full height (on the
appearance of *Childe Harold*), and the London
world pursued him with the most extravagant
homage and adulation. Moore's *Life of Byron* tells
us, indeed, more of himself at this stage of his history
than is revealed by the present publication, whilst
Lord Byron's fondness for his friend's company is
thus attested : " Moore, the epitome," writes Byron

to another friend, "of all that is exquisite in personal or poetical accomplishments."*

During one of Moore's Irish trips he formed part of that famed theatrical society which figured on the Kilkenny boards; the male actors being amateurs, and the female ones mostly, if not all, professional, having at their head the "star" of the hour, the celebrated Miss O'Neil. Moore acted well, especially in comedy, as we have been informed by one who was fortunate enough to witness those remarkable performances about the year 1810. Among other parts, his personation of Mungo in the agreeable opera of *The Padlock*, was, it is said, eminently happy.

Two sisters, both of them extremely attractive in person, as well as irreproachable in conduct, also formed a part of this "corps;" acting, singing, and ever and anon dancing, to the delight of the audience. With one of these Moore fell desperately in love, and being regarded favourably in return by Miss Elizabeth Dyke, he a few months later united himself with her in marriage, without, it would seem, acquainting his parents with his intention. The ceremony took place at St. Martin's church, in London, in March, 1811, and Mrs. Thomas Moore was introduced to her husband's London friends during the same spring. By these she was cordially received, although there was but one opinion among them as to the imprudence of the step in Moore's notoriously narrow circumstances.

Not to lose his privilege of using Donington library,

* *Life of Byron*, vol. ii. p. 95.

the young couple established themselves in a small cottage at Kegworth, within a few miles of the park, Moore working continually in the library for many months. But towards the end of 1812 all hopes of advancement through the favour of Lord Moira, after many an anxious ebb and flow, finally vanished. That nobleman, whose affairs had become irremediably embarrassed, came to a compromise, as one may say, with his political principles. Not liking to throw them overboard, by joining a government resolutely opposed to Catholic emancipation, he judged it nowise disreputable to him to accept at its hands the Governor-Generalship of India, which he endeavoured to persuade his friends to regard as more a military than a civil appointment. On learning Lord Moira's acceptance of this splendid post, both Moore and his friends appear to have cherished an expectation that his Lordship would propose to take Moore with him to India in some capacity or another, whereby his fortunes might be materially improved. One can hardly comprehend how "friends" such as Miss Godfrey and Lady Donegal, for instance, or, indeed, how Moore himself, could have failed to perceive that Lord Moira, the avowed intimate of the Regent, owing this appointment to the personal will and protection of his royal master, was utterly incapacitated from extending his patronage to the notorious satirist of that master. Without going so far as to ascribe to the Prince any *interposition* in the matter, the simple fact of Moore's having kept up a running fire of ridicule and amused the town with lampoons against the Regent, for many months previous, ought, we should have ima-

gincd, to have been amply sufficient to account for
Lord Moira's conduct.* And when we recall the
peculiarly stinging and personal quality of those
epigrammatic thrusts, we cannot but wonder at Lord
John's mild manner of characterizing them, saying,
in a note referring to the *Twopenny Post-Bag*,
that "they are full of fun and humour, but without
ill-nature!"†

But whatever he felt, or his friends thought, about
this constructive desertion on the part of Lord Moira,
the truth was that Moore found himself thereby

* The following entry, under Dec. 19, 1825, throws some illustration
upon Lord Moira's reasons for the course which he took on this occasion :—"The night before last I received a letter from Crampton,
enclosing one from Shaw (the Lord-Lieutenant's secretary), the purport
of which was, that the Lord-Lieutenant meant to continue my father's
half-pay in the shape of a pension to my sister. Resolved, of course,
to decline this favour, but wrote a letter full of thankfulness to Crampton. Find since that this was done at Crampton's suggestion : *that
Lord Wellesley spoke of the difficulty there was in the way, from the
feelings the King most naturally entertained towards me, and from
himself being the personal friend of the King,* but that, on further consideration, he saw he could do it without any reference to the other
side of the Channel, and out of the pension-fund placed at his disposal
as Lord-Lieutenant." (Vol. v. p. 24.)

† In the preface to Moore's ninth vol. of *Works*, &c., the author
takes pains to disavow having been actuated by any malignant feeling
against the Government of that day ; and, indeed, seeks to excuse
himself by saying he wrote these squibs as party missiles, without
wishing any harm to their subjects ; adding, that the late Lord Holland
also regretted the acrimony with which the Whig party waged their
warfare in 1812 and following years against the Prince, his government, and friends. We are inclined to credit Moore's assertion, that
he himself was visited with something like self-reproach, twenty years
later ; whilst, that Lord Holland, whose generous soul was incapable
of harbouring resentful emotions after the occasion was past, should
have looked back upon former enmities and political conflicts with
unaffected regret, is nowise surprising. But this admission made,
we are bound to say that the poet, as well as the peer, *were* engaged in
cordial combination for party ends, with the most violent of their
political allies.

completely cast adrift upon the waters, shipwrecked and disheartened. Nevertheless, he so far compressed his feelings of disappointment as to speak of his patron's past kindnesses and good offices as " sealing his lips" against complaint. (Vol. i. p. 323.) On quitting England for the East, Lord Moira sent Moore fifteen dozen of his choicest wine as a parting token of regard.

Nothing could be more natural under the circumstances, than that the poor poet should find in Holland House a " harbour of refuge" in his distress. Admitted to familiar intimacy with the distinguished society which habitually met within those time-honoured walls, he became more and more attached to the Whig party, and exerted his talents in its service with renewed vigour: producing at intervals (in the columns of the *Morning Chronicle*) some of the most pungent and humorous satires which political warfare has ever engendered. They were extensively circulated and relished at the time, and are perhaps destined to be remembered as *chefs-d'œuvre* of their kind, after his other works shall be forgotten.

On this passage in Moore's career much censure has been pronounced, even more than the case called for, we think; although it must be confessed, that to drive a trade in scurrility, as Moore did,—to combine party warfare with pecuniary profit,—exposes the individual who does so to a certain measure of moral reprobation. There have not been wanting, however, in our own day, examples of this twofold employment of talent in the persons of well-known characters, who have not thereby been placed under any sort of

ban for their pains. Moore himself felt at times
pricks of conscience at writing lampoons which were
to be paid for, but salved over the sore by reflecting
(and with some justice too) that his "squibs" served
to promote a good cause,—a "set-off" not *always*
within the grasp of a professional newspaper scribe.

We find Mr. and Mrs. Moore in 1813 at another
and more attractive little dwelling, called Mayfield,
near Ashbourne, at which Mr. Rogers pays them a
friendly visit. And now children begin to cluster
about the poor poet's hearth, whilst his wife's health,
being delicate and weak to a deplorable degree, gives
him much uneasiness, as, in fact, it continued to do
throughout the whole of his life. No topic, always
excepting that of Lord Lansdowne (who is the
"Protagonist" of the *Diary*), is half so often re-
curred to as the unhappiness which "Bessy's" bad
health occasions him.

Although intent upon his long-meditated task,
Lalla Rookh, Moore contrived to support himself
and his family by means of newspaper *facetiæ*, humorous satires, "Melodies," and songs (an opera was
even composed), from 1811 to 1817. His connexion
with Richard Power, the musical publisher in the
Strand, was for years his main stay, and a "bill upon
Power," to be taken up or not (as the case might be)
when due, by the efforts of his pen and fancy, was
the regular issue out of every embarrassment (and
they were not few) which occurred.

A letter written in 1812 furnishes a tolerably
clear notion of the position in which Moore's affairs
stood after the downfall of his prospects of advancement :—

"My DEAREST MOTHER,—I have not had an answer from Dalby yet, but am in the same mind about retiring *somewhere*, and I should prefer Donington, both from the society and the library. . . . .

"I don't know whether I told you before (and if I did not, it was my uncertainty about it for some time which prevented me), that the Powers give me between them *five hundred* a year for my music; the agreement is for seven years, and as much longer as I choose to say. . . . . So you see, darling mother! my prospect is by no means an unpromising one, and the only sacrifice I must make is, the giving up London society, which involves me in great expenses, and leaves me no time for the industry that alone would enable me to support them; this I shall do without the least regret." (*Memoirs*, vol. i. p. 274.)

The long-promised work, after prodigious brain-spinning and careful polishing, made its appearance in 1817, fully realizing the expectations entertained of it by the public, for a more complete success has rarely attended an author. *Lalla Rookh* was universally read, admired, and praised. It was dramatized at Berlin, and acted there by the Court itself; was translated into more than one European language, as well as into Persian, and, in short, enjoyed a reign of more than average duration in the realms of literature. The "Letters" teem with testimonies to its extraordinary attraction, and these, too, from superior judges of literary merit. This must appear surprising to the readers of fiction of the present day, for whom the adventures, sorrows, and even loves, of such fanciful and poetical beings would probably yield but slight interest: certainly less than those of the green-grocer or factory-spinner. But thirty-five years necessarily bring altered tastes upon their wing.

In one short year after this imaginative tale came out, Moore writes (under date of March, 1818) to his mother, "They will soon go to press with a seventh edition of *Lalla Rookh*." Messrs Longman paid the author no less than three thousand guineas for the copyright. It was dedicated to Mr. Rogers, to whom, indeed, it was in great measure indebted for its origin. "The subject," writes Moore to his friend Dalton, in 1814, " is one of Rogers's suggesting, and so far I am lucky, for it quite enchants me; and, if what old Dionysius the critic says be true, that it is impossible to write disagreeably upon agreeable sub-jects, I am not without hopes that I shall do some-thing which will not disgrace me."

The sum Moore received for *Lalla Rookh*, though large, did not conduce so much as might have been supposed to his independence. Writing to Mrs. Moore (his mother) in 1817, he says, " I am to draw a thousand pounds for the discharge of my debts, and to leave the other two thousand in their hands (re-ceiving a bond for it) . . . . The annual interest upon this (which is a hundred pounds) my father is to draw upon them for quarterly, and this, I hope, with his half-pay, will make you tolerably comfort-able. By this arrangement, you see I do not touch a sixpence of the money for my own present use . . ."

Ashbourne was now abandoned, and Moore took a cottage at Hornsey. " Living in London is what I do not now like at all," he says to his mother (May, 1817). About this same date he writes to her of a " dinner" he had been at; and adds, " It will amuse you to find that Croker was the person that gave my health. I could not have a better proof of the station which I hold in the public eye than that Croker should claim friendship with me before such men as Peel, the Duke of Cumberland, &c. I was received with very flattering enthusiasm by the meeting . . ."

Having, as he conceived, earned a claim to enjoy a holiday, by the achievement of his task, Moore set off, in company with his friend Mr. Rogers, on a trip to Paris. During the first few years which followed upon the peace of 1815, there was a positive dislocation of English society going on, caused by the eager rush of our countrymen across the Channel. A long privation of the delights of continental travel had whetted the appetite for such enjoyments, and the English moved off in masses, resembling, it might be said, nothing so much as the break up of the " Polar Pack." Moore, like the rest, becomes enchanted with Paris, and writes home, " If I can persuade Bessy to the measure, it is my intention to come and live here for two or three years." However, on his return, which took place a few weeks later, the loss of a child (being the second blow of the kind) checked all projects of a foreign residence. A cottage within a walk of Bowood, shortly after offering an eligible " perch," the mourners removed to that humble yet pleasant home, in which the poet was fated to end his days; the happiest of which, probably, after all, may be said to have been passed whilst master of Sloperton Cottage.

An unlooked-for calamity, which occurred in the following year, clouded over his prospects just as Moore was beginning to see his way to independence and honourable ease.* There was, indeed, one consoling circumstance which lessened the general gloom

* The Bermuda deputy absconded with the proceeds of a ship and cargo deposited in his hands, for which Moore was held answerable.

of his position, namely, the cordial and numerous offers of assistance tendered by generous friends.

But although he was, as might be supposed, wholly unequal to deal with the embarrassments he saw thickening around him, he resolutely declined pecuniary aid, and determined to work out his own redemption by the industrious application of his individual talents. (Vol. ii. p. 85.) The history of this long, though fortunately effectual, struggle, it were superfluous to recapitulate here; but the issue may be stated as having been creditable to Moore's sense of self-respect and integrity of character. The only friend who, as we believe, eventually enjoyed the privilege of contributing to his enfranchisement, was the noble editor of these volumes; the poet permitting him to apply towards the extinction of his Bermuda obligations a sum of 200*l.*, the produce of his lordship's own literary labours.

The *Diary* commences with the month of August, 1818, a few months after the Bermuda misfortune had happened; and gives indications of Moore's being already engaged upon his *Life of Sheridan.* Notwithstanding the uneasy state of mind in which he lived at this time, from apprehensions of a prison hanging over him, such was the indomitable cheerfulness of the man, that he writes to Lady Donegal from his new home (in May, 1818) :—" For nothing but to gratify my poor mother, would I leave just now my sweet, quiet cottage, where, in spite of proctors, deputies, and all other grievances, I am as happy as, I believe, this world will allow anyone to be; and if I could but give the blessing of health to the dear cottager by my side, I would defy the devil and all his works, and Sir William Scott to boot." (Vol. ii. p. 137.)

An inexhaustible flow of spirits, coupled with a boundless elasticity of character and a sanguine temper, proved through life Moore's master-key to happiness. And we shall see as his diary proceeds that few mortals have ever been so largely blest with this "sunshine of the breast." When it is considered how indissolubly men usually connect the possession of wealth with the enjoyment of existence—how we Britons "toil and moil" to acquire it, and what sacrifices we make to escape from comparative poverty—the spectacle of a man "without a shilling to call his own," flourishing in all the pride of aristocratical friendships and culling the choicest pleasures life affords, really becomes almost too much for one's patience. It may be doubted whether, at any one period of his life, Moore knew what it was to be solvent; yet he slept tranquilly, in the persuasion that he carried in his nightcap a talisman, an Aladdin's lamp, which he had only to rub to become rich; at least rich enough for his and "Bessy's" moderate wants. Nay, more, as he mounts to his garret in Bury-street, farthing candle in hand, he can dwell on the recollection of having, half-an-hour before, shone a "star of the first water" in the bright firmament of Almack's, and formed the subject of rivalry between ladies of rank, beauty, and fashion, to obtain the privilege of possessing him as their guest.

We turn now to the reverse of the picture—hard literary labour.

The *Life of Sheridan* consumed the greater portion of the author's working time from 1822 to 1825,

costing him a world of pains, and not a few disagreeable and tiresome researches. Embarrassing doubts
as to the colouring proper to be given to certain
passages, and honest disgust at the generally discreditable cast of the character he had to pourtray, were
frequently present with the biographer, who obviously
felt his task oppressive. Here is an entry of Sept.,
1818 :—" In the garden all day—delicious weather—
at my Sheridan task from ten till three . . . I often
wish Sheridan, Miss Linley, and Matthews at the
devil. This would have been a day for poetry, and
yet thus have I lost all this most poetical summer."
(Vol. ii. p. 173.)

Another entry at this period is worth quoting, as
an example of Moore's power of giving himself up to
present feeling, regardless of harassing contingencies:
—" One day so like another, that there is little by
which to distinguish their features; and these are the
happiest; true cottage days, tranquil and industrious.
. . . . Pursued my task all day in the garden," &c.

The amusing *jeu d'ésprit* which his trip to Paris
gave rise to, *The Fudge Family*, and which had considerable vogue, furnished a welcome addition to " the
supplies." By way of keeping them up, too, he ex-
cogitated another *piquant*, though not perhaps very
felicitous satire, *Tom Cribb's Memorial*, of which
Moore himself felt not, we suspect, particularly proud.
There is in the *Diary* the following sentence:—
" Went on with the slang epistle. It seems profana-
tion to write such buffoonery in the midst of this
glorious sunshine; but, alas! money must be had;
and these trifles bring it soonest and easiest." (Vol.
ii. p. 218.)

The Bermuda matter wearing a serious aspect towards the middle of the following year (1819), Moore judged it prudent to take steps for avoiding legal pursuit. He had some idea of betaking himself to Holyrood House, in expectation of which Sir James Mackintosh writes to him thus:—" You will find in Edinburgh as many friends and admirers as even *you* could find anywhere." But the prospect of going to the Continent, in company with his friend Lord John Russell, came between, and decided him upon passing a few months abroad; the rather as Lord and Lady Lansdowne were contemplating an excursion to Paris, and Moore expected to meet them in that city.

All this came duly to pass: moreover, Lord John and Moore travelled on together across the Alps, as far as Milan, where the friends took leave of each other, not without regret. Moore, full of curiosity to see more of Italy, sets off alone, in a crazy vehicle bought at Milan for the journey, and first wends his way, by Brescia, Padua, &c., to the spot where Lord Byron, who had recently achieved his most striking exploit in the paths of gallantry, was at this time residing near Fusina. To our thinking, this journal of Moore's Italian tour affords the most interesting matter of any in the volumes. We hardly call to mind any autobiography which more entirely reflects the thoughts, feelings, and foibles of the writer, so that one seems to follow him about, with a thoroughly familiar companionship, owing to the rare fidelity and candour with which he records both his proceedings and reflections.

What, indeed, can be more life-like than the details of the few days he spent at Venice, comprehending many hours passed in the company of Lord Byron? We here see these two creative geniuses *en déshabille*, and are enabled to add one more to the evidences we already possess, how completely the imaginative faculty can be cast aside, and the gross reality of human nature suffered to predominate, in the persons of great poets; as, indeed, with great orators, painters, great musical composers, and the like. It would seem that splendid gifts are frequently associated with a lively appetite and capacity for enjoyment, and that the whole Being, ardently constituted in every respect, *must* expend its various forces in turn, in order to maintain its balance of powers.*

The noble Bard at least was aroused from all *his* sentimental musings by the arrival of "Anacreon"; and this to so great a degree as to destroy all the pleasure of the latter in approaching Venice: Lord Byron's rattling ludicrous talk utterly putting to flight the whole illusion and poetic charm of Moore's first gondola voyage. (Vol. iii. p. 24.)

Five days of delightful racketing ensued: Lord Byron, although he could not quit the young "con-tessa" with whom he had but just set up house at La Mira, insisted on Moore's taking up his quarters at his palazzo in Venice, coming in occasionally himself to enjoy his friend's company. They dine together at the "Pellegrino" more than once, go to the theatre, and afterwards adjourn to a sort of public-house, "to drink hot punch; forming a strange contrast to a dirty cobbler, whom we saw in a nice room delicately

---

* The names of Raphael, Michael Angelo, Benvenuto Cellini, Alfieri, Sheridan, Mozart, Charles James Fox, Rossini, Mirabeau, Porson, Burns, &c., may in some sort serve to sustain this hypothesis.

eating ice. Lord B. took me home in his gondola at
two o'clock: a beautiful moonlight, and the stillness
and grandeur of the whole scene, gave a nobler idea
of Venice than I had yet had." (Vol. iii. p. 28.)

The two poets were not alone on these occasions,
for another Englishman, named Scott, whom Lord
Byron had requested to accompany Moore about
Venice, usually formed one of their party. By a
whimsical caprice of fate, this fortunate individual
afterwards became transformed into a Northumbrian
parson, and, to the best of our belief, still lives on
his hill top; talking ever and anon of these Vene-
tian orgies as of passages in a former state of existence.

On leaving Venice, Moore travelled, *viâ* Bologna, to
Florence, where he worked hard at sight-seeing; but,
as everywhere else, diversifying those duties by
theatres and society. Lady Morgan at this period
was in the ascendant; and through her and Lady Burghersh, Moore met all who were worth seeing in
Florence. His susceptibility to sublime emotions is
thus unaffectedly manifested after a visit to the
church of the Annunziata:—" Whether it be my
Popish blood or my poetical feelings, nothing gives me
more delight than the 'pomp and circumstance' of a
mass in so grand a church; accompanied by fine
music, and surrounded by such statuary and such
paintings, it is a most elevating spectacle."

And now the traveller reaches Rome, the ever-
longed-for goal of all sentimental pilgrims. Here
Lady Davy, who, with the Duchess of Devonshire,
appears to have shared the privilege of " lionizing "
distinguished English visitors about the Eternal City,

"undertakes" Moore, whilst Mr. Canning falls to the care of her Grace.

Nothing can be more fresh and entertaining than the record of his stay in Rome. The mingled *naïveté* and instinctive good taste with which he notes his impressions, coupled with his frank disavowal of all pretensions to knowledge in the domain of high art, remind us of the journal of John Bell, the distinguished anatomist of Edinburgh, who brought to the subject something of the same healthy, masculine judgment, unassisted by much previous study. But we must deny ourselves the pleasure of giving extracts from these lively entries, and hasten to get the poet out of Italy again, or we shall have to omit subsequent matters essential to our sketch.

He makes a brief halt at Florence, where he is forced to consent to sit to Bartolini for his bust, partly at the instance of Chantrey, who wants to make one also, and to " let Moore see the difference." Whilst here, Lady Burghersh communicated to him some particulars respecting the Empress Maria Louisa, with whom she had frequent opportunities of intercourse, passing some time with her at her Principality. Maria Louisa, it seems, " loved Napoleon at first; but his *rébutant* manner to her disgusted her at last. Treated her like a mere child; her regency a mere sham; did not know what the papers were she had to sign; never had either message or line from Napoleon after his first abdication, nor until his return from Elba; never hears from him at St. Helena," &c. (Vol. iii. p. 79.)

Moore arrives once more in Paris about the close of the year (1820); and, after a month or two, spent *en*

garçon, is there joined by his wife and family, occupying a kind of "rus in urbe" in a suburb of Paris,
called then "l'Allée des Veuves." During the period
which elapsed between their establishing themselves
here and the autumn of the following year (rather
more than eighteen months), Moore divided his life
between Paris delights and literary composition; but
candour compels us to own that the portion devoted
to dissipation and amusement formed by far the larger
one. Nothing, to be sure, was ever like it! No
wonder he originated his *Epicurean* in 1820, for
he now exhibited a thorough example, in his own
person, of one who makes self-indulgence his main
pursuit.

With every disposition to extenuate Moore's incre-
dible craving for excitement and company, we find it
difficult to excuse this incessant gratification of it,
otherwise than by the stale and well-worn plea of
"great temptations." Most of us have heard of those
to which St. Anthony was exposed, and which we are
bound to believe were overpowering in their nature,
though we never could for the life of us ascertain in
what they consisted. But the Saint could hardly
have known what it was to have Vilamils, Storys,
Cannings, Fieldings, and Washington Irvings, with
Duchesses de Broglie, Lucy Drews, and the like sirens,
all turned loose upon him, with their various seduc-
tions, offering the cup of flattery and convivial allure-
ments (to each of which Moore was so susceptible) to
his acceptance. One cannot answer for what the
result of such trials might have been to a Saint, but
with most men of lively temperament, in the prime of
life and health, dwelling under a delicious sky, re-

sistance would probably have been but ineffectually attempted.

The Paris episode, however, after all that can be urged, leaves a grave feeling of regret that Moore was ever drawn into so mischievous a vortex; though there were occasions when his time was more worthily and profitably invested. His acquaintance with Denon led to some not infructuous studies; whilst the arrival in Paris of his friends Lord and Lady Holland, around whom a certain intellectual atmosphere always gathered, seems to have strung up the Poet's mind to a healthier tone for a season, as the altered character of the "entries" in the Diary amply attests.

It is refreshing, too, amidst the whirl of daily dissipation, to find how tenderly he and Mrs. Moore continue attached to each other :—"25th March, 1821. This day ten years we were married, and though Time has made his usual changes in us both, we are still more like lovers than any married couples of the same standing I am acquainted with. Asked to dine at Rancliffe's, but dined at home alone with Bessy," &c.

Still, if justice were duly done upon mortal sinners, (which it rarely is, except by Baron P. . . .), Moore ought to have been sentenced, on his return to England, to a six months' sojourn in Baker-street or Torrington-square, without ever going to the play, and being only allowed to dine abroad once a month. At the end of such a probation (supposing him to have survived its rigours), the offender might have come out of it, if somewhat less fascinating and agreeable than before, more nearly resembling what, under the meridian of Greenwich at least, it is conceived a man blessed with a wife and children ought to be. But it is far from certain that he would have been permitted to preserve this reformed character by his numerous soliciting friends.

The Bermuda defalcation having been made up, as has been already said, partly through the friendly aid of Lord John Russell (Messrs. Longman advancing the larger portion by way of loan), the poet and his little family leave Paris, and once more "set up their rest" (if this phrase may be employed in connexion with so unquiet a spirit as his) at Sloperton Cottage. Shortly afterwards the *Loves of the Angels* came forth, for which we find the author receiving 700*l.*; and next the *Fables of the Holy Alliance*, so that we can scarcely accuse him of not working diligently at this time. Two visits to London, of a month each, succeed; during which his life was one incessant course of dining out, going to operas and plays, parties, balls, breakfasts, and so forth. His social reputation was now at its zenith, and the fashionable world opened its doors to him as to a privileged being. A delightful tour to Killarney, Cork, and other places in Ireland, in company with his noble friends of Bowood, enlivened the summer, and by the help of a subsequent visit to Mr. Benett, at Pyt-house, and the amusing sale of Mr. Beckford's effects at Fonthill, he managed to get through what remained of the year 1823, in his cottage home, contentedly enough.

Sheridan's *Life* was the task on which, as we have stated above, Moore habitually and earnestly occupied himself; that is to say, when "Phipps" did not happen to "call in his gig;" a form of seduction which, coupled with a vision of a dinner at the inn at Devizes in the background, rarely failed of its effect. It is

beside the purpose of this article to enter upon a
critical notice of Moore's writings; yet it is impossible
to allude to this particular work without observing
that in it he is justly chargeable with misstatement on
more than one point. A desire to drape the memory
of his subject (we must not term him his " hero")
with a plausible interest, had led him to cast un-
merited censure upon many who had once stood in
friendly relationship to Sheridan. It is now pretty
generally understood that the estrangement which
latterly subsisted between the Whig party and
Sheridan was altogether his own work. After the
crowning disgrace of his always discreditable career
—the getting by adroit management a sum of
400*l.* out of the hands of the party in whose keeping it was deposited by the Prince Regent, pending
its application to the procuring a seat in Parliament
for Sheridan—he appears to have felt it impossible to
face his old associates; at least he ever after avoided
the society of the eminent men of the Liberal party.
It never could be said that they neglected him; they
knew nothing, except that he kept aloof from them;
but they were far from deaf to the cry of perishing
decay when at length Sheridan permitted it to reach
their ear.* The misplaced sarcasms, again, with
which Moore seasons his dramatic detail of Sheridan's
closing days—sarcasms levelled at certain noble
persons who did violence to their feelings in attending his funeral rather than give pain to his widow—
though partially retracted in his preface to the fifth

---

* Both the Duke of Bedford and Mr. Canning, Moore afterwards
affirms (in his *Diary*), sent to Sheridan considerable sums within a
year of his death.

edition, must be regarded as a poor device, resorted to by way of turning the reader's attention from the character of the man, and fastening it upon the condition to which he was reduced by the imputed inconstancy of his " great" friends.

There have been, perhaps, few examples of so prodigious an abuse of the disposition in human nature to tolerate vices and defective moral feeling, in behalf of brilliant talents, as Sheridan's character and conduct furnished. That there should be a limit, beyond which an admiring sympathy could not secure even him against disapprobation and contempt, ought to be subject for gratulation, not for querulous complaint. But a biographer, like a barrister, feels bound, we presume, to present the best case he can for his client; and this must be Moore's apology.* The statement concerning the Prince's indifference was not less unfounded; for it has been satisfactorily shown that George IV. entertained, for this pitiable wreck of a once cherished associate, sentiments more kindly than his conduct deserved; and further, that he would gladly have mitigated by his bounty the sufferings he compassionated.

The book we are speaking of, with all its faults, had also great merits, and was (like everything Moore wrote, indeed) eagerly welcomed on its appearance in the autumn of 1825.

The first edition sold rapidly, and Moore felt him-

---

* In confirmation of this view of the matter, we may quote a passage from a book recently published:—" On my complimenting Moore," says Sir Robert Heron, " on his impartiality in the *Life of Sheridan*, he told me he regretted having suppressed many facts, and represented his character much too favourably." (*Notes*, 2nd ed. 1851, p. 254.)

I

self relieved of a load of obligation, for the publishers were generous enough to superadd the sum of 300*l.* to the original price of the copyright, in consequence of the extensive sale which it met with at the very outset. A tribute of admiration from Lord John Russell, on reading it, is thus couched:—

"I am all astonishment at the extent of your knowledge, the sound-ness of your political views, and the skill with which you contrive to keep clear of tiresomeness, when the subject seems to invite it . . . . .

"I dined at Wimbledon yesterday, and all the Spencers sang chorus in praise of your book." (Vol. iv. p. 323.)

When we run our eye over the entries in Moore's *Diary*, we are apt to take comparatively little heed of those which relate purely to work. Yet they really are numerous, though a fortnight is commonly in-cluded in a line; such as "3rd to 17th. At work;" "Rest of this month hard at work." Hence we are unconsciously led to regard the labour as nothing in the scale, when weighed against the indulgence of the gregarious propensity. The *Diary*, in fact, taken in its general character, might bear to be prefaced by an inscription which we remember to have read upon a sun-dial near Padua, "Horas non numero nisi serenas."

As a holiday, after being so hard at work, was indis-pensable, Moore rushes off to Scotland, and pays a visit to Sir Walter Scott at Abbotsford, a brief account of which is among the pleasantest passages in the book. Scott's conversation about his own productions is curious, showing that he rather stumbled upon his talent than cultivated it originally. " Had begun *Waverley* long before, and then thrown it by, until having occasion for some money (to help his brother,

I think), he bethought himself of it, but could not find the MS." (Vol. iv. p. 333.) When he *did*, "made 3000*l.* by *Waverley*."

Moore goes to the theatre (need we say?) at Edinburgh, of which his brother-in-law, Murray, was manager. Jeffrey, Sir Walter, and Mr. Thomson are there with him. The enthusiasm displayed by the audience is quite extravagant (for us Scotchmen), and delights Sir Walter, who exclaims, " This is quite right. I am glad my countrymen have returned the compliment for me."

Moore also visits Mr. Jeffrey at Craigcrook. On the morrow of his arrival, he writes :—

"After breakfast, sitting with Jeffrey in his beautiful little Gothic study, he told me at much length his opinion of my *Life of Sheridan.* Thinks it a work of great importance to my fame . . . . . ' Here,' (said Jeffrey) ' is a convincing proof that you can think and reason solidly and manfully, and treat the gravest and most important subjects in a manner worthy of them . . . . . I am of opinion that you have given us the only clear, fair, and manly account of the public transactions of the last fifty years that we possess.' " (Vol. v. p. 7.)

On his return from Scotland, Moore is called to Dublin by the illness of his father, who expires shortly subsequent to his son's arrival. Through the kindness of Messrs. Longman, who, although Moore is so heavily in debt towards the firm, permit him to draw upon them, he discharges all outstanding obligations, defrays expenses of his father's funeral, and supports his mother with all the comforts and attentions the occasion calls for. The Lord-Lieutenant proposes to arrange that the half-pay enjoyed by the late Mr. Moore should be continued, under the form of pension, to his daughter. Moore peremptorily declines the offer.

"All this is very kind and liberal of Lord Wellesley; and God knows how useful such an aid would be, as God alone knows how I am to support all the burthens now heaped upon me; but I *could not* accept such a favour." (Vol. v. p. 25.)

It would seem that during the year 1826, Moore's talent for facetious and satirical verse-making was placed at the service of the *Times* newspaper, and, as has ever been the practice with that Journal, was amply remunerated. In fact, looking on the one hand at the large sums realized by everything he produced, and on the other at the very modest scale on which his *ménage* was conducted, together with the well-attested frugality and self-denial of his excellent partner, we have found it difficult to explain the state of chronic insolvency in which Moore obviously lived. His children were, it is true, always ailing, his wife never well. But then their medical attendant, Dr. Brabant of Devizes, having a cordial sympathy for genius and virtue in difficulties, would accept no fees. Moore himself seemed to have had no expensive habits, except that he never refused himself a hack post-chaise; that luxury which Dr. Johnson so feelingly prized! His "junketings" in London were usually enjoyed at the cost of others, and his garret to sleep in seems to have constituted almost his only expense. The solution must lie in the fact of his having twice had to overtake a considerable sum by his unassisted exertions; his own maintenance and that of his parents needing to be provided at the same time.

The history of the gift, sale, and ultimate destruction of Lord Byron's *Memoirs* has been so much canvassed, and versions so various have circulated concerning Moore's conduct on the occasion, that we are thankful to find much circumstantial information to guide us to a safe conclusion, though the *Diary* contains only a part of what Moore left in elucidation of this complex affair. The rest has been withheld by the noble editor, and we are bound to say without, as far as we can discover, satisfactory reasons for its suppression. Enough nevertheless remains wherewith to frame an accurate summary of this case—an indispensable item in a retrospective sketch of the Poet's life.

The *Memoirs* were given to him, without reserve, as without directions, by Lord Byron; but were unquestionably intended partly as a justification of himself, and partly as a means of enriching his friend. Moore, pressed for money (as usual), made over the MSS. to Mr. Murray for the sum of 2000 guineas. He subsequently modified the transaction by ordering a clause to be inserted in the deed, by which he, Moore, should have the option of redeeming the *Memoirs* within three months of Lord Byron's death.

When that unlooked-for event occurred, in 1824, the family and personal friends of the deceased nobleman urgently sought to possess themselves of the manuscript, with a view to its destruction. Moore, conceiving that in yielding it up for that purpose he should be defeating the intentions and wishes of his friend, demurs to the request. He pleads earnestly for its publication, proposing to suppress all matter calculated either to wound the feelings of living persons, or to shock public taste. But the Byron family, Mrs. Leigh, Sir John Hobhouse, and Mr. Wilmot Horton, are inexorable; and so much im-

portunity is addressed both to Moore and Mr.
Murray, by various distinguished parties, that they
at length consent to place the *Memoirs* in the
hands of Mr. Horton and Colonel Doyle, as the
representatives of Mrs. Leigh; who forthwith
commit the same to the flames at Mr. Murray's
house.

Mr. Murray, of course, stipulates to be repaid his
money with lawful interest, which is accordingly done,
by a draft drawn by Moore on Mr. Rogers.* (Vol. v.
p. 224.) Much persuasion is used to induce Moore
to accept of compensation at the hands of the Byron
family—even his most valued friends, such as Lord
and Lady Lansdowne, Mr. Luttrell, Lord John
Russell, with Mr. Rogers and his sister, concur in
the opinion that he ought to do so. Moore's high
sense of self-respect is, however, a match for all, and
he steadily refuses. Indeed, for some time after the
destruction of the *Memoirs*, his mind is uneasy, lest
he should have committed an act of constructive dis-
loyalty towards his departed friend and benefactor.
Ultimately he learns from Sir John Hobhouse that
Lord Byron, when remonstrated with by himself as
to the indiscretion of placing such a MS. out of his
own control, had replied, " that he regretted having
done so, and that delicacy towards Moore alone
deterred him from reclaiming it;" on this Moore is
reassured, and whilst regretting the loss to the world,
rests satisfied with the course which he had himself

---

* This loan, or accommodation, on the part of Mr. Rogers, was
subsequently repaid out of the profits of *The Loves of the Angels*
and *Fables of the Holy Alliance*. (See Preface to vol. viii. of
Works.)

pursued. It has been objected, that at the time
Moore made this reluctant cession, the *Memoirs* were,
strictly speaking, the property of Mr. Murray, and
that Moore had consequently no claim to merit in
making the sacrifice; the rather, as he foresaw that a
round sum might hereafter be gained by his becoming Lord Byron's biographer, on a new footing.
The truth is that, by the negligence of the draughts-
man or the attorney, the clause providing for the
redemption of the MSS. by Moore was *not* inserted
in the body of the deed, and thus the property
formally remained with the bookseller. But nobody
was cognisant of this fact till after the deed was
virtually cancelled by the destruction of the *Memoirs;*
so that Moore's proceeding is entitled to whatever
credit may be thought to attach to his resigning his
share in them. At the same time, Mr. Murray must
be held to have acted with perfect good faith, and
strictly business-like correctness, throughout the
affair.*

A contemporary remarks on Moore's cupidity in
his dealings, and on this feature of his character a
brief commentary seems called for. "The warmest
admirer of Moore's talents, we apprehend, cannot
dissemble from himself that the main business of his
life was to 'keep the wolf from the door.' The

* There occurs at page 315 of vol. iii. the following passage, which
is worth quoting in reference to the foregoing transaction :—

"April, 1822. Ought to have mentioned that soon after my arrival
I spoke to Murray upon the subject of Lord B.'s *Memoirs;* of my wish
to redeem them, and cancel the deed of sale, which Murray acceded to
with the best grace imaginable. Accordingly there is an agreement
making out, by which I become *his debtor* for 2000 guineas, leaving the
MSS. in his hands as a security, till I am able to pay it I
know I shall feel the happier when rid of the bargain."

steady eye which he kept upon every transaction connected with literary profit, it would be distasteful to observe, unless we bore in mind the anxieties which he habitually endured respecting his daily subsistence. One cannot deny that he read but to reproduce—that he listened but to borrow—that he caught at 'tunes' to work up into 'melodies'—that he sang in drawing-rooms to give circulation to his wares. Nay, he even ransacks his Bible, in church, for dramatic subjects, to weave into musical expression; (finding one too, in Jeremiah, of all authors!) in short, the fact is clear that Moore's thoughts mainly alternated between his amusements and the shop."

But the public ought by this time to have learnt (if it ever cared to learn anything except what suited its convenience), that the greater portion of the labours of literary men, even some of the highest productions of Genius, have been extorted from their authors by the pressure of necessity.

It would appear invidious to run over the long catalogue of gifted writers from whose pen and brain little would ever have descended to us but for the temptation offered by money gains; large or small as the case might be. The class of men who are mentally qualified to produce, are commonly more disposed to enjoy than to work, and hence it is that, with a few remarkable exceptions, we owe the great mass of our literature to the necessitous student. Even our greatest poet of the century, Lord Byron, confessed that but for the sake of gaining money *he* should be too lazy to write poetry requiring effort. No, the rare endowments which are fitted to contribute

to the delight of our fellow men are seldom brought
forward by any inducements except those of profit;
nor, in fact, will their possessors be persuaded to go
through the severe probation needed in order to shine
in any sphere of art, if blessed with fortune and the
means of living at ease.

The following extracts will afford a sample of the
familiar conversation of Bowood, where Moore was now
continually a guest:—

"1824. Oct. 23rd. Dined at Bowood: company, Grosetts and
Clutterbucks, Mrs. Clutterbuck looking very pretty. Clutterbuck's
story of the old lady (his aunt) excellent. Being very nervous, she
told Sir W. Farquhar she thought Bath would do her good. 'It's very
odd,' says Sir W., 'but that's the very thing I was going to recommend to you. I will write the particulars of your case to a very
clever man there, in whose hands you will be well taken care of.' The
lady, furnished with the letter, sets off, and on arriving at Newbury,
feeling, as usual, very nervous, she said to her confidant, 'Long as Sir
Walter has attended me, he has never explained to me what ails me.
I have a great mind to open his letter and see what he has stated of
my case to the Bath physician.' In vain her friend represented to her
the breach of confidence this would be. She opened the letter, and read,
'Dear Davis, keep the old lady three weeks, and send her back again.'"

"1825. Jan. 3rd. Walked over to Bowood: company, Mackintosh
and his daughter, Mr. and Mrs. Vernon Smith and Lewson Smith.
. . . . . A good deal of conversation about Burke in the evening.
Mentioned his address to the British colonists in North America.
'Armed as you are, we embrace you as our friends and as our brothers,
by the best and dearest ties of relation.' The tone of the other parts,
however, is, I find, moderate enough. Burke was of opinion that
Hume, if he had been alive, would have taken the side of the French
Revolution. Dugald Stewart thinks the same. The grand part of
Burke's life was between 1772 and the end of the American war;
afterwards presumed upon his fame and let his imagination run away
with him. Lord Charlemont said that Burke was a Whig upon Tory
principles. Fox said it was lucky that Burke and Windham took the
side against the French Revolution, as they would have got hanged on
the other. Windham's speech on Curwen's motion for Reform—an
ingenious defence of parliamentary corruption—like the pleading of a
sophist. Burke gave the substance of the India Bill, and Pigot drew
it up."

"1833. Feb. 6th. An excellent *mot* of somebody to Fontenelle, on the latter saying that he flattered himself he had a good heart,—'Yes, my dear Fontenelle, you have as good a heart as can be made out of brains.'

"In talking with Hallam afterwards, I put it to him why it was that this short way of expressing truths did not do with the world, often as it had been tried, even Rochefoucauld being kept alive chiefly by his ill-nature? There was in this one saying to Fontenelle all that I myself had expended many pages on in my *Life of Byron*, endeavouring to bring it out clearly; namely, the great difference there is between that sort of sensibility which is lighted up in the heads and imagination of men of genius, and the genuine natural *sensibility* whose seat is in the heart. Even now in thus explaining my meaning, how many superfluous words have I made use of? Talking of the Brahmins being such good chess-players (nobody, it seems, can stand before them at the game), Mrs. Hastings' *naïveté* was mentioned, in saying, 'Well, people talk a good deal about the Brahmins playing well, but I assure you Mr. Hastings, who is very fond of chess, constantly plays those who come to the Government House, and always beats them.'"

For three editions of the *Epicurean* (which first came out in 1827), Messrs. Longman, we find, credited the author 700*l.* In 1828 Mr. Murray finally concludes a bargain with him to write a *Life of Lord Byron*, for which he is to receive 4000 guineas. Moore begins this in February, after having paid a visit to Newstead Abbey, and to Colwich, the residence of Mrs. Musters (formerly Miss Chaworth), with whom he conversed respecting Byron, as he has related in the *Life*. The usual gaddings, excursions, and pleasure-hunting characterise these years, the record of which is, however, interspersed with amusing notes of conversations, held chiefly at Holland House and Bowood; often valuable, though brief, from the light they shed upon transactions regarding which public channels of information have been of necessity imperfect ones. Many little touches reveal the state of political parties, too, in a way no out-of-doors organ could possibly do. The ill-assorted combinations of 1826-27-28, which succeeded on the break-up of Tory ascendancy, are curiously commented upon; and some good stories also find a place in the *Diary*.

The sixth volume opens with 1829, and the death of his amiable daughter Anastasia, which plunged both her fond parents into deep affliction. The notices of the *Life of Byron* came out in the following year, after which Moore set to work to collect materials for that of Lord Edward Fitzgerald; in fact, he seems to have been more than commonly industrious about this time. He and his wife made a journey to Ireland in August, mainly on this errand, but also to visit Moore's mother once more. At a great meeting of from two to three thousand people, Moore being induced to make a speech on the subject of the late French Revolution of "the three days" (Bessy present among the auditors), it proved one of the happiest efforts in oratory that he ever essayed.

"From this on to the end my display was most successful, and the consciousness that every word *told* on my auditory, reacted upon me with a degree of excitement which made me feel capable of *anything*. The shouts, the applause, the waving of hats, &c., after I had finished, lasted for some minutes. I heard Sheil, too, as I concluded, say, with much warmth, 'he is a most beautiful speaker!'" (Vol. vi. p. 140.)

The enthusiasm felt for Moore by his countrymen is, indeed, universal, and proclaimed; and many of his admirers endeavoured to persuade him to try for a seat in Parliament for some Irish constituency. This temptation, which is renewed after his return to Sloperton, he steadily resists (although his inclination would have strongly urged him to accept the offer), on the ground of his utter want of fortune.

Of " adventures" there are, properly speaking, none
in the whole six volumes; Moore's movements being
chiefly from Devizes to Bath, from Bath to Farley,
from Farley to Laycock, from Laycock to Bowood, and
so on,—much after the style of Major Sturgeon's
campaigns. But although his person revolved in a
limited orbit, his mental activity, and frequent unre-
served commerce with the class in whose hands the
government of the nation was now vested, caused him
to feel no want of more enlarged experience of the
world. Indeed the privilege which he enjoyed, of
intimate and habitual intercourse with the Marquis of
Lansdowne, was of itself an equivalent, or more than
an equivalent, for a wide range of ordinary social
advantages.

Moore's political feelings partook all through life of
the early impressions derived from his boyish connexion with certain friends who were forward in the
organization of Irish resistance to the Government in
1795-96. Though a mere youth, his ardent attachment to Ireland led him to yield the fullest sympathy
to those efforts, and from that period downwards he
never spoke or wrote about his native country save in
a strain of mournful resentment. He was himself,
whilst a college student, subjected to an examination
before the formidable Chancellor Fitzgibbon, and displayed a self-possession, we might even say an heroic
fidelity to his associates, highly praiseworthy in one
so young. The scene is related in the first vol. of
the present publication, and repeated by Moore in
the preface to his *Works* in ten vols. 1840. His
Letters of Captain Rock likewise displayed his
views and feelings on Irish politics. But although he

held opinions of a strongly democratic cast, he seems to have been less cordial in his wishes for reform in Parliament in 1831-32 than might have been expected. This is to be ascribed partly, as he confesses, to his having reached the age of fifty before the Reform movement became effectual, and partly to his comparatively slender interest in English politics, with which he rarely meddled, whilst with Irish affairs he maintained a constant sympathy. (See his Letter to Electors of Limerick, vol. iv. p. 305.) The "wrongs of Ireland" lay at the bottom of his heart, and tinged his views on most public questions. It is honourable both to himself and to his noble associates, that Moore's extreme opinions, though openly maintained and ably defended, never interrupted the friendly relations in which he lived with the leading statesmen of the Liberal party. His out-spoken objections to the course pursued by the Whig Government, after 1831, towards Ireland, would infallibly have offended any minister but the nobleman who bore him a friendship so warm as to be proof against the shocks of dissent when coming from his privileged neighbour.

A recent newspaper criticism has laboured to fasten upon Moore the imputation of having " dangled upon the great;"—one more groundless could scarcely be adduced. " The great" ran after Moore, not he after the great. If there be one fact more abundantly attested than another by the *Diary* it is this. And among the rare instincts which his nature revealed was the perception of that nice medium between familiarity and humility of demeanour, which he so admirably hit in his intercourse with the nobility of both sexes. He was treated like a spoiled child; yet he conducted himself like a well-bred man. He might assuredly feel a pride in reflecting that he could reckon among his intimate friends the names of Walter Scott, Samuel Rogers, Crabbe, Bowles, Sydney Smith, Lord Byron, Francis Jeffrey, Lord Holland, Luttrell, Lord John Russell, Lord and Lady Lansdowne, with those of other eminent and estimable persons of both sexes; and he did feel it. But no one, we venture to affirm, could charge Moore with presuming upon the favour with which they regarded him. What he seems to be most severely reproached with is, having been inwardly elated, flattered,—made happy, in short, by it. On this manner of construing the revelations comprised in these volumes, we will, even at the risk of appearing sermonic and tedious, venture to offer some remarks.

The general reader of memoirs seems to require before all things, the gratification of his curiosity. But one would think that, this primary object being attained, the next would be to acquire an accurate knowledge of the inward mind and thoughts of the author, particularly if he be a person of eminent and renowned character; and so it is in a measure, for everybody takes pleasure in diving into the soul of genius, and prying into the laboratory of a poet's fancy. If, however, the writer record for posthumous publication feelings which he would or ought to have dissembled during life, such is the inveterate, the all-puissant influence of conventional habits, that, instead of thanking him for his candour and veracity, the public positively blame him for not disguising his genuine emotions, for not counterfeiting to pos-

terity indifference both to high reputation and to
homage from his fellow-creatures. The very quality
which is understood to bestow a value on autobiography
—viz., the presenting the writer's real mind and
thoughts to the reader,—is lost sight of in the abhor-
rence which the public entertain for what they term
"ridiculous personal vanity!" They shrink from
everything which is not disguised and "dressed up,"
—from the real mind, as from the naked body. The
public have, indeed, so long and peremptorily prohi-
bited all external signs of self-satisfaction, or self-love,
that at length they have come to believe in the Latin
apophthegm, that what does *not appear*, does not
exist; and thus, when an idol is caught in the fact,
through his private closet avowals, they regard him
as a rare instance of depraved morals, and fall to
abusing him as such. For in our artificial society,
everything is made to give way to conventional forms
and usages, and neither mind nor matter dare wander
beyond the prescribed despotic circle.

To be sure, if a writer of autobiography has died in
want and misery, if *his* vanity have been never so misplaced, offensive, or egregious, we can afford to be
more indulgent; the mortification and humiliation he
has endured have the effect of neutralizing the ascetic
element within us, and we feel comforted, as it were, by
the spectacle of expiatory justice. But let not the successful or *happy* man lift the veil, and reveal the
pleasure with which a life of labour and poverty was
sweetened when he was praised, flattered, and loved
by his contemporaries. In vain would his apologists
plead that vanity, under profuse homage, is at once
natural, just, and innocuous. Our excellent commu-

nity seldom travel so far as the domain of ethics for their standard of judgment. They take a shorter cut; *what they dislike* is odious and reprehensible, and the converse,—and from this there is no appeal.

A great deal has been said, also, respecting Moore's neglect of his domestic hearth; so much, indeed, that it would be unbecoming, in presenting even this slender portraiture of the man, to pass over such a feature in silence. He certainly enjoyed mingling with his friends and acquaintance when his work was done—sometimes, indeed, when it was not done—and it is not disguised in the pages before us that Mrs. Moore felt his frequent absences from home. On the other hand, it should be borne in mind that, whereas cerebral labour, especially that of the inventive faculty, exhausts the individual more than any other occupation, so it is of the last importance to him to seek occasional, even frequent, renovation by some external agency. The spirit-stirring action of pleasant and distinguished society, the expansion of his peculiarly happy talent for conversation, the exercise of his almost magical gift of touching the feelings by musical expression*—all these recreated the man, and replenished the springs of those powers by means of which the poor *poet* was expected to produce his page of the morrow. The physician, the lawyer, the minister, the sharebroker, the soldier, and others, necessarily pass their lives *from* home, a return to

---

* No person was ever gifted with a more perfect organization for music than the deceased Irish bard. Had he received a thoroughly sound musical education, it is difficult to say whether he might not have produced some great composition as gorgeous in melody and harmony as the Eastern imagery of his *Lalla Rookh.*—ELLA, *Musical Sketches,* 1853.

which constitutes a welcome change and relief. But
the laborious man of letters spends his working hours
alone, in silence within his own four walls; when the
sand of his intellectual hourglass has run out, he
needs variety, and the reviving influences afforded by
social and festive pleasures. If the Irish temperament happen to be superadded, the want is, by so
much, intensified. Again, the strongest endeavours
were used to prevail on Mrs. Moore to accompany her
husband into the world; to Bowood especially, the
house at which he was the most frequently himself a
guest, Moore often strove to persuade her to accept
Lord and Lady Lansdowne's many cordial invitations,
but to little purpose. We cannot wonder at this.
Mrs. Moore wanted the inclination to mix in the
society of persons with whom she had no familiar
acquaintance, and she was too proud (Moore says) to
be at her ease with such as she knew and felt to be
her superiors in birth and education, though not in
personal beauty or native talent. And farther, she
could afford neither fine clothes nor carriage; she
was the habitual nurse-mother to sickly children,
whilst her own health gave her but too frequent cause
for failing her social engagements. Thus Moore must
have gone into company without her or stayed by
her side; an alternative which, as a rule of conduct,
both he and Mrs. Moore knew and felt to be far from
advantageous to either, however glad he might feel
to fly back to it when the needful stimulus was over.
Moore might be said to belong to a numerous "pro-
prietary," among whom his wife unquestionably held
the greatest number of "shares." But Mrs. Moore
had far too much sense and feeling to wish or expect

K

to monopolise so gifted, so mercurial a being. She was, nevertheless, throughout life, the *chief* object of his tender, admiring affection, as well as of his grateful esteem; and this must have consoled her (as it has doubtless done other women, also united to men of genius) for not being the whole and *sole* occupant of a large, impressionable heart, and a restless imagination.

The duties of editorship of these volumes have been apparently limited by Lord John Russell to the handing over the manuscript to the printer (after making a tolerably free, though insufficient use, we think, of the scissors), and the composing a friendly introduction to the first and sixth volumes. What additional value might have been imparted to the book by judicious commentary and interpretation, we will not inquire too curiously; since, if a man will have a minister of the Crown, and nothing less, for his executor, it is not to be expected that his " remains" should be so expertly, or so carefully, prepared for publication as by a practised literary hand.

But it has been remarked, and we think justly, that some key ought to have been furnished to the numerous acquaintances in whose society Moore passed so much of his time in the country. It would have been easy to append, in foot-notes or otherwise, a slight indication of their personal history, and their provincial standing and connexion, and thus have enabled us to follow with greater interest the records of many happy days spent among "Houltons," " Fieldings," " Douglasses," " Smiths," " Phipps's," " Storys," and others, whose names figure so prominently in the *Diary.* Whilst neglecting to supply useful information such as this, the noble editor thought fit to insert a note which has had the effect of involving him in an acrimonious correspondence with an eminent literary character, wherein, we regret to own, the latter seems to us to have the advantage over his Lordship.

The "note" in question was, in truth, a gratuitous personal sarcasm against Mr. Croker: and the manner in which this has been repelled certainly leaves both Lord John and his friend Thomas Moore on lower ground than it is at all agreeable to us to see them occupy.

It would also have been a useful exercise of editorial industry, had Lord John afforded us some explanation respecting Moore's sudden change of tone towards the Regent: passing from the relation of almost familiar intimacy to an attitude of hostility. Moore gives none himself, whilst his disappointment in not going to India with Lord Moira occurred, not before, but after, he had assailed the Regent with such felicitous acerbity.

Still, notwithstanding these deficiencies, the book, as it stands, will be gladly accepted as a microcosm of a social world concerning which tradition is becoming daily less and less distinct, and whose parallel, it is probable, will never be reproduced; whilst those individuals who are yet living, and who took part in it, will find many a delightful reminiscence of bygone days preserved in the pages of one of their most brilliant, as well as most popular, contemporaries. Some excellently engraved "illustrations" confer a welcome additional attraction on the work.

SOME ACCOUNT

OF

THE HAMLET

OF

EAST BURNHAM:

Co. Bucks.

BY A LATE RESIDENT.

PREFACE.

THE following pages contain what to many readers may appear prosaic and tedious details of a purely local character. To some others they will offer an interest, as affording a glance into the inner relations which subsist between the humbler members of the rural population, and the owners of the land which *they* till. In the picture I have endeavoured to present of the hamlet in question, a general sketch of the past and present condition of the peasantry will be found, together with a view of the general bearings of the relation between rich and poor, and the effects of one or other course of conduct on the part of the former class; I trust with no invidious or prejudiced statements, or partial colouring. Entertaining a deep interest in the welfare of the working people, I have studied their modes of feeling with attention; and feel persuaded that the best forms of beneficence consist in encouraging domestic virtues and whole-some instincts among them, and in fortifying their respect for those who of necessity control their collective social destiny. In connexion with these views, I have thought it not an idle employment to trace the mutations of ownership, and the personal history of the place, as well as to depict the moral and social aspects of an obscure district of my county.* Let me hope that some of those who may honour my little work with a perusal, will learn from it to appreciate the utility, if not the duty, of attending to

" The short and simple annals of the poor."

H. G.

Nov. 1858.

---

* I say advisedly " my county," for my ancestors belonged to it two centuries since, residing at Middle Claydon and Steeple Claydon, Bucks, up to the beginning of the present century.

SOME ACCOUNT

OF

THE HAMLET OF EAST BURNHAM.

The Hamlet of East Burnham is situated about
half-way between Beaconsfield on the north and
Slough on the south. The land and houses—the
far larger portion, at least—were for centuries the
property of one family, the last male member of which
died at East Burnham as long ago as the year 1810.
Up to a recent period few visitors ever wandered into
this hamlet, unless it were now and then a sportsman.
The old forest, called "Burnham Beeches," composed
chiefly of aged and hollow-trunked trees, forms a
part of the Manor of "Allards" (otherwise East
Burnham), in which the scattered hamlet is situated,
and a wild open heath, called East Burnham Common,
adjoins the same. But a small number of persons
seem to have known anything of this picturesque
tract, although the poet Gray speaks of it in his
letters;* the road communicating between Windsor
and Beaconsfield—never much travelled—passing at

* Mr. Gray used often to ramble into this forest from Stoke
Poges, and compose poetry therein. Some of the lines in his
Elegy may fairly be taken as descriptive of the scenery of this
spot.

some distance from it; but after the year 1840, when
the railroad came into use, the neighbourhood became
somewhat more resorted to, and the "Burnham
Beeches," hitherto almost a sylvan solitude, gradually
became the favourite resort of summer pleasure-
parties from the surrounding districts.   Tourists and
book-makers likewise began to talk of this singular
and picturesque spot, so that now there probably are
few persons residing within twenty miles of the
"Burnham Beeches" who have not either visited or
heard of them.   The ancient tradition of the locality
has it, that the Beeches were *pollarded* by the Parliament army, which encamped here during the civil
wars of Charles I.   That they ever were pollarded
at all has, however, been doubted.   Be this as it may,
the appearance of the trees is precisely such as would
be presented had they been subjected to that process
in the year 1645.   A person who has resided at East
Burnham for the last twenty years, or thereabouts,
has taken the trouble to collect (from living testimony
chiefly) the following particulars relating to this
sequestered region.

Up to the middle of the last century, the possessors
of the estates of Huntercombe and East Burnham
habitually resided at the ancestral mansion known as
Huntercombe House, situate a short distance from
Burnham on the old London and Bath road; the last
male representative of the Eyre family who lived
there being Mr. Thomas Eyre, who was born, it would
appear, about the year 1661.   This gentleman had
two sons, besides daughters.   For his second son,
Charles, he obtained the place of secondary in his
Majesty's Exchequer, a lucrative post at that time.

The eldest son lived with his father. Mr. Charles
Eyre, the secondary, bought a house at East Burnham, with some land round it, situated in the centre
of his father's estate, which estate he was one day
destined, though the younger son, to inherit. At
this house he established his *ménage*, which comprised within it a pretty housekeeper of the name of
Green (a native of Stoke, hard by), by whom he had
two children, both girls. He lived in good style,
received his male acquaintance there hospitably,
and was considered to be what was called a "man
of pleasure." It is related that the elder brother
of this Mr. Charles Eyre was, or pretended to be,
scandalized at his brother's free way of life, and was
wont to say "that he would take a wife himself, if
only to get an heir who should keep Charles out of
the estate." Nevertheless, he died a bachelor, and
Mr. Charles Eyre accordingly succeeded to these
ancient possessions, about the year 1745. But he
let the house at Huntercombe, and continued to live
at his own house at East Burnham, his eldest daughter,
Elizabeth, residing with him (bearing his name)
until his death, at the ripe age of eighty, in 1786.
She used to assist him in his business as "Secondary,"
the greater part of which he transacted in the country;
boxes of papers, coins, tallies, &c., being sent from
the Exchequer to East Burnham by official messengers for that purpose. His youngest daughter,
Arabella, was sought in marriage about the year
1770 by a Captain John Popple, a young gentleman
in the regular army, without any fortune : the captain
probably calculating on that deficiency being supplied
by his wife's expected inheritance. He continued

in the army, living in quarters, accompanied by his
wife, on a very small income, up to the death of Mr.
Eyre, when that gentleman leaving his daughters
each a comfortable fortune, Captain Popple quitted
the service, and went to live at a place called Bury
Hill, in Hertfordshire.

Mr. Charles Eyre dying without legitimate issue,
the paternal estate, manors, &c., passed to his nephew,
a Captain Sayer, the son of one of his sisters, who had
married a Mr. Sayer, of London, drysalter. This
gentleman accordingly came to reside on his estate;
but he could not well live where Mr. Eyre had done,
seeing that Mr. Eyre had bequeathed that house to
his eldest daughter as part of her inheritance: East
Burnham House, and about forty acres of land adjacent, not forming any portion of the Eyre estate.
Captain Sayer took up his abode in a small house (at
that time almost a cottage), pertaining to the Eyre
estate, adding a few rooms to make it suitable for a
gentleman to occupy. There was another house
belonging to himself, called the "Manor House," of
much better appearance, also situate in East Burnham : but this was sadly out of repair, and decayed,
so that Captain Sayer preferred to live in the house
above mentioned, situated on the verge of the common.
Here he kept a pack of harriers, and lived like a
gentleman, though from having delicate health he
went rarely abroad. His hounds were maintained
more for his country neighbours' amusement than
his own, since he, poor man! was all but blind, and
could take therefore very little share in any kind of
sport.

Mr. Sayer had been in the army, and had received

a bullet wound at the battle of Minden, in 1759. The belief entertained by his friends was, that he had contracted an injury to his sight by sleeping on the damp ground, in the campaign in Germany; he was never married. At the time of his residence on the estate (which embraced a span of twenty-four years), a vast deal of game was spread over the manor. Mr. Sayer was a justice of the peace, and persons who trespassed on the manor and killed his game were often caught, and brought before him by his own gamekeepers: yet he never would punish them, but used to reprimand them gently, telling them " they must not repeat the offence;" after which, he would order them into the servants' hall to get victuals and drink. Before Mr. Charles Eyre's death, the cottage, to which Mr. Sayer afterwards made the addition I have spoken of, would seem to have been occasionally let for the summer, for it is well remembered in the neighbourhood that, to this cottage Mr. Richard Brinsley Sheridan brought his charming young bride, Miss Linley, on returning to England from Flanders after their stolen wedding; and here, therefore, may be supposed to have been spent their real " honey-moon." In Moore's *Life of Sheridan* will be found letters from Sheridan written from East Burnham Cottage.

To return to Mr. Charles Eyre. He left the bulk of his personal property—which was considerable—to his two daughters. The eldest was, a year or two after his death, united in marriage to Mr. Coxe, a gentleman of fortune in the county of Gloucester; he was nephew to Mr. Charles Eyre, through his mother, and consequently cousin german in blood, though

not in title, to Miss Elizabeth Eyre. She bore him
no children, being no longer young at this period,
and in the sequel (as will presently be narrated) she
managed to enrich his descendants by a former wife
with her own money.

After her marriage, Mrs. Coxe let the house in
which she and her father had so long resided, and
took possession of her new home at Lippiat, in
Gloucestershire. I cannot make out the names of the
parties who thenceforth tenanted " the great house"
at East Burnham, except that of a Mr. Sturt, and a
Mr. Stevenson, of Coxe Lodge, Co. Northumberland,
whose daughter became Countess of Mexborough,
and, with the Earl, also resided some time at East
Burnham. A Mr. Parry lived and died (in 1812)
at the *Manor House*, the site of which was many
years since converted into a market garden, let to
Thomas Buckland, (formerly gamekeeper to the lord
of the manor,) where a noble cedar of Lebanon
remains and flourishes still, a vestige of the character
of the residence in bygone days. I am unable to
say who lived there after Mr. Parry's death, although
doubtless the books of the collector of rates and
taxes of the period would furnish the names, if
referred to.

During the reign (as we will call it) of Mr. Sayer
—viz., from 1786 down to 1810—the hamlet of East
Burnham seems to have been profoundly tranquil and
stationary, the agriculture eminently primitive and
unskilful, the habits of the people rude and uncon-
trolled; the labouring class less depressed, perhaps,
than in many other districts, since Mr. Sayer was
liberal-handed, Mrs. Coxe extremely kind and generous

towards them, and the farmers held their land at an
easy rent.   Mr. Sayer must have lived much within
his income, passing his days as he did in quiet retire-
ment, occupying his own house, and keeping an establishment of a moderate size.   He seems to have had
a sister about his own age living with him, who died
one year before him, unmarried.   An old man now
alive, named William Buckland, at the age of eighty-
four, relates that his father was gamekeeper to Captain
Sayer, and was also general overlooker of the woods
and the manor of East Burnham (or " Allards".)
He himself (the deponent) knew this place during
fifty years, never knew an instance of a tree standing
on the waste or forest being cut down, but sometimes
the wind would blow one down, or part of one, on
which occasions the lord of the manor always had
them cut up by his own men : often distributing among
the poor people the wood so obtained, but not invari-
ably.   Sometimes took it home for his own use.
Had heard it said by many persons that Mr. Sayer
had no legal rights over the manor, not having inherited through the male line; still, nobody ever
contested it, Mr. Sayer being well liked by his
neighbours.

Another man, named Slaymaker, related to the
writer some particulars concerning this hamlet, in
December, 1856, he being then eighty-five.   He came
first into this neighbourhood about the year 1792;
he was farm servant, or husbandry-labourer, and
shepherd, many years with a farmer named Edward
Goldwin, who then held the farm now occupied by
Mr. William Watkins.   During the eleven years of
Slaymaker's service with Farmer Goldwin in East

Burnham, the cottagers of the hamlet enjoyed the liberty of entering the woods belonging to Captain Sayer, at felling-time, and carrying away quantities of "rough wood," or "lop and top." They were never obstructed by the wood-cutters—indeed, Slaymaker has often seen them assist the poor people (most of them women) to cut up the large pieces: lending them their hatchets occasionally, to facilitate the removal of such wood as they could carry away on their backs. The farmers in the immediate vicinity were in the habit of sending their carts to fetch home to the respective cottages the wood thus collected. Farmer Goldwin, Farmer Bonsey, and Farmer Taylor, all of East Burnham, frequently lent their horses and men for this purpose, so that most of the cottagers possessed a tolerable stack of firewood, to which they added sometimes a little peat, which they cut un- molested when and where they liked, on the common. But as wood was so easily obtained, peat or turf was comparatively little used. Slaymaker mentioned, in relation to these facts, the following anecdote. His master (Goldwin) being then eighty years old, was apt to be somewhat "short" in his temper, and one day a woman named Plumridge coming to his house to beg "that he would be so good as to send a cart to draw home a load of wood belonging to her in Captain Sayer's copse," the old man refused her request.

After a pause, he told her to go and ask some other neighbour—naming Farmers Bonsey and Taylor— adding that "he (Goldwin) could not do it;" on re- ceiving this rebuff, the woman went her way, when the old man called after her and said—"I'll tell you what! good woman; you *shall* have my cart and horses, provided you give my men a drop of beer and a bit of bread and cheese for their trouble, and that is all it shall cost you." Slaymaker witnessed this colloquy, and recollects it distinctly, though at a distance of some forty years. Slaymaker confirms Buckland's statement that the game of Captain Sayer's manor was very abundant. The whole district was at that time (Slaymaker says) exceedingly retired and unfrequented. Such a thing as a carriage was never seen; poaching was habitually practised, though (as Buckland likewise related) Mr. Sayer would never proceed against the offenders. The wonder is, that the game was not altogether destroyed! Slaymaker's wages, as labourer in husbandry, were 10s. per week; he occupied a cottage, known as "The Orchards," on the skirt of the common; it belonged to the Hutchinson family at Beaconsfield, by whom it was afterwards sold (about the year 1844) to Mr. Grote. While Slaymaker occupied this tenement, he paid a rent of 12l.; keeping a cow, sometimes a few sheep, and always some pigs, all of which he pastured on the common and waste.

I pause here, to note the evidence furnished by another old inhabitant of East Burnham, named Plumridge (December, 1857). This man, being now eighty years of age, tells me that he in his youth cut wood for Captain Sayer; that it is true that the cottagers fetched away "rough wood" and "notch ends, and such like," not being saleable as faggots, stakes, or heathers; but, he adds, this wood so fetched away was not had for *nothing*; it was valued to the woodcutters themselves, and "set off" as part payment of their work; they settling accounts in their turn with the cottagers.

I come now to the period which succeeded to the reign of Mr. Sayer; that gentleman dying, at the age of eighty, in the year 1810. But I must first relate what befel Mrs. Coxe, who came to be an important personage in the locality.

Mr. Coxe died, advanced in years, towards the close of the last century, leaving Mrs. Coxe his estate of Lippiat. She soon found it an unsuitable residence for a single woman however, and, within a brief space, quitted Gloucestershire, making over the house and landed property to Mr. Robert Gordon, M.P., who had married the granddaughter of her late husband by his first wife.

Mrs. Coxe, ever attracted by early associations to the place of her birth, now resumed the occupation of her mansion at East Burnham: spending the greater part of the year there, but repairing to Bath (where she had purchased a house) for the winter months.

With Captain Sayer, who, as has been related, lived at East Burnham during the whole period of his possession of the estates, Mrs. Coxe was on friendly and familiar terms. He used to say to her, "Cousin, I intend to leave you this house and land, and the adjoining wood (Tomkins' Wood); and Popple shall have the estates, and shall inhabit your large house."

In conformity with this assurance, Mr. Sayer made a will, in which the whole of the Eyre estates, manors, &c., were bequeathed to Mr. Popple, for life, and in which the house and land above specified was left to Mrs. Coxe for *her* life. The whole to revert to the wife of Mr. Robert Gordon, absolutely.

Mr. Sayer being the last male heir of the long line of Eyres, whose property he enjoyed, was, it would appear, master of the same, and competent to will it away to whomsoever he thought fit. The heir in remainder, Mrs. Gordon, was related by blood to the testator, as has been already mentioned; and it was believed that Mr. Sayer had been influenced by personal liking for Captain Popple and his lady in making *him* his immediate heir; the rather, as he had little or no acquaintance with the legitimate branch of his uncle's family.

Captain Popple, on finding himself invested with the possession of this fine property, came to reside at East Burnham: obtaining permission from Mrs. Coxe to inhabit the house belonging to her (where Mr. Eyre, her father, had lived), as being a more capacious and gentlemanlike residence for the "Squire" of the place. During the first years of his tenure, Captain Popple exercised his rights over his newly acquired property very much to the satisfaction of the neighbourhood;* his steward, a Mr. Hall, held his "courts" at the Manor House, and attended to the maintenance of the roads and highways, the gates upon the waste, and all matters concerning the general interest of the inhabitants. At the courts, "presentations" were made of any neglect of duty on the part of the surveyor of roads, or of nuisances in the hamlet. William Buckland, of whom I have already spoken,

---

* Towards the latter period of his life, Mrs. Coxe used to reproach her brother-in-law with neglecting his duties as Lord of the Manor, and with allowing the highways and other matters to fall into bad order: Mr. Popple always replying, "Yes, yes, I know it—I will have it done"—and so forth.

told me that his father passed into the service of
Captain Popple at the death of Mr. Sayer, as gamekeeper and overlooker of the woods. In Mr. Popple's
time, all the woods belonging to the East Burnham
estate, except "The Beeches" proper, were fenced
about, but never locked. That in winter season all
the cottagers used to go and fetch away, at falling
time, as much "rough wood" as they chose for firing,
without molestation; he, Buckland, confirms Slaymaker's statement in every particular as to the practice of the woodcutters permitting this to be done,
lending their hatchets, &c. &c.

Mrs. Coxe having consented to allow her brother-
in-law to occupy her house (whether rent free, or
otherwise, I am unable to say), Captain Popple be-
sought her to grant him an assurance that in case Mrs.
Popple should die before him he should not be disturbed in his occupation as long as he lived; to this
request Mrs. Coxe most kindly acceded, though not
without some reluctance, having a local attachment
to the spot where she had been born and bred. Mrs.
Coxe herself took possession of the house and land
which Mr. Sayer had left to her, where she spent the
greater part of the year, diffusing her bounty over the
humble inhabitants of the place, and influencing them
in every good direction by her precepts and example.

Now the heiress in remainder to all this fine
Eyre property was the wife of Mr. Robert Gordon,
M.P., sometime Secretary of the Treasury. (Her
grandmother was the first wife of Mr. Charles Coxe,
the husband, by second marriage, of Mrs. Coxe, late
Miss Eyre.) Mr. Robert Gordon wishing to realize
by anticipation a portion of his wife's prospective

inheritance, sold to lord Grenville* his wife's reversionary interest in the estate; which transaction coming to the knowledge of Mr. Popple, he began cutting the timber growing in the East Burnham and other woods, which he had a right to do as life tenant. Lord Grenville, fearing to become a loser by the bargain if this was persisted in, found himself compelled to pay a considerable sum to Mr. Popple in order to protect himself by a lease for seventeen years, as I have been told.† Slaymaker stated that, from the time of the said woods being leased to Lord Grenville, the ancient practice of fetching out firewood by the cottagers was put a stop to. Buckland affirmed this also; adding that compensation was granted at the time, in money, at the rate of 5l. to each cottage. As the occupants of these cottages successively died off, such payments ceased, and their successors thenceforth took to cutting peat or turf for their firing. Buckland adds, that up to this period but little turf was used by the labouring people.

Soon after his accession to the property of Mr. Sayer, Mr. Popple, effecting an exchange of lands with the Eyre property, enlarged the little domain around East Burnham House, by stopping up a road called " Hagget's Lane," which formerly led from the hamlet to Slough : and, throwing the land on either side thereof into one undivided plot, he obtained an area of about ninety acres, which received the appellation of " Popple's Park," and is so called in the parish " Terrier " to this day.

---

* At the price of £54,000.

† Some persons state the price of this lease to have been 300l.; others, rather less.

I have been told that Mr. Popple gave up a wood
called " Moswells," and also some land in Burnham,
afterwards occupied by a farmer named Crocker, in
exchange for the ground contiguous to his residence.

It has already been stated that Lord Grenville, in
the year 1812, bought the reversion of Robert Gordon
at the price of 54,000l., and as regarded the woods,
having obtained a lease of them from Captain Popple
(paying smartly, however, for this), he awaited the
period of Popple's death, when he would take possession of the whole estate, manors, and privileges, of the
late Captain Sayer.

But Captain Popple "held on" till an advanced
age, not dying until 1830, when he had reached his
eightieth year.*   Accordingly, Lord Grenville came
into the property under circumstances disadvantageous
to the purchaser.   He had waited no less than
eighteen years or so for the falling in of the reversion
of Captain Popple's life tenancy, and *then*, as might
have been expected, he found the buildings, fences,
and general condition of the farms deplorably dilapidated, and needing a vast outlay to put them into
anything like order and substantial repair.   For this
outlay Lord Grenville was ill disposed, as may be
imagined.   And an event took place, within a short
space after Mr. Popple's decease, which gave to the
transaction I have recorded an aspect of yet more
complete disappointment.

The dominant idea of Lord Grenville's whole life

---

* Each of the three last possessors of this property lived to the
age of eighty : one among many other evidences of the salubrity of the
place.

was to secure political influence for the family of
which he was a member. The Marquis of Buckingham, the head of that family, may be said to have
dreamed of little else: his mind was vastly inferior to
those of Lord Grenville and the third brother, Thomas
Grenville, and his claims to political office and power
arose almost entirely from the extent of his territorial
possessions, together with the pressure which he could
exercise at elections, over the tenantry of his lands,
and over the residents in his boroughs. Accordingly,
the aim of Lord Grenville, for many long years, was
to lay hold on every estate in the *south* of the county
of Bucks which came into the market, in the view of
strengthening the Grenville interest in the elections,
especially of the two members for the county. By
the aid of Lady Grenville's large inheritance (which
unexpectedly fell to her by the death of Lord Camel-
ford), and his own emoluments as one of the auditors
of the Exchequer, Lord Grenville managed to add
very largely to his landed possessions, and doubtless
to his political influence. Still, from the important
acquisition of the East Burnham and Huntercombe
property much less advantage resulted, either as an
investment, or as a means of multiplying dependent
voters, than his lordship had expected when effecting
the bargain in 1812. Not only were the buildings on
the farms found to be quite decayed, and the labourers'
cottages half in ruins, on the Sayer estate; but the
Reform Bill swept away, two years after Lord Grenville came into the enjoyment of the estate, a large
portion of the advantage to be derived from the voters
living upon it. However, the distinguished statesman
himself closed his mortal career almost at the same

period, leaving to his widow the charge of setting to
rights the dilapidations consequent upon five-and-
forty years' neglect and apathy, on the part of the
two aged predecessors, Captain Sayer and Captain
Popple.

On the death of Captain Popple, Mrs. Coxe thought
fit to remove to the house in the Park, wherein, by her
indulgence, he had resided up to his death in 1830.
The house which she now vacated was soon after let
to a clerical gentleman named Joyce (formerly of
Henley-upon-Thames), who received young gentlemen
in it as pupils. A Colonel Trant also rented the
house for a year or so.

The good and kind lady lived at the paternal mansion for about five years more, and died, regretted and
mourned by all who knew her, in 1835; she, like her
predecessors in the hamlet, having reached a ripe and
healthy old age.

During the tenure of Mr. Popple, the house had
been enlarged, at the joint expense of himself and Mrs.
Coxe, and was at this period a handsome, spacious
mansion, containing twenty-eight rooms. The plea-
sure-grounds were suitably kept up, and the walled
fruit gardens were extensive and productive.

From 1836 to 1838 the house in which Captain
Sayer had lived remained unoccupied. The land was
let to neighbouring farmers, whilst the garden was
suffered to go to ruin.

The mansion in "Popple's Park" was offered in
vain to be let. Dancer refusing to relinquish his lease
(except upon extravagant terms), no gentleman would
take the place. Mrs. Coxe had bequeathed the house
and land, together with 10,000l. in money, to Mrs.

Gordon; but she left the furniture, and "personals" belonging to her, to a young man (her godson, I believe), named Philip Shepherd, whom she had brought up, and to whom, moreover, she left the bulk of her funded property, which was considerable. To this gentleman—who was her residuary legatee—was also left the reversion of an annuity of 50*l.* a year bestowed upon Mrs. James Dancer,* during long years the faithful attendant of the testatrix.

In 1837, Mr. Robert Gordon, finding no one disposed to rent the great house, proceeded to pull it down, and sell the materials: whilst the old Manor House which, from long neglect, was in bad condition, underwent the same fate by order of Lady Grenville.

Thus it came to pass that the hamlet of East Burnham, which, during perhaps a century, had possessed three opulent families, now found itself all at once without either a gentleman or lady resident. The only gentleman's house left standing was that in which Captain Sayer had resided. Besides this there was a small but genteel cottage, standing in a plot of some eight or nine acres of ground, near the old Manor House, and now inhabited by Mrs. Elizabeth Dancer and her husband: the land had been given to her during Mrs. Coxe's lifetime, and the cost of building the dwelling-house had likewise been defrayed by that benevolent lady. Mrs. Dancer (whose husband was brother to the lessee of "Popple's Park") afterwards bought the small cottage and garden situate

* Now living in the village of Burnham.

on the verge of her own ground, paying for it 200*l.*
to Mr. Gordon.

Such was the condition of the Hamlet of East
Burnham at the period when accident led me to
become acquainted with this "out-of-the-way" spot.
I had for some time been on the look-out for a rural
dwelling in some healthful, retired district, where the
air and water were good, and where I could find
facilities for walking and rambling about, on ground
other than a dusty high-road. These conditions
appearing to be realized by the district in question, I
opened a negotiation with Mr. Gordon, which resulted
in a purchase, by Mr. Grote, of that property which
Mr. Sayer had left, for her life, to Mrs. Coxe: consisting of the house and land, a labourer's cottage
and garden (let to G. Taylor), and a wood, of about
eleven acres, called "Tomkins' Wood." We took
possession of this little estate about the month
of June, 1838, but found that extensive repairs
must be undertaken, which were effected in time to
enable us to establish our residence therein during
the course of the same autumn. It would have been
wise to have pulled down all the older portion (or
"Sheridan's Cottage," as Mr. Sayer used to call it),
together with the stabling and out-buildings, and to
have rebuilt these. However, my state of health
was at this time too delicate to allow of my post-
poning the occupation of our country retreat, and we
accordingly contented ourselves with mending up
the old concern so as to be "habitable;" removing
to our London house about Christmas, 1838-9.

Within a year of our establishing this *ménage* at

East Burnham, we made an exchange of lands with
Lady Grenville, which conduced sensibly to the comfort of our occupancy. The adjacent orchard and a
cottage, together with a close lying north of this
orchard, and bounding our garden on the east, were
conveyed over to us by Lady Grenville, along with a
slip of land through which a public footpath ran from
East Burnham to the common-side.

In return for this lot of land, we gave up to her,
first, a cottage and garden on the north edge of our
meadow (called the Captain's Meadow); secondly,
two very good meadows, called respectively " Dod's
Meadow" and " Appletree Close," situate on the east
side of the slip on the slope of the hill, containing more
land than the lot which we obtained; and over and
above this exchange, we paid Lady Grenville in
money the sum of 200*l.*   The object we considered so
desirable, of possessing the ground abutting on our
garden, that we willingly consented to this arrangement, which certainly left her ladyship a clear gainer.

On Lady Grenville's coming into the exercise of
her rights over the property and privileges of East
Burnham, I have understood that " a court" was held
at which (among other business) it was laid down as a
regulation that no person should be permitted to cut
turf for firing on the common except the inhabitants of
East Burnham proper, and that such inhabitants were
to limit their cutting to 2000 turves for each cottage, or,
as the phrase ran, for " each chimney."   Now, as I was
anxious to be informed how the matter stood in regard
to the lord of the manor and the occupiers of houses
in the " Liberty," I asked Mr. Bowman (the steward
of Lady Grenville) to state the footing on which this

privilege was placed. The steward told me that I was at liberty to cut turves for my own house, and turves for my cottage at the end of the orchard, at the rate of 2000 each tenement.

I caused turf to be cut on this understanding from 1838 till 1851, when I quitted my original residence in East Burnham. My successor and tenant did the same; no hindrance or objection ever arose on the part of Lady Grenville, to the best of my knowledge, nor were the labouring people ever interfered with in cutting and carrying away *their* parcels. It was universally believed that this right belonged to the inhabitants, in the same way as the right of turning out animals to pasture and hogs to fatten on the acorns and beech-mast—a right, subject, of course, to restrictions against injury to the property of the manor, or to the persons and property of other parties, or the general interests of the public frequenting the district.

I shall return to this subject by-and-bye, but meanwhile I must say a word or two upon the general character of the population of East Burnham, such as I found it in 1838, and during many following years. In the first place, the inhabitants earned their living almost entirely by husbandry labour. Neither a tailor, shoemaker, plumber, or, in fact, any kind of skilled artisan, was to be found in our hamlet. One old man, of the name of Hughes, lived by working as a bricklayer; and a young man, named John James, bred to the trade of a wheelwright and cart-maker, could also act as carpenter, bricklayer, or in almost any handicraft connected with country life. He, however, did not at first live in East Burnham, but occupied a tenement in Farnham parish, until I

" located" him, a few years later, in a house which I
caused to be built (on the ruins of another cottage)
on a croft adjoining the common, bought in 1844 of
a family living at Beaconsfield.

Besides Hughes, there was the landlord of the
little alehouse called " The Crown," and a man named
Ryder, who got his living by attending markets, and
again selling by retail various produce, such as oats,
bran, flour, poultry, pigs, and pigmeat—keeping a
horse and cart; and also a huckster's shop on an humble scale. These formed the exceptions. All my
other neighbours followed husbandry in all its
branches, including woodcutting and hurdlemaking,
thatching and sheepshearing, &c. We could not
even boast of a smith in " the Liberty," though one
lived hard by, in the adjoining parish of Farnham;
neither had we a baker!—the Burnham baker regularly bringing bread on stated days, to supply the
dwellers in East Burnham, only a few of whom adhered to the old practice of " baking" at home. The
women were, here and there, in the habit of hawking
small wood, in donkey carts, to Eton and Windsor,
distant four to five miles—buying wood in the copses,
fetching it out, and cutting it up at home in little
faggots, called " pimps." Sometimes, I am afraid,
the faggots were made not wholly out of such wood,
but out of wood stolen by the urchins out of the
copses, at dusk—at least so said the wood-overseers
in the service of the proprietors. Again, a few of
my cottagers' wives would have a lace-pillow, which,
during winter, they would work at—lace being a
traditional occupation in the county of Bucks. But
after the year 1844, or thereabouts, lace-making

dropped out of the list of industrial occupations—machine-made lace completely supplanting "pillow-made" by its low price.

The women of East Burnham were, for the most part, hard-working, decent, and good-hearted creatures, and friendly neighbours: labouring in the fields at stone-picking, weeding wheat, reaping, gleaning, &c., and going out to help wash at farmers' and gentlefolks' houses, as occasion offered. For the male portion of the community there was, commonly speaking, a constant round of employment—somewhat more, indeed, than it is usual for rustic labourers to obtain. The vast extent of woodland in that neighbourhood created a constant demand for woodcutters when hard frost and snow forbade farming operations. Thrashing machines obtained but slowly among the farmers round East Burnham, who thus furnished long thrashing jobs, at piece-work (or "by the grate") to their men in hard weather. The immense amount of hedge-rows required a considerable outlay to keep them and their ditches up; the preserving of the game on the manor absorbed many of the men as watchers and under-keepers; and furthermore, at a season which often leaves the farm hands slack of work—namely, whilst the crops are ripening after midsummer, and haymaking is pretty well over—then would our people fall to at "cherry gathering;" a business which, in a good "bearing time," keeps scores of "hands" fully employed. The country teems with fruit in every direction, and some idea may be framed of the magnitude of the dealings in the article of cherries alone, when I state that John James (the man already mentioned) has for some years past found it answer to spend five or six weeks in Liverpool, selling to retail fruit-vendors the produce of the district round East Burnham—his father buying up the orchards, distributing his "gatherers" among them, and dispatching nightly by the railway well-packed baskets of cherries to his son at Liverpool.

The women meanwhile earn a good penny at strawberry and raspberry gathering in the market gardens, chiefly to supply the demand for these favourite fruits on the part of the eight hundred Eton boys. Many of the cottagers keep bees, and turn another penny in this way at Michaelmas.

As to the boys of our hamlet, *they* need never be at a loss for work. At some seasons one cannot obtain a boy "for love or money," as the saying goes. The parents usually send their children to the school (founded by the generous Mrs. Coxe for the benefit of the poor of the hamlet of East Burnham) from the age of six to eight or nine years, when the boys go forth to farm service, seldom, however, quitting the parental roof; for the modern practice of farmers is to hire boys at weekly wages, not "boarding" them in the farmhouses, as was the usage some fifty years since.

Boys are, however, hired for a specified term, occasionally, receiving a certain payment weekly for victuals until the end of the term, when the residue is paid in full. This arrangement is made only with the *best* boys of the place, because the employer wishes to make sure of their services—the final sum being conditional on the boy's completing his time as agreed; usually one year.

The girls continue at school longer than the boys,

although what they *learn* is worth mighty little.
After they are able to read, write, and cast up a sum,
little more is gained, except a slight knowledge of
Scripture history, and, perhaps, the elements of
needlework. The mothers, however, enjoy the advantage of being "rid" of the children for many
hours of each day, and are freed from the necessity
of staying at home to look after them, instead of
going out to work. As the girls approach the age of
fourteen or fifteen, they get out to service, chiefly in
that of the middle classes, such as farmers, tradesmen, and innkeepers; passing, as occasion offers,
later in life, into wives of young men of their own
station, frequently of their own parish. Of the
chastity of this part of East Burnham population I
may not boast. As in most other rural districts, the
young women were, in some instances, mothers before
they became wives; nevertheless, the young men show
a *preference* for correct females in selecting their
partners for life, and I am warranted in adding, that
the larger number of my poor neighbours possessed
the merit of being honest, well-conducted wives and
careful mothers, as they likewise were hardworking,
sober women.

Now, having given a general sketch of the industrial condition of "my hamlet" (as I used to call it),
the reader will perceive that this condition placed
the labouring folk somewhat high in the scale of
comfort. To the advantages I have enumerated, of
sufficient and diversified employment, of cheap firing
(for the wooded district around East Burnham furnished a constant supply of broken and drift wood
for the women to collect, and the woodcutters always

carried home a load of faggot wood, on leaving work, from the copses in winter), must be added the annual distribution of clothing made to the inhabitants of East Burnham at Christmas, to the amount of perhaps 3*l*. to 3*l*. 10*s*. per cottage, in pursuance of a bequest made by the kind lady so often named in this memoir, Mrs. Coxe. She left a sum of some 2660*l*. Consols, as a fund wherewith to enable certain trustees to distribute clothing and linen to her poor neighbours and their posterity.

This bequest, however, although affecting the interests of the labouring people beneficially to a certain degree, has proved less advantageous to them than might have been expected; and this owing to two causes. First, the cottages which (to use the phrase current in the hamlet), "carried the gift," were sought after so eagerly, that the rents demanded of the tenants have all along been higher than the tenements would have fetched under ordinary circumstances. Accordingly, the benefit accruing to the cottagers is divided between them and the owners of their tenements. The larger number of these is the property of Lady Grenville: two or three belong to the family at Beaconsfield before mentioned.

I had built three, on the site of as many ruined dilapidated abodes which I found in the place, and one belonged (and still belongs) to Mrs. Dancer. But Lady Grenville has suffered no less than five tenements to tumble down, from sheer decay, since my first acquaintance with the hamlet—three in the lane near "Lock's Bottom," one near the "Crown," and one in the way to Up-end Farnham, not far from "The Conduit." I am inclined to think that *more* than five have ceased to exist since Lord Grenville came to the property, but of this I am not quite certain.

Now the loss of five cottages out of the small number composing our hamlet, has had the effect of driving the young couples to settle *out* of it, and to obtain a dwelling at a distance; also, it has deprived five labouring men's families of a welcome help; throwing into the lap of the actual recipients a greater share than they ought to receive, and, in fact, a greater share than they really require: inasmuch as Mrs. Carter told me, in 1857, that she had been led to exceed the limits of her legal power, and thus to bestow *blankets* upon some of the poor who stood in need of no farther supply of *clothing*. The terms of Mrs. Coxe's bequest being thus in some sort infringed.

Again, for want of cottages, the farmers are compelled to engage farm-labourers living at a considerable distance from their fields, by which much time is lost going to and from work, and additional fatigue is laid upon the working man, who, after a long summer's day, has to trudge two miles or more to reach his own roof-tree.*

Three very small tenements, containing as many families, were erected by Lady Grenville, about the year 1838, one of which is devoted to the holding of the day school, endowed by Mrs. Coxe, for the gratuitous instruction of the poor children of the hamlet.

---

* It ought not to be forgotten either that of late years, our farmers having improved in their knowledge of the science, more hands have been needed to carry on farming operations than formerly.

The interpretation put upon Mrs. Coxe's will by Mr. Carter, the respected vicar of Burnham, and "*ex officio*" one of the trustees under the charity, was entirely arbitrary; some cottages lying on the skirts of "the Liberty" not being admitted to share in " the gift," although others, equally distant, received it. One rule, however, was laid down, which has been acted upon undeviatingly—viz., that no new tenements should be entitled to the charity, unless built on the ruins of one in existence at the period of Mrs. Coxe's decease.

Now, the cottages being, as I have stated, almost all Lady Grenville's, and some of them old decayed, half-rotten dwellings, unfit for a decent peasantry to inhabit, the question naturally arises,—how is it that Lady Grenville permits the hamlet to become, as it were, depopulated, by the disappearance of its cottages, and that she suffers those which remain to fall out of repair, although the rent which is paid for them is what would be considered " high"?

This question, however, is only one out of many which suggest themselves to whoever happens to take notice of the general aspect of things in the Liberty of East Burnham. With equal, if not greater, reason would the visitor ask why all the " Common gates" have been suffered to disappear, so that cattle turned to pasture on the common stray beyond the Liberty, and trespass on private lands? Why the " pound" was absolutely useless for many years, for want of the trifling expenditure which it was the duty (as it was the privilege) of the Lord of the Manor to bestow upon it? Why the dams or " pond-heads" on the manor were left to fall in, letting the water rush out, and so destroy the passage across for horse or foot wayfarers, and losing a store of water useful to the residents? Why the farm buildings were not repaired, the fences made good on the roadsides, the stiles maintained on footways—the tenants enjoined to keep their ditches scoured and to keep the highways of the Liberty in a creditable state? Why—but I should never finish were I to go through the series of "acts undone which ought to have been done" in reference to this neglected district.

The current impression in the place was that Lady Grenville entertained a feeling akin to spite and aversion towards this portion of her estates; and certainly, if such was the case, no one could wonder at it, after learning what I have related, concerning the mistaken calculation which her husband fell into in purchasing the reversion of it at so high a rate. Her ladyship very rarely visited the hamlet, and I never heard of her setting foot in any one of the cottages or farms upon this estate during the twenty years of my connexion with East Burnham.

I hardly exchanged a word with her steward, Mr. Bowman, from 1839 to 1851. I frequently *tried* to see him, for the purpose of asking his assistance in repairing parts of the causeways, in repressing the abuse of pig depasturing, in keeping up pond-heads, in preventing injury being done to the old trees, in relieving stoppages of the " conduit" or reservoir, and many similar matters; but on no occasion could I obtain his personal co-operation. The pigs were suffered to disfigure the whole neighbourhood, being turned out loose without rings in their noses. It was the duty of

the steward to compel the owners to put rings in them
if turned loose, and to cause the hogwarden, or " hay-
ward," or " howard" (as this ancient function has come
to be designated), to impound the ringless hogs. No
heed was taken of my repeated applications for the
steward's interference on this point, and the pigs ran
riot over " the Beeches," ploughing up whole roods of
close green turf every autumn. Not only hogs belonging to inhabitants, but droves of these animals,
brought from miles around, came grunting into the
forest, searching for the beech-mast for weeks together, unchecked by the manorial officers. The
roads in the Liberty were neglected, and suffered to
become disgraceful, both from the accumulation of
mud and from deep ruts. The charge of them lay
with the surveyor of the highways of East Burnham
Liberty, or " Hallwards," as it was frequently called,
after its ancient name. This officer was chosen
annually, or bi-annually, by the parishioners of Burnham in vestry, by vote. But there was no " gentleman" living in East Burnham after Captain Popple's
death, and accordingly the office fell into the hands
of one or other of the three occupiers of land in the
" Liberty;" farmers all, who " served" in rotation,
levying a rate upon the inhabitants for the expense of
keeping the roads in repair. The rate was chargeable
on land and houses, woodland not paying highway
rates. Accordingly, the weight of the charge lay
upon the farmers themselves, the houses contributing,
of course, far less than the land. The few acres belonging to us formed but a slender exception, the
whole of the lands being rented under Lady Grenville, except the woods, which were in her own hands,

and, as has already been observed, paid no rate to the highways.

Now, the interest of the farmer being to keep the expenses as low as possible, and to pay as little towards them as he could, the roads became hopelessly bad, in all parts except on the high road between Windsor and Beaconsfield, which was maintained in tolerable order, out of respect to " the parish," which would have complained of any short-comings on *that* portion of our district.   In vain have I remonstrated with the surveyor upon the condition of the roads.   So long as there was nobody but the farmers to serve the office, so long was it useless to strive for an improved management.   The ditches, rarely "scoured," stood full of stagnant water, the water ran over the roads, and wore "gutters" in them, though an hour's work would have cleared a passage down the ditch at the side; the mud was " overshoes" deep, the hedges were never trimmed, the trees dripped upon the roads (Lady Grenville's steward prohibiting their being "lopped"), the ruts were deepened by the heavy-wheeled wains, and in short there was widespread indifference to the condition of all the bye-roads around East Burnham. This was just a case in which the interposition of the owner of the lands would have proved beneficial to the inhabitants at large.   But the saying, " Property hath its duties as well as its rights," found no confirmation at the hands of Lady Grenville.   And, as far as my information extended, the steward confined his labours to the producing of as much rent and profit as it was possible to extract from this much neglected estate.   Not only were new tenements not

built in the place of old ones, but space was grudged
for pigsties, which, in the case of the dwellers in the
"courtyard," were placed close to the cottage doors,
forming an *ensemble* strictly resembling a cluster of
Irish "cabins."

The only really active exertions made by Lady
Grenville's steward were directed to the repression of
poaching, which practice was visited with constant
penalties; offenders being summoned before the
justices on every occasion of detection, and punished
accordingly. Lady Grenville deriving a considerable income from the shooting on her manors, she
naturally sought to secure the exclusive right over
the game, which, however, subsisted upon the neighbouring lands; the lessee of the manor being understood to pay the value or damage of the same to the
respective occupants.

Again, in the village, or rather hamlet, of East
Burnham, stood an alehouse, which in the days of
" Squire Popple," sold wholesome beer, being a " free-
house," as it is termed. The labouring folk say that
the beer was usually very good, and sometimes home-
brewed. When Lady Grenville took possession of
the property, this alehouse was let on lease to a
brewer, who naturally offered more rent than a
private individual could afford to pay; and from that
day to this (1858), the poor people have had nothing
but inferior, and in some sort unwholesome, beer
supplied to them. A beer-shop on the "common
side" sells beer of similar quality, neither better
nor worse: both being tenants under two different
brewers, and obliged to vend *their* "mixture," and
nothing else. A real advantage would be gained

by the cottagers at East Burnham, were Lady
Grenville to let "The Crown" to a tenant paying
his yearly rent to herself; but she might not obtain quite so high a rent in this way, and thus the
poor people feel and say that they must drink bad
beer, in order to profit the Lady of the Manor. I
know that one of the most general complaints against
this lady's management has always been, that she
let the only public-house to a brewer, and deprived
the cottagers of the chance of good liquor.

I have already stated that, when we took up our
quarters in East Burnham, no other "gentlefolk"
resided in the Liberty. There subsequently came to
live, in Mrs. Dancer's cottage, a retired military
officer, named Rivers; but he was an invalid, and
scarcely made an exception to my statement.

I lived in the house, formerly Mrs. Coxe's, from
1838 to the end of the year 1850, when we resolved
to give up this residence, letting the house to the
widow Lady Shadwell, and her daughters. Lady
Shadwell dying in 1852, the house reverted to our
possession, and in 1853 we sold it, along with the
twenty-four acres of land, three cottages, and the
timber, to Mr. Ludlam, who shortly after came to
reside upon the same with his family.

"The Park" had been purchased by us from Mr.
Robert Gordon in the year 1844: we buying up the
remainder of Mr. Dancer's term, and thereby acquiring full possession of the estate. There was no house
whatever on this little property, consisting of eighty-
seven acres in a ring-fence. A market-gardener,

named John Timblick, lived in what had once been
an "orangery," which was situated in the old mansion's kitchen-garden. This he rented under Mr.
Gordon, and continued to rent under me: cultivating
fruit and vegetables for the supply of Eton and
Windsor demand.

But in 1852 I caused a small Elizabethan house
to be built in this "Popple's Park," and also a range
of farm buildings and a labourer's cottage; and
letting the land for seven years to Mr. Wm. Webster
(a farmer already occupying a farm in our Liberty,
under Lady Grenville), I came myself, in January,
1853, to this house, where I passed (at intervals)
about the half of every year. During the period
of my absence from East Burnham—viz., from
January, 1851, to January, 1853—there had arisen
some circumstances which somewhat disturbed the
relations between the inhabitants and the Lady of
the Manor. Much of the heath and turf on East
Burnham common had been cut and carted away
by persons living out of the Liberty, for sale. The
practice at length became so notorious, that the
steward interfered to prevent it, placing watchers
for that purpose. He next proclaimed a regulation
that no turves should be cut, even by the cottagers,
except in boggy, swampy places. Since these turves
cost much more labour, both to cut, to dry, and to
cart off, than the turves cut on solid ground, this
regulation was very loosely observed, and in consequence, matters were already growing uncomfortable
on this point when I resumed my intercourse with
the hamlet. In 1854, I ordered my usual lot of turves
to be cut, by a labouring man accustomed to the work,

and these were duly brought home and housed.   In
1855 I proceeded in like manner.

About that period Mr. Bowman, the steward, was
dismissed from his office, and we were informed that
in his stead a new steward had been appointed, who
was to live in Cornwall, and only visit Dropmore occasionally : to hold courts, receive rents, and the like.
Meanwhile, a youth named Forbes announced himself to the inhabitants as acting steward, or deputy,
whose duty it was to watch over the interests of the
manor, but who was bound to refer all important
matters to the gentleman at the " Land's End."

In the summer of 1856 I ordered a man named
Armon (one of our husbandry labourers in the
Liberty), to cut 1000 turves for me, in the parts
prescribed by Lady Grenville's steward, on the
waste.

Not long after these turves were cut and set up to
dry, my gardener came and told me that Mr. Forbes
had caused my " lot," together with turves cut by
some other parties (cottagers), to be carted away and
burned.   This proceeding, taken without any notice
or remark as towards myself, I regarded as offensive
in itself; and it further occasioned me to institute
some inquiries among the elders of the hamlet, relative
to the ancient practice of " the Liberty," and the
supposed rights of the ratepayers and freeholders
living within the Manor of Hallwards.   The result of
these inquiries I have embodied in a former portion
of this memoir.   (See page 155).

Among the inhabitants of our hamlet, a very general
feeling arose against the arbitrary acts of Lady Grenville's steward, and I was strongly tempted to endea-

your to obtain some redress on behalf of the cottagers. Although I cared little or nothing for the
privilege of cutting turves myself, it seemed to me a
fit occasion to interfere, if only to arrive at a more
definite understanding as to what rights belonged to
the Lady of the Manor, and what rights belonged to
the inhabitants; especially the owners of land in the
Liberty, or freeholders, of whom there were three or
four besides myself.

I accordingly drew up and forwarded a memorial to
Lady Grenville, stating the circumstances which had
occurred, and requesting her ladyship to communicate
to us the exact conditions which she considered herself
justified in claiming, in regard to the inhabitants, on
the subject of turf, sod, peat, sand, and the.like;
the memorial was signed by Mr. Grote, and by some
other parties, occupiers of land, interested in the
question.

After the lapse of a fortnight we received a reply,
penned, as we understood, by the steward who lived
at the estate belonging to Lady Grenville in Cornwall,
of which reply I here annex a copy:

Boconnoc, 12th August, 1856.
GENTLEMEN,—I am authorized to say, that Lady Grenville has
received the Memorial, dated July 28th, 1856, signed by certain
"inhabitants and occupants of land in East Burnham," in which
the memorialists state that certain lots of turf, cut by some of them
in the exercise (as they say) of their long enjoyed rights on East
Burnham Common, having been recently removed and burnt without
any previous notice to them that such a step would be taken, they ask
on what grounds it proceeds?

And then, supposing the grounds of the recent proceeding to
have been, that turf has been cut either in greater quantity than the
understood rights of each occupant warrant, or by persons not duly
authorized, or in an unsuitable and unusual portion of the common,
the memorialists "submit that the limits which her ladyship (as Lady

of the Manor) is disposed to prescribe ought to be distinctly specified and made known."

Before answering the question as to the grounds of the recent proceeding, Lady Grenville begs to remind the memorialists, that East Burnham Common is not a common of turbary. No one, therefore, in virtue of his being an inhabitant and occupant of land in East Burnham, has any right to cut turves on the common without permission of Lady Grenville (as Lady of the Manor): that permission, within certain limits, has been accorded to the cottagers of East Burnham, to whom a little peat-turf for fuel was a great boon. The limit, as regards place, was confined to the bogs, and as regards quantity, it was not to exceed annually, to each cottage, two thousand turves, each turf to be not more than 12 in. long by 6 in. wide by 3 in. thick; and her ladyship is surprised to learn that the memorialists should be ignorant as to what those limits were, as one or more of them, she believes, was present at a Court Baron when the limits prescribed were distinctly specified and made known.*

Some of the parties, however, to whom the before-mentioned privilege was accorded, and possibly others to whom it was not accorded, instead of confining themselves to the bogs for peat-turf, have at various times of late gone on other parts of the common, and have skimmed off the surface, to the great injury of the pasturage of the common; and on one of the aggressors being summoned before the magistrates for the trespass, he set up a claim, as of right, to do what he had done.

Under these circumstances it was that the turf found upon the common, not on bog ground, was removed; and Lady Grenville cannot but think that the memorialists themselves must consider the act perfectly justifiable.

There was no intention of withdrawing the privilege which has been accorded to the cottager, so long as he did not abuse it; but that which was permitted as a favour, must not be claimed by the recipients as a matter of right.

I am, gentlemen,

Your obedient servant,

WM. PEASE.

To Messrs. W. Bayley, W. Williamson, and others.

The tenor of Lady Grenville's reply gave us to understand that she acknowledged no right or privileges as regarded the waste land in East Burnham, on the part of any one but herself. That she did not

* See page 155.

intend to forbid the practice of cutting turf, subject to the stipulations already laid down, but would continue to permit turf to be cut for fuel, in the proportions which had for many years been allowed to the inhabitants of East Burnham. The document declares the common not to be a "common of turbary," and Lady Grenville assumes the exclusive jurisdiction over the whole district, to the entire abrogation of all other rights or privileges on the part of any one else. If she grants leave to take away any portion of the soil, such as turf, sand, gravel, peat, or the like, it is as a matter of favour, which may be annulled at pleasure.

This construction of the rights pertaining to the Lady of the Manor was far from being satisfactory to the memorialists. Few or none of the neighbours yielded their conviction to Lady Grenville's assertions of unbounded and undivided legal right over the common; but since she had declared her readiness to allow of the turf being cut and used for fuel, we judged it on the whole better to suffer the question to rest where it was. When the summer of 1857 drew nigh, I directed my gardener to get 1000 turves cut as heretofore. The people on the common-side informed him that the young man who acted as deputy to the steward had recently laid down a new regulation: namely, that no one should cut turves except such men as were in the employ of Lady Grenville, and, as such, responsible to the steward. I accordingly employed a man coming under that category, and in due course carted home my turves.

In a few weeks after this, I sent a cart and horse to bring in a small number of green turves for my

garden edging, which I had had cut on a corner of
the common. Whilst my people were loading the
turves, they were accosted by the young man, Forbes,
who said that "Madam Grote had no right to take
turf off the common," and that "he had a great mind
to seize the cart, and to take the men employed therewith before the justices for trespassing," and so forth.
However, he limited his proceedings to angry talk,
and the men carted home the turf. A few days after
this, Mr. Forbes came to my residence, and inquired
for me. I happened to be out, but returning within
a short space, I found the young man awaiting me in
the garden next the road.

He said he was come to complain of my cutting
turf without asking his leave. I replied that I did
not conceive it at all necessary to ask leave every
time I required a few sods of turf; that Lady Grenville had, many years ago, sent me her authority to
cut turves, sods, to take peat, sand, or gravel off the
common; that I had never abused this licence, but,
on the contrary, had taken very moderate advantage
of her permission in every respect; and that I did not
deem it my duty to send and ask leave to help myself
on every occasion which might arise. Mr. Forbes
rejoined that Lady Grenville was now resolved to
enforce strictly her manorial rights, and that "he
should fine me on her behalf for having committed a
trespass." I answered that he had better try to fine
me, and that it might perhaps lead to a legal investigation of her rights, which would be attended with
useful results. Mr. Forbes was civil, and nowise
wanting in respectful manners, and appeared to be
acting simply in conformity with instructions received

from his principals. I heard nothing more from this quarter, but was informed by a person whose authority was undeniable, that Mr. Forbes was of late in the habit of affirming " that Mrs. Grote now *bought the turf from him*, and thus acquiesced in the absolute right of the Lady of the Manor over the soil."

Whilst Mr. Forbes was within my gates, on the occasion above referred to, he passed into the stable-yard, and looked into the wood-house. Seeing the turves stacked up therein, he asked Howlett, my gardener, " Whose turves are these?" " Mine," replied Howlett. " Ah! they are yours, are they? that's all very well, but Mrs. Grote has no right to any turves for herself. Only the poor are allowed to have them."

On the gardener's reporting this conversation to me, I blamed him for saying that the turves were his, which was speaking wrongly. The turves were cut for me, paid for by me, and carted home by my people, and I used a portion of them for my green-house stove-fire. Howlett, like all the common folk, standing in fear of Lady Grenville's displeasure, had said what he did in the amiable design of shielding his mistress from it.

After this incident, which seemed to me to require some notice, I conversed with more than one of the inhabitant householders of East Burnham, in the view of ascertaining the sentiments of the hamlet in re-ference to the enlarged claims recently advanced on the part of Lady Grenville over " the waste." I found that but one feeling existed on the subject, which was that of extreme dissatisfaction, and sense of injustice towards the general interests of the resi-dents, as attempted to be practised by Lady Grenville's steward. The cottagers complained also, that carts belonging to persons living at a distance were continually sent to carry away from the common quantities of peat, sand, fallen leaves, and turf, by permission of the steward. They specified several parties, among whom were the Duchess of Sutherland, Sir Richard Colt Hoare, Mr. Bragg and Mr. Brown (both nurserymen, of Slough), and others. They complained that these parties were allowed to benefit by the common, although they contributed nothing to the " rates," or to the maintenance of the roads, gates, or fences in the Liberty, whilst one of *them*—being ratepayers—could not take a single barrow-load without going to Dropmore to ask leave. They felt, in short, that Lady Grenville was seeking to establish an *absolute* rather than a manorial property in the soil : giving away the same out of the parish, in any quantities she thought fit, and preventing any one but herself from using the soil unless specially authorized by herself. Coupling the information thus collected with the evidence I had already obtained as to the old usages and practice of the manor, I felt a certain impulse to probe the case further, and to endeavour to put Lady Grenville on the necessity of proving the right she claimed over the common and "waste." I found, moreover, that a " court" had been held out of the limits of the manor, that is, at her own farm at Brookend; and that at this same court (held in 1857), though the jury was composed of persons entitled to be upon it, viz., occupiers of land in East Burnham, the business was carried on within closed doors. I have been informed that both these facts were contrary to law, and would invalidate and nullify any rule or orders passed at this same court.

At a court held in 1855, in "The Crown" ale-house, at East Burnham, Mr. Grote officiated as foreman; two or three other occupiers of land in "The Liberty" serving also as jurymen. Mr. Bowman attended, as representative of Lady Grenville, and opened the court in the customary manner. This, I believe, was the last court held by Mr. Bowman for and in the Hamlet and Liberty of East Burnham.

To return to my purpose of pressing this question —so important to the humble inhabitants—I would willingly have taken steps to this end, but I found myself deterred by the fear of bringing down upon their heads the vengeance of the steward. He had lately, it seems, explicitly given them to understand that whoever moved in the matter, or furnished in-formation tending to call in question Lady Grenville's supremacy, should be immediately turned out of their tenements. This menace had the effect of tying up the tongues of all her tenants, and of inducing them to wish that no farther " stir" should be made. The whole of the inhabitants, it may be said, rented cot-tages under Lady Grenville, with the exception of my gardener, Mr. Ludlam's three tenants, "The Stag" beer-house, and one or two cottages on the common side. Under these considerations, knowing how grievous a penalty the quitting a tenement would be to any East Burnham resident, I was obliged to lay aside whatever intention I had before cherished of seeking to aid my poor neighbours in this matter: and this brings my history to the close of the year 1857.

N

It may be asked, why did I not make a direct appeal to Lady Grenville in person and invite her to state her own view of the respective rights in question? The reason was, that Lady Grenville had reached the age of eighty-four years; an age at which it would have been indiscreet to attempt to open up a discussion involving a variety of small particulars, and relating to long bygone days, and in which, moreover, she probably would have felt disinclined to engage.

The situation in which the large estate of Lady Grenville found itself at the period of which I have been treating, is one not unfrequently exhibited in England, but which is not only unfavourable to the interest of the parishioners, and of those who are in any way dependent upon the property, but is in a minor degree inconvenient to all residents in its vicinity. An aged landed proprietor, delegating her authority over her lands and manors to persons of an inferior station in life, who cannot take the same view either of public interests or of the credit attaching to the condition of a gentleman, as the proprietor herself—such proprietor, I say, is often construed to behave in a way which she would not sanction if she were in full possession of her active faculties.

Thus it was with Lady Grenville. Her steward not unfrequently acted on her behalf in a manner to draw upon her most unpleasant animadversions; among which instances I might adduce the affair of the annual payment of 25l. out of the Huntercombe estate for the use of the poor; the upshot of which was, to compel Lady Grenville, who had resisted such payment for years, to make it good, with arrears, to

the parish authorities, about the year 1852. I cannot suppose that Lady Grenville would have sanctioned the acts which produced so much ill-will in my
district, had she been informed of what was going
forward. On the few occasions when I have taken
the liberty of communicating directly with her Ladyship, she has always shown a polite readiness to forward my wishes, and an obliging disposition. In the
matter of the water supply, for example: a few years
ago her steward repeatedly promised that repairs
should be made in the conduit pipes on which we
depended for our water. But month after month
passed over without even a move on his part, and I
had no resource but to address a remonstrance to
Lady Grenville herself. She replied without delay,
in a business-like, courteous letter; ordered the work
to be executed, and it was put in hand forthwith, at
her cost. This was in Mr. Bowman's time.

Of the young man who acted as subordinate
steward I never had any cause to complain personally. When I have represented to him any abuse
of the privileges of the inhabitants of the Liberty, he
has endeavoured to correct it, especially in the case
of the herds of hogs which latterly overran the Burnham Beeches, rooting up (as I have stated) many
roods of turf in search of beech-mast and acorns,
befouling the pathways with their filth, and even
molesting timid people by their audacious, defiant
approach. Mr. Forbes did try to impound many
pigs which were found to be without rings; but the
difficulty of driving them out of the woodland was
well-nigh insurmountable when once they had got in.

The origin of all this lay in the destruction of

N 2

the eight or ten gates which formerly protected the Liberty against intruding animals, many of which were extant when I first came to East Burnham.* Gates having sufficient latches or nooses would have kept out all unauthorized pigs. It was the duty of the ratepayers to compel the surveyor of the roads to uphold these gates. But as the surveyors were tenants of Lady Grenville, so were the ratepayers, with hardly an exception. Accordingly, every item of expenditure which could be evaded, *was* evaded: Lady Grenville could have compelled the surveyor to do his duty, for he held his farm as tenant at will. The parish might have appointed a surveyor other than one of Lady Grenville's tenants, it is true; but there was only Mr. Grote who was eligible, as a rate-payer of any consequence. He, however, naturally shrank from this sort of trouble, being, moreover, only an occasional resident in East Burnham; and there remained no other individual at once eligible and capable of discharging the office.

Thus the whole system under which the district was administered revolved round Lady Grenville, represented by a paid steward (living 300 miles away in Cornwall), and he again by a young deputy, instructed to keep down expenses above all, and to maintain "rights." The poor were left without any-body to care for them, except an occasional visit from the curate, all trembling at the nod of "the steward;" whilst the farmers, backed by this functionary, managed the whole of the affairs of the hamlet between them. The labouring people entertained an unpleasant feel-

---

* Five of them were, certainly, perhaps more.

ing towards the farmers, who, as they considered, disregarded their interests, and discharged their men at short notice whenever it suited them. Some of the farmers even gave no "harvest supper;" and I am afraid it must be avowed that between these classes no great friendliness subsisted. That the men frequently gave their masters cause for dissatisfaction there can be no doubt; still, as a body, I really cannot rate the character of the husbandry labourers of our hamlet at a low level, compared with those of other districts of this county. "Drink," of course, formed the leading vice of the class; but it should be remembered that the working men in general have no amusements (cricket, even, being forbidden on Sundays, their only leisure day), and that the gossip and chatter of the alehouse are the only agreeable excitement which their ignorant minds receive, from one year's end to another."*

I may say, for my own part, that whatever kind-ness, and care, and good offices, I bestowed upon my

---

* For several years after I first settled in East Burnham, cricket was regularly played during the summer on Sunday afternoons, by all the men and lads of the vicinity. The common, indeed, presented a lively and pleasing aspect, dotted with parties of cheerful lookers-on, with many women and children and old persons, among whom we ourselves, and our servants, not unfrequently mingled. But about the year 1842—3, some boys of our hamlet, having been taken up and carried before the Beaconsfield Bench, for playing cricket on a Sunday, and fined "fifteen shillings each, or six weeks of Aylesbury gaol," the practice of playing cricket was effectually checked in East Burnham. The young men and boys, having thenceforth no recreative pastime, spent their afternoons in the beershops, or played at skittles in public-houses, or prowled about the lanes looking for birds'-nests, game-haunts, hare "runs," and the like; while the common was left lonely and empty of loungers.

humble neighbours, during the period of my residence among them, was gratefully felt; that they bore me unfeigned respect, and would, I think, have repaid my interest in them by any services in their power to render me.

When I quitted the cottage in the Park, never more to return to it, the cottager women were prone to exclaim, "Ah! there will be no one left to care for *us* when ' Madam' is gone !"

I disposed of my little property, called (by courtesy) East Burnham Park, in the spring of 1858, after having resided in the hamlet—with one short interval—for twenty years.

The oft-recurring vexations incident to the position I occupied—viz., that of a lady residing in the centre of a population dominated by a young servant, armed with the authority of the owner of all the land, manorial privileges, and cottages (nearly all) in my district : from whose arbitrary control no appeal could be made, on account of Lady Grenville's advanced age;—these oft-recurring vexations, I confess, made me feel, latterly, uncomfortable. Being of a temper liable to fret under the spectacle of wrong-doing, without having the smallest power to prevent it; the invariable opposition offered by Lady Grenville's Steward to my endeavours to effect measures of public utility—the grievous neglect of the highways precluding me from taking walking exercise in winter, and the advance of years rendering me less disposed to exert myself, as formerly, in behalf of the general welfare of the place,—all this concurred to make me resolve to retire from the neighbourhood: at the same time, I retain a sincere interest in the prosperity and well-doing of the inhabitants, among whom so large a portion of my life has been spent.

A feeling naturally suggests itself, after learning the circumstances which have been here related (concerning an obscure fraction of rural life in an agricultural province of England), that surely some remedy ought to have been available for the evils set forth! I am afraid there was none.

Mr. Eyre was eighty years old when he died.

Mr. Sayer, or "Captain Sayer," as he was styled, was unmarried, had infirm health, and led a secluded life: letting everything "go its own way" till his death, also at an advanced age.

Captain Popple latterly grew full of years, and having only a life-interest in the estates, he, in his turn, cared mighty little about keeping them in order. Thus, for forty years and more, the duties of administration, in regard to this large property, were neglected; mainly owing to the incapacity and indifference of its two last possessors. Then comes Lady Grenville, winding up the list with a hireling superintendence, and a nominal government,* resembling that of Irish "absentees" under the old *régime.*

Among the numerous blessings attending on free institutions in a country, some defects naturally co-exist. An unbounded control over land or house property possessed by individuals, leads to equally

----

* The responsible " deputy" living at the " Land's End."

unbounded power over those persons who occupy and
rent such: often comprising the whole, or nearly the
whole, population of a district. When the proprietor
devotes his (or her) attention to the general direction
of affairs on their estate, both the tenantry and the
neighbours have usually reason to be content; but
when a proprietor is obliged to entrust such superintendence to servants, and is unable or indisposed
to listen to complaints of mismanagement, *then* the
general welfare of the estate usually suffers. Parish
authorities may in certain cases offer resistance.
Burnham parish actually did so in the year 1836,
when they went to law with Lady Grenville, carried
it against her at the assizes, and obliged her to repair
a certain roadway near her residence. Nevertheless,
since parish officers in rural districts are commonly
composed of occupiers and cultivators of land, for
the most part "rented;" so their interest leads them,
as a general rule, to pay obedience to the will of the
owners of property in their neighbourhood. The
Liberty of East Burnham was not, I regret to say,
under the *general* administration of the parish. It
paid its own rates, contributing nothing to the highway rate of Burnham Parish. Its officers, accordingly, were of necessity occupiers of land within the
Liberty. In point of fact, Lady Grenville stood in a
relation all but *seignorial*, or feudal, to the Hamlet and
District of East Burnham.*

There is at present no help for such a state of things.
But a time must and will come, as society becomes

---

* So did the former "Lords," only that *these* resided among, and
cared for their "vassals."

more exigent as to "rights" and "duties," when owners of real property shall be brought under some kind of legislative control, so far as regards the public interest. Acts of Parliament will ere long, I expect, establish authority to quicken the activity of rural functionaries on matters involving health, convenience, morality, and decency in village communities; and although I myself regard the principle of "centralization" with anything but favour, yet I cannot but think it must sooner or later be invoked, if English landlords will not arouse themselves to a more conscientious discharge of their social obligations.

CONCLUSION.

Among the most salient points of difference which are traceable between the former and the more recent condition of East Burnham, is to be noted the lessened reliance of the poor upon their richer neighbours. I entertain little doubt that, formerly, the opulent occupants in East Burnham not only bestowed largely of their abundance upon the labouring people, but that the relations between these two classes were both familiar and kindly, as was the case in bygone days in most country places. Yet I am by no means sure that the cottagers are less *well off* now than they were formerly. In fact, the comfort of the labouring man is *better* attended to in many ways at the present time;* and, 'bating the difficulty of obtaining good

* The parochial provision for medical attendance, since 1835, counts for much in the present condition of the poor.'

beer to drink, perhaps his material condition is higher in most respects. I should say that the thing to be regretted is, the absence of the ties of social contact between rich and poor,* which absence has led to a bad state of feeling in the minds of the latter, and has fostered a jealous mistrust on their parts of the class above them. But again, I say, for *this* I can see no remedy. The beneficent dispositions of the *smaller* gentry can operate to but little advantage amongst the poor, beyond the mere temporary increase of their comfort. To influence the labouring class, you ought to have the power to raise their moral condition, to improve their habits, to encourage reasonable requests, to show them a kindly interest, and to foster justice between labourers and their masters; all which the possession of landed property enables you to do, if the Will exist. But so long as the poor feel the pressure of property privileges, unaccompanied by compensating benefits, no efforts on the part of individuals can alter their mode of viewing the relations between themselves and the rich. What that mode is, most residents in rural districts can tell; but it varies according to the character of the " Lords of the soil," by which the behaviour of poor residents is more influenced than it is often conceived to be.

I forbear, however, to open up a question, the bearings of which are too wide-spread to be considered here. Every half-century brings with it some modification of the framework in which society is encased,

---

* Mainly owing to the circumstance of there being no resident owner possessing the power of which I speak below.

and we ought to endeavour both to preserve unim-
paired such portions as are fitted to all times, and to
adapt our changes, as far as possible, to the immu-
table principles on which human society is based. And
perhaps the most important of these is, the maintenance of a cordial amity between the employers of
labour and the labourers themselves.   I have a
sincere value for the character of our husbandry
labourer, and believe that, under ordinary good treatment, he fulfils his duty with conscience, and even
zeal for his master's interest. Moreover, he is sensible
to acts of kindness and sympathy in a greater degree
than it is usual to give him credit for—more so, in
fact, than to acts of charity, in the common accepta-
tion of that word.

ON ART, ANCIENT AND MODERN.

ON ART, ANCIENT AND MODERN.

Tnis vast theme, to the illustration of which the finest intellects and the most assiduous study have been for ages directed, can hardly be approached without temerity by an amateur, whose knowledge must be, necessarily, superficial and incomplete, compared with that possessed by professional students. As, however, I have been invited to aid in weaving a " garland" of literary leaves, destined to be laid at the feet of our illustrious sovereign, I will do my best to justify the compliment.

Whilst renouncing the pretension to offer any novel or striking views on the subject, I propose to take a short survey of the comparative position occupied by the arts, and of the character imparted to them by cotemporary influences, at different stages of the history of mankind.

That the function of art is to act upon the imagination through the senses, is a proposition familiar to all of us. The precise form, however, in which this action shall exert itself must depend upon the state in which the popular imagination of the period happens to be. In an early stage of social development the prevalent ideas are few, simple, and deep-seated. The ancient architecture of the world accordingly combines grandeur and simplicity with

perfect adaptation to its ends. In pictorial efforts
the primitive features of interest ever present in early
societies constitute the subjects; as war, hunting, and
pompous ceremonials. In proportion as the course of
human thought advances, subjects multiply. The
introduction of female figures attests a certain improvement in the social habits. Farther on, a conception of grace united with strength is engendered by
the habitual contemplation of the unclothed human
body; and the portrayal of this, under diversified
action, comes to be regarded with pleasure. It was
among the small Greek communities that this power
of producing, in marble and on canvas, examples of
the finest forms of both sexes reached its climax. An
attentive study on the part of their artists of the
living beauty and symmetry continually present to
their eye, was of incalculable importance in the culture
and practice of imitative art. To this they superadded the closest devotion to the technical branch of
their art; the " treatment," the disposition of drapery,
the composition and character of their figures. The
minute study of external configuration did, in fact,
with the Greek sculptors, supply the absence of ana-
tomical science; and it may admit of a question
whether a knowledge of this would have enhanced
the effect or the accuracy of their delineations; such
was the familiarity of their eye with the situation and
functions of the muscles, and with the mutual relations of the osseous structure. The sources from
whence we derive our widest acquaintance with the
pictorial genius of the ancient Greeks, are their vessels
of earthenware, to which may be added a small
number of fresco paintings. In the urns and vases,

of which innumerable specimens are to be found in public collections, and many in private dwellings, the subjects almost exclusively consist of men, women, and animals, of which endless groups are arranged, illustrative of habits, manners, and, sometimes even, of passions; not unfrequently the mythology of the heathen world furnishes the matter of the composition, and nothing can surpass the charm which is present in these poetical representations when executed by the best artists of the period.

In the relics of ancient Greece, then, are to be found the highest examples of that branch of art which is devoted to the human form and its attributes. That nations, sprung into existence since that time, have reached considerable excellence in art, is indisputable; but not one has arrived at equal mastery with the Greeks, in the creative vein of sculpture. To enter upon a speculative disquisition, as to the causes which gave rise to this acknowledged supremacy, would be a task too comprehensive for the present occasion. If I may be permitted to express an opinion, it is that the two main sources whence this supremacy took its rise, were—1. The peculiar cast of the Greek mind, demanding, as it did, to be occupied with the study of man, to the exclusion of the rest of creation, and thus craving, at the hands of art ministers, exhibitions of the human effigy under interesting aspects, suggestive of some dominant sentiment, whether heroic, religious, or amorous; and, 2. The advantages enjoyed by the artists of constant, familiar observation of the nude figure, whether under the excitement of active games or in the varied attitudes of repose and recreation.

The Greeks, it must be remarked, took no delight in contemplating the beauty of the external world, or in what is commonly termed the " Poetry of Nature." Man, in his corporeal and physical aspects, and Man, as a social and intellectual being, seem to have absorbed the attention of artist, dramatist, and thinker respectively, among that remarkable people.

Under the Roman dominion, the character of the arts of sculpture and painting lost much of their dignity, becoming subservient to the degraded tastes and corrupted manners which prevailed among that people. When, in the fourth century, the pro-tection of the Roman Emperor was accorded to the Christian form of worship, the artists from various quarters who flocked to the new capital, Byzantium, shared the patronage of the Pagan with that of the Christian world; so that, for some con-siderable time, a mixed style of art obtained the ascendancy : blending the still extant, though impure, types of Grecian civilization with the Oriental style of treatment; and pictures and frescoes abounded, blazing with colour and glittering with meretricious, and even with metallic, ornament.

After the sixth century, the gradual increase and spread of Christianity enabled its professors to substi-tute paintings illustrative of their own sacred origin and history for the representations of subjects familiar to the older world. Such few vestiges as remain to us of these primitive efforts are, of course, injured and defaced; but, viewed as paintings, they could never have been other than barbarous productions. Passing over the feeble endeavours made during the dark ages to keep alive the embers of art, as serving both to kindle and to propagate the religious sentiment, we find so early as the eleventh, and notably in the twelfth century, a marked progress, of which the Church was naturally the chief promoter, in the form and character of Christian, or Pure Art.*

The subjects on which the painters of this period occupied their skill, partook of the religious feeling to an almost exclusive degree. And this concentration of the powers of the pencil on one vein of sentiment, produced in these works a simplicity of design, and profound devotional expression, together with a certain *naïveté* of composition. Qualities which have always commanded the homage of connoisseurs, although not generally attractive to the unlearned.

Through successive phases, such as an inquiring student will find no difficulty in tracing from Cimabue onwards, the capacity for expressing deep sentiment gradually allied itself with an improved faculty of composition and skill of hand, until the Umbrian and Florentine painters carried this divine art to a point of perfection never since attained; their works having continued to be regarded as models of excellence, with admiration and emulous imitation, by each successive age.

* In a work on Italian art, recently published in Paris, the author, M. Charles Clement, mentions, as being among the most striking efforts of the eleventh century, some of the mural pictures in mosaic work, especially those of Sicily and Venice :—" Ces gigantesques figures à demi barbares, dessinées sans art, qui n'ont ni modèle ni perspective, placées contre les parois, et dans le fond de vastes édifices obscurs, les remplissent de leur présence. Elles resplendissent, sur leur fond d'or, d'un éclat mystérieux et terrible ; et si le but de l'art religieux est de frapper vivement l'imagination, je ne pense pas qu'il l'ait jamais plus complètement attient que dans les mosaïques,"

Although painters of unquestionable genius and wide-spread fame continued to enrich European edifices and galleries during a considerable number of years, it is generally admitted that Italian art, after the sixteenth century, underwent a gradual decline; insomuch that the glories of the pencil and the chisel were, in the seventeenth, assigned to other lands.

The sculptors of Germany, and the painters of the Low Countries, together with a few eminent masters among the French, took a prominent lead in their respective departments, producing works which continue to enjoy a deservedly high repute to this day. And it is easy to understand how that the arts, no longer exclusively devoted to the sustentation of religious faith, but encouraged by the laity with liberal hand, broke into a variety of channels—secular, historical, voluptuous, architectural, festal, and the like. Landscape painting, too, assumed a more important character, and began to display the charm and captivation of which it is avowedly capable. Thus, the increase of wealth, the multiplication of objects of curiosity, and of means of enjoyment, contributed to diversify the productions of art, and to engender new styles; at the same time, by this active movement, the earnest, meditative compositions of the early painters became much less sought after. The tone of the period was changed.

During the eighteenth century no country would seem to have produced better painters than the British; our native artists maintaining a creditable position in that walk of art, though the sculptors of the Continent were confessedly superior to our own, and, I am afraid, continue to be so. The works produced in the latter portion of the century seem to rise, rather than decline, in public estimation, especially in respect to portraits, a branch of art in which the moderns scarcely reach the standard of their predecessors. However, the rich products of the easel in the nineteenth century surpass, in most other respects, those of the previous period. Stimulated by the growing appetite of the community for art, accompanied by an extraordinary increase of the purchasing power, the painter of modern days has invented new methods, employed the science of chemistry to improve his colours, and cultivated fresh fields in choosing his subjects. The foreign schools have likewise developed considerable activity, and many of their professors exhibit a dexterity of handling, a correctness of drawing, and a finish which command unqualified admiration. Yet, with these painters, as with us, high art is in some sort eclipsed by general subjects and, especially amongst the French, by such as are connected with battles and victories.

As to the predominant taste of the English in matters of art, it would puzzle the most attentive observer to characterize it suitably; so multiform are the fruits of the pencil in our day. I will venture, nevertheless, to employ one epithet, (which indeed seems applicable to modern feeling in general,) and say that it inclines to the *realistic* in art. Even in pictures of a religious class, we may observe how far this element has superseded the ideal and the pathetic. Pious ecstasies, eloquent agonies, are no longer in demand; the sober Protestant form of faith, conjoined with amiable and homely forms of sympathy—

domestic incidents and every-day interests—such are
the subjects which command the attention and ensure
the gaze of "the multitude," rich and poor, of our
time. And these predominate through the range of
modern artistic productions, reflecting indeed very
correctly the tone in which popular serial literature has, for some ten or twenty years back, been
composed.

"The applause of the exquisite few," said Wilkie,
in one of his published letters, "is better than that of
the ignorant many. But I like to reverse received
maxims. Give *me* the many who have admired, in
different ages, Raffaelle and Claude." On which
passage, Mr. Leslie, in his own memoirs, published in
1860, comments thus :—" But have *the many*, in any
age, admired Raffaelle and Claude? I certainly
believe not." . . . And again, Leslie remarks that,
" Wilkie's works were popular from the first, because
the public could understand his subjects, and natural
expression is always responded to. But the beauty of
his composition, the truth of his '*effects*,' the taste of
his execution, were no more felt by the multitude
than such qualities are felt in any class of painting, by
any but those whose perceptions of art are cultivated.
. . . An artist must belong to the multitude to
please the multitude."

In these remarks I own I am disposed to concur,
whilst guarding myself against being supposed to dis-
parage the taste of "the multitude." It is certainly
a most pleasing circumstance that so large a portion
of our countrymen and countrywomen should indulge
a liking for art. Nevertheless, a faculty of nicely
discriminating between true and false greatness in

painters can only, in my judgment, be exercised by a comparatively small class amongst us—composed of individuals who possess leisure, opportunities of travel and of study, aptitude for observation and comparison, and a natural disposition to derive enjoyment from the contemplation of objects of art. On them the duty rests of upholding the eternal principles on which true art is based. English amateurs—from Royalty downwards to the merchant—have always fostered the arts; not alone encouraging living artists, but coming forward, with alacrity, to possess themselves of really valuable specimens of bygone times, when offered, at intervals, in the market. And the English Government also displays unremitting zeal in the acquisition of works calculated to encourage the public to interest themselves in the higher excellences of painting. It would be matter of real gratification to feel that these could be exemplified in the performances of modern professors. Let us hope that such will be forthcoming at no distant day.

The very narrow space into which it has been requisite to compress this sketch, precludes the addition of farther remarks suggested by the actual condition of art, and the influence of opinion bearing upon it in this country. I must content myself with saying that if, indeed, " the many," now form the bulk of the purchasing class, and bestow the widest fame upon professors of art, it may safely be added that never were " the many " so well served as now. For every variety of taste, a painter brings the supply; (often, indeed, creating it;) yet the teeming abundance of artistic talent—diffusing itself, as it does, along countless channels, and offering meritorious and attractive works in all styles,—seems destined, in some degree, to supplant the cultivation of the noble and elevated type. If each period of history bears its characteristic stamp, surely in none has the impress of contemporary feeling and thought been more discernible than in the art, and I must permit myself to add, the literature of fiction, of our own era.

It may be fairly presumed, I think, that the important step taken in a high quarter, within these few years, to improve the means of art education among the people, was owing to a perception of the tendencies above indicated. To furnish to the humble youthful student, gratuitously, assistance in forming a taste for the higher attributes of art, and, next, in carrying even into the material products of the country some traces of their refining influence, was, indeed, a project dictated by a discerning comprehension of the value of sound elementary study. The foundation of the South Kensington Museum, due in great part to the Prince Consort's agency, may, it is to be hoped, operate as a counterpoise to the causes which for some considerable period would seem to have modified and, in a measure, vulgarized the character of British Art. That relish for striking effect, both of colour and expression, for exquisitely high-wrought finish, and for melo-dramatic composition, which now pervades the community, may possibly be one day superseded by a preference for loftier qualities in painting. Should such a change arrive, we may safely ascribe much of it to the salutary, the instructive, study of the masterpieces of all kinds and all countries, ancient and modern, which are to be seen in our principal

national depositories: accompanied and seconded by
the lessons of competent professors under the direction
of the managers of the Kensington Museum, working
in harmony with the great schools of the Royal
Academy.

August, 1861.

[Reprinted from the " Victoria Regia."]

VARIOUS PAPERS

CONTRIBUTED TO THE

"SPECTATOR" WEEKLY NEWSPAPER.

1845—1852.

POMMERSFELDEN.

Coblentz, September, 1845.

I WANT to tell you about Pommersfelden, a place I alluded to on a recent occasion ; and which is not one of the " King of Bohemia's seven castles," but one among several real chateaux belonging to the noble family of Schönborn,—a name widely reputed in Bavaria, or, to speak more precisely, in old Franconia, where it is situate.

About seven or eight English miles out of the main road leading from Wurtzburg to Bamberg, and in a direct line between the last-named city and Neustadt, there stands a vast and imposing edifice, built about the commencement of the last century by Lothair Francis, Count Schönborn, Bishop of Bamberg, and Archbishop of Mainz, Chancellor of the German Empire, and Lord knows what beside; who, in addition to the princely revenues derived from these high offices, inherited the estates of Pommersfelden from a Count Truchsess, his kinsman, on the death of this nobleman in 1710. Lothair Francis was a man of remarkable abilities, and enjoyed a high reputation as a statesman, jurist, and patron of the arts; with which he was himself extremely well acquainted, especially with architecture. Desiring to apply a portion of his wealth to the erection of a palace, or " schloss," suited to the dignity of his family, of which he found himself the leading member—a monument

that should honour the memory of his generous kinsman, he commenced this undertaking, in 1711, after
the design of Loyson, a Jesuit, doctor and professor
of philosophy, and Chancellor of the University of
Bamberg, an eminent *dilettante* of the period. The
style of architecture employed is of the character
which was then coming into vogue, and which had
recently been introduced by Louis the Fourteenth in
building his palace of Versailles. The plan of the
edifice may be described as that of the letter E. In
the hollow of the centre is placed the magnificent
entrance-hall and staircase, which for lofty proportions and elegance of design may challenge any vesti-
bule in Europe. The size of this truly regal residence
may be guessed at when I mention that we passed
through four large rooms occupying a part of the
principal floor on the Northern front (the other part
being appropriated to the library)—making, I should
say, one hundred feet in length—and next, through
twelve rooms on the West front, one of which was a
splendid banquet " salle," floored with marble, forty
feet high, and not less than sixty feet long. To add
that there is a chapel attached to the " schloss," were
needless, Franz Lothair being an ecclesiastic of the
highest rank. But the circumstance of its containing a valuable collection of pictures constitutes the
prominent attraction of Pommersfelden; and it is to
this I wish to invite your attention.

The palace once built, its distinguished possessor
bent his endeavours to the acquisition of a gallery of
paintings fitted to adorn its interior, as well as of a
good collection of books. Lothair Franz was on familiar terms with the eminent artists of his times; and,

by his own discerning judgment, as well as by the
able assistance of his " hofmaler" or court painter
(in fact, he had two in his pay, *Byss* and *Cossian*), he
speedily got hold of a considerable number of precious works,—chiefly, however, of the Flemish school,
in which our Prince-Bishop especially delighted. Herr
Heller, of Bamberg, in his interesting little notice of
.this chateau, published quite recently, states the
number to have been 480, as early as the year 1719.
The heirs and successors of Lothair pursuing the
design of enriching the gallery with choice pictures,
it became, towards the middle of the eighteenth century, amply stored; and critical catalogues and notices
upon it began to be published by the connoisseurs of
that period. In 1759, the invasion of Franconia by
the Prussian troops engaged in the Seven Years'
War, occasioned the pictures to be hurried off to a
place of safety; and again in 1802, when the French
overran this country, the treasures of Pommersfelden
were a second time dragged across the heart of Germany to another and distant residence of the Counts
Schönborn, in Bohemia, there to abide the course of
events. When they were finally replaced in their
wonted positions, a regular keeper was installed to
watch over them, named Joseph Dorn ; who lived
into the year 1841.

Although, as has been said above, the collection is
more richly furnished with Flemish works than with
the productions of the Italian masters, yet are there
many of the latter to be found here which may fairly
be classed as superior pictures. Of these, the leading
specimen is a painting by Leonardo da Vinci (long
attributed to Rafaelle, however, and by Byss, among

the rest), of the Virgin and Child, than which I have seldom seen a more charming production. The Virgin, whose left hand and arm hang over a pedestal, is exquisitely painted; her right arm encircles the babe, who is sitting in her lap, and pointing to a vase or urn in the background. I should not wonder if this picture alone were found to be worth from one to two thousand guineas. It is of the size of life, and three-quarter length. It has undergone some injury by being carried to Munich, to serve as a model for the students in painting there: the journey has damaged the impasto in places, and this has been repaired somewhat unskilfully,—a sad return for the generous proprietor's kindness in allowing this valuable picture to go to Munich. A naked Venus, by Titian, is perhaps next in point of merit to the Leonardo; whilst a portrait of a young officer in armour, by the same master, near it, challenges the warmest admiration. A Carlo Dolce (Mater Dolorosa, according to the received pattern of this painter) is of very high quality, perhaps equal to Sir Thomas Baring's. A Magdalen, by Guido, in his brown manner, is rich in colour, but voluptuous in character; an Assumption, by Giovanni Bellini, is interesting, though not in the artist's best style; a large allegorical piece by Paul Veronese; a St. Sebastian, by Carlo Dolce (of a truly celestial expression); Tobias and the Angel, by Murillo; Isaac blessing Jacob, by Annibal Carracci; and several subjects by Tintoretto, Spagnoletto, and Domenichino, are all more or less worthy of honourable mention. In passing to a description of the *chefs d'œuvre* of the other schools of art, I am apprehensive of falling into

superlatives: so perfect, so matchless are many of
the pictures, that you get into a *fever* of admiration
as each gem occupies your eager attention by turns.
Where shall I begin?—with the Vandycks?—but the
Rembrandts—yes, the Rembrandts! what a feast
had we in his "Saul gazing upon the Shade of
Samuel evoked by the Witch of Endor." The
language of praise is pale in presence of such a
masterpiece—I dare not attempt to use it, but must
content myself with saying that the picture is in the
finest *condition;* about three feet high; and the figures
larger than common in Rembrandt's compositions.
But the glorious colouring and effects of torch-light—
ah me! There are several Rembrandts besides this,
two of which are of high merit,—viz., an old woman
reading at a large open book, called the Prophetess
Johanna; and a man sitting in an easy-chair: there
is also a Dutch baker blowing his horn at his shop-
door, an excellent work. By Rubens, a Christ on
the Cross, in his finest manner, about two feet and a
half high; a magnificent composition called Charity,
with four lusty naked boys—a large canvas, the
flesh incomparably fine; a St. Francis, vigorously
painted, life size; a lady seated, a whole-length
figure—capital; an Entombment; David playing
upon the Harp. But I must here pause. More
remains to be told of the rarities I beheld in this
palatial residence; but they must form the subject of
a future letter. So prepare for fresh rhapsodies on
the part of your humble servant and subscriber.

CHARACTER OF THE REV. SYDNEY SMITH.

March 10, 1845.

THE comment on the Reverend Sydney Smith's character and writings, which appeared in the *Spectator* of 1st March, struck me as being at once accurate and discriminating, in so far as it took a view of both, such as a thoughtful observer of his times might well arrive at, having no personal feeling towards or even private acquaintance with the eminent divine lately lost to the world. But those who enjoyed the privilege of private intercourse with this remarkable man must feel that quite as much remains to be said of him under that aspect; and I venture to speak as one of them, although admitted within the circle of his familiar associates only during the latter years of his life, when, of course his beams must have been shorn of a part of their former splendour. Still, the setting glories of Sydney Smith were more brilliant than most other men's meridian rays.

In the varied flow of his conversational powers, the point of his playful satire, and the force and vivacity of his illustrations, few, if any, have ever approached him: added to these, there was a natural buoyancy of temper, and genial aptitude for mirth and for the enjoyment of society, which had so exhilarating an effect on those around him that no one ever felt reluctant to be made the subject of his pleasantry. His attacks were indeed like summer lightning—they never harmed the object illumined by their flash.

But not in the convivial hour alone was Sydney Smith qualified to bear a leading part. In temperate and philosophic discussion—on topics embracing the substantial interests of the human race—on ethical questions—he was luminous in his remarks, large and liberal-minded, and even patient of contradiction. In fact, he had read much, and always with the sincerest desire to arrive at truth; and if he lacked that quality of intellect which is capable of imparting original views on profound subjects, no man was ever more successful in possessing himself of the results of other men's thoughts, and in diffusing them in a form suited to the apprehension of ordinary readers. A distinguished scholar now living, writing of Sydney Smith to a friend in 1840, observes—" Ridicule seems to me to be admirably fitted to confound fools, and to destroy their prejudices. It is not needed in order to recommend truth to wise men; and indeed, from its generally dealing in exaggeration and slight misrepresentation, is likely to offend them. It is his mastery of ridicule which renders Sydney Smith so powerful as a diffuser of ideas; for in order to diffuse widely, it is necessary to be able to address fools. His powers as a *diffuser*, as compared with the powers of a great *inventor*, who was latterly altogether wanting in the diffusing power, are well shown in his article on Bentham's *Book of Fallacies*. Indeed, as a diffuser of the good ideas of other men, I do not know whether he ever had an equal."

When the imaginative faculty was in question, however, Sydney Smith was creative and original enough, God knows. When in good spirits, the exuberance of his fancy showed itself in the most fan-

tastic images and most ingenious absurdities, till his
hearers and himself were at times fatigued with the
merriment they excited. He had the art, too, of
divesting personalities of vulgarity; and not unfrequently was the luckless victim of his wit seen to
enjoy the exercise of it quite as much as others. In
fact, many persons rather felt it as a compliment
when Sydney singled them out for sport. And he
was so universal in his sympathies, that he did not
require a select or distinguished circle in order to be
incited to display. His rich resources flowed so freely
forth, that I have heard some of his happiest inspirations uttered to persons of comparatively humble pretensions either to intelligence or fashion. The presence of men and women—so they were but of the
educated class—always unlocked his sympathies, and
he expanded without difficulty as without vanity. Not
that he was insensible to the value of choice society—
none knew better how to prize and enjoy it. But
he had such a store of kindly benevolence in his
heart, that he liked to contribute to the happiness of
whomsoever he found himself in company with.
Nobody too obscure, in fact, for Sydney to put into
good humour with themselves. Nay, I have seen
him brighten the countenance of his poor parishioners, for the day, by a captivating phrase or two,
when he met them, or visited their cottage in quality
of "doctor," as he was wont to do at Combe Florey.*

---

* On one occasion, his parish-clerk being laid up with a broken shin,
Sydney called round to know if *his plaster* had wrought benefit. "I'm
getting round, Sir; but I doubt I sha'n't be fit for duty by Sunday
next." "Sorry for that, David, indeed; we shall miss you at the singing." Then turning to me, "You can't think what a good hand David

It has been objected, that his temperament unfitted him for the clerical profession.   It certainly did
not prevent his active discharge of those duties which
belong to the office of a parish-priest; and I have
heard from good authority, that during his long residence (of sixteen years, I believe) on his living in
Yorkshire, no clergyman ever performed those duties
with better effect.   *I* know how he performed them
at Combe Florey, and recollect it with admiration
and respect.   Such village sermons are rare; such
pastoral protection and care not frequent; whilst his
medical knowledge (which was purposely acquired at
Edinburgh in this view) was always available to his
poor neighbours' comfort and relief.   But he indulged
in levity, it is asserted, on religious topics.   To this
I reply, that, whatever may have passed in the familiar confidence of his intimate society, nothing that
the public have a right to deal with is obnoxious to
this cavil.   Professionally speaking, Sydney Smith
was without blemish; and this is saying much.   Let
such dignitaries as are without spot throw the first
stone.   He did not, moreover, choose his profession;
and the most that can be said, therefore, is, that being
made a priest by his father's will and desire, he did
not compress and subjugate the original man into the
ideal of a churchman.   Yet it has been suggested, on
the opposite view of his character, that he used his
powerful pen in behalf of his corporation interests!
(Letters to Archdeacon Singleton, to wit.)   The
truth is, that Sydney conceived it to be his profes-

is at a psalm—you should hear him lead off *the Old Hundredth.*"   At
which the old clerk's eyes fairly glistened as he stammered out, " Ah !
your honour's only saying that to cheer me up a bit."

sional duty to espouse the corporation interests; and
accordingly he sustained them by his one-sided professional remonstrance against Lord John Russell's
interference with its rights. But it is difficult to
please all objectors, and even Sydney Smith could
not hit the mark,—too catholic for some, too clerical-
minded for others; the only sure course being a blind
and steady party-zeal: and this was just what my
revered friend could not practise. He aided the
Whigs prodigiously when they figured as the apostles
of the principles he had at heart; for he wrote with
the force of conviction. At a later season, they were
in the ascendant, and he wielded his pen in the clerical service as the paramount obligation of his later
days. That he should have been something more—
or something less, as you will—than a member of the
sacerdotal corporation, seems to me inseparable from
the enlarged and beneficent character of Sydney
Smith's mind: and I can only add, would that the
Church were never worse served than by my lamented
friend!

FRENCH POLITICS.

January, 1850.

LA PRESSE is distinguished among Paris journals for an undaunted self-reliance, and together with the vices of audacity it possesses not a few of the good qualities of courage. It can, when so pleased, be candid; and it has thus given circulation to a remarkable and interesting series of letters, by an American gentleman, on the Political Constitutions of England, the United States, and France under the actual Republic.

Compared with the wearisome and pompous declamation of the Democratic organs, or with the mystical and high-flown homilies of Legitimacy, these letters claimed a marked attention; coming as they do from a citizen of the greatest Republic ever organized since the world began; from one schooled in its discipline, familiar with its machinery, and extensively conversant with its doctrines; accustomed also to compare them both in their theory and in their practice with the old institutions of Europe. Mr. Henry Wikoff has lived much with the French; he admires their nation, and loves to dwell among them: hence his earnest longings to be useful, according to his ability, in assisting them to arrive at that most important blessing, a solid and well-constructed form of government. Taking as the text of his first letter " the Constitution of the United States," he expounds the action of its respective forces in securing the

nearest approach to liberty and equality ever beheld
in the social state, coincidently with that security to
life and property without which any government were
a worthless pageant. We hardly know in what shape
instruction on political philosophy could be rendered
more available to the people than in the one Mr.
Wikoff has chosen. His exposition of the American
apparatus of government is delivered in an unpretending simple style, such as might characterize the
descriptions of machines or instruments in the pages
of a scientific treatise. One is made to see so clearly
the relation between the several parts, that ideas of
mechanical laws unconsciously rise to the mind, and
we half expect to see an illustrative cut, with " A the
cylinder, C the fly-wheel, F the revolving pinion, H
the valve-index," and so forth. Once familiar with
the structure of a political constitution sanctioned by
experiment, the French people will be furnished with
a model according to which their own may be made
to fit its purpose; although, starting from a condition
less favourable to constructive organization than the
colonial architects, some compromises must be made
with ancient principles. It depends upon the French
people, as a nation, how far these shall extend; and
they may thank the author of the letters to *La Presse*
for lending them a helping hand towards a better
comprehension of their interests in respect to the
nature of such compromises.

The striking feature, we repeat, of these letters, is
their transparent clearness; a feature in which the
writers of the day in France, with all their talent,
certainly do not shine. The view Mr. Wikoff has taken
of the English constitutional course may be pronounced

sagacious on the whole; and it is instructive, as
tracing the conflict between the mighty elements of
English life, Aristocracy and Democracy, through a
long historical period, till the curious and indescri-
bable thing which the English government has come
to be, got into operation, to the despair of foreign
statesmen and the misleading of foreign imitators.
The New Yorker, however, is not quite so much at
home in his subject when writing upon England; but
is hardly open to censure for incompleteness, seeing
that he has treated a prodigious subject within the
space of a few columns, and that without violating
any important historical sequence, although he has
necessarily overlooked a vast number of intermediate
and connecting links.

But the really essential lesson to be inculcated on
the French nation is, not so much how their new
framework of civil government should be put together,
as how it should be worked and applied to its purpose
when set up.   For here lies the formidable difficulty
with that people, so insidiously cheated of their hopes
by each successive dynasty, and so unfairly reproached by lookers-on for manifesting discontent
under their disappointments.

It is to no purpose that the French people make
revolutions, since the government which succeeds
contrives to get back into the vicious track of its ex-
pelled predecessor; or, if not into the same, into a
course no less fatal to national credit and tranquillity.
The moral to be deduced from this is twofold.   Some
will choose to affirm that this fact proves how much
wiser the people would show themselves if they would
let revolutions alone, and submit to the unavoidable

evils of bad governors.   Others, more keenly alive to
the principles of equity and the reciprocal duties of
governors and governed, will adopt the maxim that
care must be taken in reforming a government to put
at the head of it persons interested in its going on
successfully and healthily.   But this is just what
cannot be hoped for in the case of the present
Republic of France.

In that beautiful country, rich in all the elements
which can constitute earthly happiness and solid
prosperity, there unhappily wants a steadfast desire
for the growth and permanent establishment of the
actual government.   The whole of the upper class of
Frenchmen, from the President down to the Lecturer
on Botany at the Academy of Dijon, are in a tacit
league to the end that the Republic shall *not* stand.
In the face of such a coalition, what are the working
classes to do?   Is it conceivable, we would ask, that,
under the original American constitution even, a
republic could have got on its legs, if Washington, if
Jefferson, Adams, and Franklin, and that class of
political men, had looked unkindly upon its birth?
What made the infant republic spring to vigorous
life? what made the constitution gradually evolve
itself into effective operation after the Convention
of 1787-8-9?

It was the cordial patriotism of the American
statesmen, principal no less than secondary, which
mainly brought about the success of that memorable
experiment: it is the absence of this element in France
—patriotic singleness of purpose, and a disposition to
accept the present fabric as her permanent destiny—
which, it is to be feared, will hinder it from taking

root in her soil, or in the attachment of her sons.
Can anything be more disheartening than to see a
noble man-of-war betrayed by her officers? Yet
such will be the spectacle offered by the Republic of
France, unless some means can be found to frustrate
the combination formed against it by every cluster of
parties engaged in public life.

It is not difficult to specify in what consists the
disposition to abolish this government. Every attentive observer can see that it is not rich enough to
corrupt the hungry harpies who supported the late
system. Their support is withdrawn, whilst that of
no other party can be relied on; simply because they
desire and hope to establish each their own idol, on
the ruins of the Republic. The President, weak in
his personal following, is thus obliged to play the
game of attracting the favour of the working classes
and of the army. And a game more destructive, in
respect to permanent popularity with the nation at
large, there cannot be. With Mr. Wikoff's aid we
may recur to the leading points which bear upon the
difficulties of the French nation in getting even a
good constitution into work. Meanwhile, let us
refrain from those too common accusations against
the people, as such, for allowing no government to
stand, whilst as yet they have destroyed none which
has deserved to endure.

Should the present one perish, it would certainly
owe its destruction, not to the "Republicans of the
streets," but to the conspirators of the salons; to the
very class from whom we have heard such unmea-
sured revilings against the "restless discontents" of
the lower orders. The Republic, it is manifest, suits

neither the aristocracy nor the office-seekers; the Monarchy did not satisfy the people. Shall we never get beyond a choice between one class interest and another?

The third letter addressed by Mr. Wikoff, the American, to the Paris journal *La Presse*, deals in a sort of historical *résumé* of French internal changes, from an early period; the drift of which would seem to be the illustration of Mr. Wikoff's favourite dogma, that without a due proportion of the three elementary principles—monarchical, aristocratical, and democratical—no nation can expect to flourish, or even to avoid political tempests. We suspect that a good many other reasons, besides the defective operation of "the balance," may be assigned for the frequent intestine commotions of our neighbours; and what is more, we doubt whether "the balance" has been the secret of our own tranquil progress since the expulsion of the last Stuart. It is true that a belief in the theory of mutual checks in the English constitution has been widely circulated, and treated as a reality by eminent publicists and professors of jurisprudence. De Lolme, for instance, built a name upon an elaborate exposition of its admirable structure, which for years served for a text-book on Government. But whoever studies the operation of English institutions attentively, seldom fails to discover that there are, in fact, only two forces at work,—the monarch and the aristocracy, covertly united, on one side; the popular will on the other. Even the memorable project of the Reform Bill was but a sacrifice on the part of one section of aristocracy to gain the advantage over a rival section, in which the reigning monarch lent them his aid. The pure element of aristocratical power, the House of Lords, was then seen to exert its separate will and interest. But the " balance" was, like the scales of Brennus, falsified by an unscrupulous use of the royal prerogative. The king, having the people at his back, for once showed the value of the pretended " balance," when compared with the *reality* of a popular determination: an instructive lesson, not often permitted to the lookers-on, so plausible is the fiction, and so useful to the governing powers.

After all, we have no objection to the theory, as such; and if Mr. Wikoff succeed in engrafting it upon the French mind, it is quite conceivable that he may be doing them a service. For as the Democratic party in the French Chamber seeks to render itself predominant by means unbecoming a deliberative assembly, it would seem but fitting that those members who belong to a class habituated to the restraints of genteel life should be allowed to exercise the function of legislators in peace and with decorous forms. And to this end, as Mr. Wikoff urges, two Chambers are indispensable,—a bear-garden for the " Montagne;" and a Senate (or " House of Lords") for educated men of business, where public discussion should be carried on with some chance of profit to the country, by those who under an unitary representative system would be condemned to inaction.

But in order that a nation should consolidate its public institutions, it must positively resist wanton changes. " Le mieux est l'ennemi du bien," it has been happily said; and the existing French constitution, with all its faults, offers so much of what is essential to a good one, that, having got it into

operation, the nation ought to endeavour to keep it
going at least for some years, by force of good citizenship, and a firm will to resist the provocations of
dissatisfied and restless partisans of a monarchy: and
thus, since the existing law forbids the re-election of
the President, so ought it to stand, although it may
be one of questionable wisdom.

It strikes us as a most discouraging fact, that an
able and influential writer like M. C. Dunoyer should
at this time of day, constitute himself all at once the
apostle of Legitimacy. In a pamphlet recently put
forth, he distinctly calls upon his countrymen to
throw aside all this wicker-work of a government,
and to recall Henri Cinq, with the whole tissue of
exploded sentiments and traditions, as being the only
chance for the French nation to regain her character
among the powers of Europe. It reminds one of what
takes place after the curtain has fallen at the theatre
upon the final scene of a tragic drama: every leading
personage being killed or exiled, and the "moral"
left to operate on the spectators, forth steps the
manager, and announces that the play will be acted
again the next night. So with M. Dunoyer: the
terrible efforts by which the French have sought to
escape from the abuses of kingly government are
treated like the acts of players; whilst the King is
behind the scenes, ready to step on to the stage once
more, wholly regardless of the sanguinary lessons
which have been inculcated on his predecessors.
But the French people cannot be desirous of re-
establishing a Bourbon dynasty. We agree with
Mr. Wikoff, that they are not justly chargeable with
fickleness or with a blind love of revolutions. They

have proved that they could resent the faults of bad governments, and also that, sixty years ago, they could be led to commit furious excesses in their vengeance: but what centuries of oppression had they not endured? Now, however, the nation, as such, is disposed to check all attempts at violence, and might be readily brought to co-operate in the organization of provincial and local systems of government, were its rulers but honest enough to afford it the means. We fear, however, that the passion for centralization, so rife among political leaders, will continue to paralyze a tendency which, if encouraged, might beyond all else promote the internal tranquillity of France, as well as afford a counterpoise to the mischievous ascendancy of its metropolis.

THE CITIZEN PEER.

February, 1850.

ONE of our most distinguished fellow citizens is, we understand, to be speedily advanced to the honours and dignity of the Peerage, by the title of Baron Overstone. The road by which Mr. Samuel Jones Loyd will have arrived at this dignity is one which is seldom travelled,—namely, that of individual merit. It is indeed probable that the vast wealth of which he is reputed to be the possessor, counts for much in the calculations of those by whom he has been invited to assume the coronet; but we believe that the personal qualities of the eminent ex-banker, his accurate knowledge of some of the most difficult subjects which the Legislature is called upon to consider, coupled with a rare talent for lucid and condensed exposition of his views, have supplied still more weighty motives for placing him in the House of Lords. The acquisition, by the party in possession of office, of a recruit of so valuable a quality, is matter of congratulation to all their friends, whilst the country may well regard with satisfaction the presence in Parliament of a man of large possessions, combining talent of no common order with a sincere love of progress, and a sound appreciation of the public interests.

For many years past, the friends of Mr. Loyd have regretted that the sphere of his influence should be so limited, and that the confidence felt in his sagacious counsels should be shared by those alone to whom his society was accessible. But to the House of Commons he was little suited. He regarded that assembly as one in which a man's capacity to be of service to the public was more than counterbalanced by the extreme annoyance to which the licence permitted there to personal attacks subjects him; especially after the period of youth is past, and the habit of self-respect has become comparatively sensitive.

In the Upper House, to do it justice, more attention is given to expository speeches; a greater decorum prevails; and, what is of still more value to an advocate of farsighted principles in any walk of legislation, the speaker is unfettered by the control of constituents. And here, in fact, lies the important distinction between the debates in the respective Chambers. The standard by which a member of the House of Commons adjusts his discourse is necessarily kept down to the quality which suits his supporters in the borough or county he represents. That of a peer needs to be adjusted by no considerations except such as belong to his theme, unless perhaps we admit party motives as likely to influence his arguments. From party motives, however, the new peer will probably derive but slender inspiration; although doubtless his inclinations will lead him to put out his strength, when occasion and conscience concur, in favour of the Whig Government.

The reasons in support of a double chamber of legislation would seem to be sustained by the experience of recent Continental events. If, in truth, we hold by the old song, " Crabbed age and youth cannot live together," and farther, if mature age and property are to be allowed their fair proportion of influence in the national councils, then must an Upper House be maintained for its exercise. For since the changes in the Lower House, brought about by the infusion of a class somewhat addicted to infringe upon polite rules and customs, it cannot be disguised that the well-bred and more instructed section of that body feel themselves unequally yoked; whilst their taste is offended, and their health impaired, by a profitless attendance in a heterogeneous assembly, of which the greater number are indifferent to the real merits of the questions debated before them.

Viewed under this aspect, therefore, the present House of Commons would seem to retain its attraction for gentlemen of large stake in the country, chiefly as offering the means of maintaining their political influence, and as a step towards the Upper House. And it is creditable to the Government that it waived this customary probation in the case of Mr. Jones Loyd. To have bestowed the character of a legislator for life upon an independent and un-political commoner, of the commercial class, falls in with the temper of the times, and is likely to give general satisfaction out of doors.

A GLANCE AT MODERN EUROPE.

November, 1850.

THE events of the day, notified as they are by the various organs which the ingenuity of man now devotes to the business of supplying "news" all over the world, are enough to occupy most persons' minds during the hours which business or the cares of life leave us for the indulgence of reading. So rapid, indeed, is the sequence of incidents which pass before the eyes of Europe, that few people can discern in the facts such a connexion as may afford a clue to the really pervading influences at work on the old frame of society. That there is such a connexion may nevertheless be affirmed; and one which it is amply worth while to watch and trace, were it only for the sake of curiosity, but which it more behoves us to detect and interpret in the hope of turning our knowledge to wholesome profit for the coming time.

The lower classes of the people of Europe may in these days be likened to a child who has become possessed of a watch. He sees the dial, and the hands at work; it performs certain processes with given results; his curiosity impels him to break open his machine and examine the structure and contrivances; whereby he destroys it, and the watch ceases to go. The old governments of Continental Europe have been in like fashion exposed to view; broken into by popular curiosity, prompted by popular displeasure; and the actual result is, that they, like the watch,

Q 2

have one and all ceased to perform, or at least have
come into so dismal a state of confusion that everywhere is found consternation, disunion, vacillation,
and alarm. One power alone may be said to have
got "on her legs" once more, which is Austria; and
that *she* is insolvent is admitted even by her stanch
supporter the *Times* newspaper. But Austria, at
least, "knows what she would be at," which is more
than can be predicated of any other European cabinet.
She wants to bring matters back to a position nearly
resembling that in which governments stood prior to
the revolution of 1848. With Russia at her elbow,
Austria is therefore labouring in her vocation, and
has recently shown her sincerity by aiding one of the
lesser German states to resist manifestations of dis-
affection among its subjects. On the other side, the
King of Prussia, with characteristic weakness and
incapacity of foreseeing political results, has been
worse than a nullity in regard to the advancement of
Liberal doctrines in Germany. By his trimming
and dissimulating conduct, he has forfeited all claim
to confidence on the part of the friends of progress,
whilst he has become odious in the eyes of his more
consistent and clearsighted fellow monarchs. His
pretended demonstrations in behalf of the *people* of
Hesse have been proved insincere; and the King of
Prussia is now, although wielding an immense
military force, completely at sea as to how to play out
his own foolish game. I need not particularize the
sources of this embarrassment, which must be patent
to the eyes of such as have observed passing events
with any attention of late. But the combination of
Austria and Russia against the growth of popular

institutions is too formidable to leave room to doubt that, in countries subject to their influence, very little progress can be made for the present: coupled with this, the resistance on the part of the higher classes to popular sentiments, in countries not comprised under this leaden despotism, may be considered as forming nearly as potent an obstacle to the growth of freedom as the resuscitated remnant of the Holy Alliance itself.

If I am not misinformed, the bulk of the richer inhabitants and noble families in the leading states of Germany (certainly in Prussia, Hanover, Saxony, and Bavaria) entertain a decided aversion to admitting the element of "representation" into the machinery of state government. Now, therefore, when we hear of certain kings being disposed to grant concessions to popular demands, it should always be borne in mind, that in doing so they alienate the main body of their adherents among the upper ranks in the country, and find, in these, unwilling ministers of any line of policy tainted with the sin of a democratic tendency. When this general fact is remembered, together with another, namely, that the mass of the people in Germany is both untrained to political action and ill-provided with individual organs or leaders, it must appear hopeless to expect German social amelioration to proceed, save at a terribly slow rate. Still, I believe it does proceed, and that in spite of Austrian influence; and now the question suggests itself, why is Austria suffered to weigh like an incubus upon civilization and human development? Has she a friend among the Western family of Europe? No, I answer; not one at heart. But her position in *the map*, involved as it is with everlasting traditions of bygone transactions, treaties, "understandings," protocols, &c., mixed up with indefinable apprehensions of "losing the key to the East" if Austria ceased to bar the road to Constantinople,— all these and many more mysterious associations have so hedged the old empire round about, in the minds of red-tapists of the highest order, that her genuine character, or the mischief her rule generates to the millions subject to it, never counts for anything in discussions bearing on Continental polity, among her contemporaries.

This ancient, time-honoured nuisance, thus continues to bear sway; thanks to the superstitions embodied in her existence, and to the instinct of sympathy which enlists every lover of absolute government in her preservation. Nay, her very resurrection, after the expulsion of her presiding genius Prince Metternich, in 1848, was the fruit of too respectful an attachment to ancient rights and forms on the part of popular chiefs, who were thereby withheld from pushing the advantages they had gained.

Among the motives, however (for they are multiform), which concur in maintaining the power of Austria, is the desire to keep on foot an antagonist force as against France in Europe. Whatever one may wish as regards the maintenance of good and amicable relations with that near and powerful neighbour of ours, nothing is more clear than that we ought "never to trust her out of our sight." The extreme sensitiveness of the French people on the side of national importance, not to say vanity, enables their governors to turn to account their foible, on occasion, often at perilous cost: with such a weak side, it is natural to apprehend that our neighbours would clap up an alliance with any power who should offer them the tempting bait of an "arrondissement de frontière," or who would do homage to their "greatness" in any other, even less substantial way. The fact is, that the French nation is in too unsettled a state to be counted on for any purpose beneficial to the interests of mankind. They will be persuaded to do anything—march anywhere—repudiate no matter what principles of political morality—if they but hear the old watchwords "French influence," "legitimate ascendancy," "glory of the French arms," and so forth. For who can ever forget, much less forgive, the monstrous application made of newly-established republican powers, on these pretexts, to the extinction of nascent independence and republican government in Rome?

That unpardonable act of the French rulers was, indeed, I much fear me, far from offensive to the nation itself: at least, I know that some of its most estimable citizens, including, for instance, M. Léon Faucher and M. Alexis de Tocqueville, viewed the employment of French bayonets to force the Pope upon an unwilling people as a suitable, nay, a praiseworthy act, even of a government owing its existence to the popular breath.

But to return to the general aspect of the European world as it now stands. From France small anticipations are to be cherished of co-operation in the work of progress. Whatever disposition may animate *the masses* of that nation, her present ruling classes have too great a fear of the encroachments of

the popular element to encourage new efforts at reforming social abuses. They would rather, in fact,
accept the friendly support of some old despotism
than that of a republic of any kind. It is tolerably
evident, then, that from no existing government
can the partisans of political reformation look for
support, or even countenance. From England it is
not likely to attend them—and I say this without
meaning to cast blame on this nation for withholding
it; the peculiar position in which she is placed in
reference to France being of itself a serious ground for
observing a discreet neutrality in the affairs of other
countries. France and England might, indeed, new-
model the greater portion of these, if they could
cordially agree upon fundamental principles. But
how can this be hoped for, after the hateful crusade
of the former in behalf of a crumbling priesthood,
whose rule, already fallen into contempt and odium
among its own subjects, was confessedly unsuited to
the altered tone of sentiment prevalent in the modern
world? What common action can there be on the
part of the French and English people, after such a
manifestation of attachment to the old doctrine of
"divine right" on the part of a government of
yesterday? There is no knowing on what mutual
foundation we are to base our alliance, in short. And
thus the idle dream of a cordial co-operation between
the two countries melts away into thin air; and
England turns to the more comprehensible, though
ugly-looking partnership afforded by the alliance of
Austria, as better calculated to help her in maintaining order in Europe.

The two great elements now arrayed against each

other are, democratic doctrines, and resistance by the actual depositaries of power to their encroachments.

How the conflict will finally end, is perhaps not difficult to foresee. But the phases it may have to pass through before the opposing forces come to a stand-still, will derive their complexion and importance from the individual actions of existing governments. And the interest one feels in the progress of this vast struggle arises from watching the conduct of these, month by month. The popular party naturally make blunders, and will commit more; whilst the reigning parties divide their tactics between concession and duplicity: and concession oftentimes proves an illusion; witness the Austrian and Wurtemberg Governments' retractation of those which were made in order to recover their position in 1848. If the French Revolution gave, as it seems it did, the first shake to absolute government throughout the Continent, it is not from that quarter that any farther help is to be expected to the Liberal cause; and though its enemies the sovereigns are alarmed, and their fears lead them to make terms with their subjects here and there, the powerful armies of Russia and Austria will probably overwhelm all resistance, should the spirit of revolt become sufficiently general to call for the employment of so extreme a measure.

The hopes of advancing in the path of reformation, then, depend on the peoples keeping within the limits of this necessity their manifestations of dissatisfaction. And thus a grumbling underground portentous note of change *may* be all that the present generation are destined to witness. A silent revolution, however, which in any case must be achieved, has its advantages, though it is difficult to appreciate the gain of what is not patent and tangible. And whether Europe shall become much the wiser or happier for the great organic modifications which are impending over her society, must in the end depend upon the character of those few leading minds who rise to influence under a new form of government. That some men worthy of their sublime mission will come out of the mêlée, can hardly be doubted; when they must take heed lest they lose the fruit of sacrifices, always serious, often ruinous to a nation in revolt, by the fatal process of conciliation of enemies: a process which infallibly leads to the necessity of beginning the work anew. In conclusion, the sad truth must out, that England and France never can " row in the same boat:" we may be thankful if neither nation launch their " boat" at all upon the ocean of strife, for the chances are that they would be found on opposite sides of the dispute. This reflection, however, need not prevent our remaining on friendly terms with our great neighbour during the prevalence of peace in Europe: for which let us heartily offer up our prayers to Heaven.

THE "SITUATION."

Paris, Nov. 1851.

A FRIEND now in Paris has given us the aid of a graphic pen to realize the "scene" in the French Assembly, on the proposition of the Questors to place an independent army under the command of President Dupin or his nominees; and has added some specula-tions on the position of political parties in Paris. As a description, the letter speaks for itself: as an observer, we know that our correspondent's opportu-nities and faculties of interpreting the true political aspect are equally of the best—(*Spectator.*)

"You will have seen the accounts given by the journals of the agitated *séance* of the 17th instant, which is acknowledged to have been one of the most exciting performances of the year. I was fortunate in obtaining an excellent seat, where I could hear almost every word, at least when the orator's voice was not drowned in clamour or laughter. The Chamber was excessively full; seven hundred or more Deputies being present, besides numerous clerks, officers, and attendants : the tribunes crowded to in-convenience, and the interest taken in the debate unusually keen. After General Leflo's speech, which was listened to with great attention, a hubbub arose, the like of which is seldom witnessed even in the National Assembly. I noted the duration of this disorderly tumult (for such one may term it), and it was precisely half an hour. The President, M. Dupin, sat passively in his curule chair, gazing on the surging waves below, ever and anon giving a shake of the piercing but ineffective brass bell at his elbow; the ushers shouting, so as to be heard above the storm, ' A vos places, Messieurs!' ' Silence!' ' En place!' &c.; but the eager and confused masses engaged in talk, chiefly in the middle of the salle, and round the President's seat and tribune, heeding nothing thereof; almost every member of the Gauche quitted his seat and rushed down to the floor. The Faucher section, as I may call it, or those of the Majority who were resolved to resist the proposition of the Questors as leading infallibly to some overt rupture between the powers of the state, remained mostly in their seats, awaiting the subsidence of the uproar. The noise was so great that you could hardly make yourself heard by your next neighbour in the tribune. You need not to be told that the appearance of M. Thiers at the rostrum was productive of fresh clamour and furious demonstrations of party feeling. Thiers himself seemed choking with rage, as he bandied sarcasms with his skilful opponent Jules Favre; who dexterously turned upon him the ridicule of the Mountain and the contempt of the Faucher party, feebly redeemed by a few straggling cries of ' Très bien!'

" The words ' Comédie de la peur,' and ' Réunion nocturne,' were used in an allusion to the farce played off by M. Thiers and a few of his adherents on Thursday night the 13th instant. They affected to believe that a violent attack on the independence of the Assembly was in contemplation, and accordingly thought proper to *bivouac* there all night; sending messengers to members of the Gauche in all directions, to urge them to repair to the Assembly to aid Thiers and his party in defending their sacred rights, &c. Some of the Gauche complied, and have since laughed at their own credulity.

"This move of the Questors, you must know, is universally believed to have been the work of M. Thiers; who, being now the bitter foe of the Elysée, wanted to force on a conflict, which would either put the President of the Republic in the wrong, or, in case of his compliance, enable him, Thiers, and his party, to nominate to the command of the guard at the Chamber a man understood to be favourable to their political purposes. General Changarnier, if so nominated, would not scruple, it is thought, to use his authority to repress the pure Republican party, and possibly to exalt that of the Royalists.

"The Montagne, on their side, discerning pretty clearly the drift of this scheme, have taken part with the Executive, and, with a few exceptions, resisted a proposition which, if followed out, might possibly throw up unforeseen difficulties in the way of the repeal of the law of May 31, the favourite object of this section of politicians. Again, the Moderate party, laying aside their enmities and wounded *amour-propre* (the effect of the President's offensive message), took counsel together on Saturday evening last, and determined on a combined opposition to the proposition, as reported by M. Vitet, Vice-President of the Chamber; and this for the sake of maintaining, as long as it should be feasible, a decent accord, or semblance of accord, between Louis Napoleon and the Assembly, in the obvious interest of the country in general.

" Now the upshot of this cross action among the
sections of the Assembly is somewhat curious to
contemplate. The picture is placed in a very
different light since last August. Then, the President
had managed, through the address and unwearied zeal
of M. Léon Faucher and his colleagues, to make up
his quarrel with the Majority, and to keep the
Montagne at least in check. The actual position of
affairs throws Louis Napoleon upon the Montagne for
support, and arrays the two sections of the Majority
against each other; thus, practically, annulling the
formidable combination which lately threatened to
close the door against his re-election.

" But, whilst it is undeniable that, *pro tanto*, he
has gained by the dislocation of parties till now
concurring in enmity towards himself, yet his new
allies can be viewed as no better than casual supporters, who will desert him so soon as he has
served their immediate turn. The President, therefore, must be considered in the light of a desperate
gamester, who accepts any sort of chance of bettering
his fortune, come from what source it may. On the
other hand, the Chamber may be said to have lost
ground by the late exhibition, and to have furnished
another proof of their entire inability to pursue any
course of combined action. So far, indeed, Louis
Napoleon may be considered as benefited by the
passage in question: his opponents are discredited,
and are more disunited than before; whilst the
Montagne, which on most questions votes as one man,
will bear him through the impending struggle for the
repeal of the unpopular law.

" The President seems to have sunk extremely low

in public opinion, as far as I have had opportunities
of observing; and if he succeed in getting himself
illegally re-elected, it can only be through the absence
of any more acceptable candidate; since the ignorant
or blind Napoleonist votes of the masses, which
would remain after deducting the voters for the
(inevitable) Red candidate, could hardly outweigh
the votes of those who would support an eligible
Republican name (if proposed) rather than elect a
non-eligible candidate. Still, there is always the
prodigious advantage on his side of being a prince,
strange though it sounds; for each eminent public
man feels jealous of an equal in rank, and grudges
his vote to assist in his elevation, whilst a prince is
already placed far above him, and *his* farther exalta-
tion excites no sense of humiliation in the unsuccess-
ful party.

"The Parisian citizens take scarcely any interest
in the squabbles of their governors. The shopkeeper
hopes to see his candidate, if possible, succeed; but if
not, I really believe the French mind is become so
much more reasonable than it was, that he will
accept a legitimate defeat without being roused to
anger. The longing for quiet, and to be allowed to
drive their trades their own way, is become a
dominant feeling, as I am told, with all ranks of
Frenchmen."

A RURAL EXCURSION IN FRANCE.

Versailles, Sept. 1, 1852.

THE weather has been so fine during the last fortnight, that to pass one's day out of doors, like "the natives," has become well nigh a habit with strangers. By way of turning one of these beautiful days to account, we set out yesterday on a little excursion; of which I proceed to give you a brief sketch.

Quitting Versailles by the Porte de Satory, you ascend a hill, from which the traveller obtains a noble prospect over the town and surrounding country. The railroad to Chartres passes under this road; on the top of the hill stretches a wide and extensive tract of level ground, called the Plaine de Satory, well known to fame, and which certainly offers unusual advantages as a field for military displays. The road leads from this height down a pretty dell into La Minière, a narrow gorge richly wooded, forming the limit of the old Parc de Versailles of Louis Quatorze's creation. We next traversed the dull but productive Plaine de Saclé, reaching about four miles to the south-west; the whole surface being under the careful culture of large occupiers, and evidently of a fertile quality. Fruit-trees, in abundant bearing, border the road the whole way, and in some measure compensate the eye for the absence of hedges. When we had passed over this region, we found ourselves on the verge of a small but richly-wooded valley, divided by a streamlet and green meadows, with a few farm-buildings, old garden walls, and a large round structure, denoting a " colombier," on its Northern slope. A more charming site could not have been chosen for the retreat of those who once illustrated this obscure spot. We left the carriage, and, walking a short distance, entered, not without pilgrim emotions, within the precincts of Port Royal des Champs! The destroying spirit of Persecution* has done its work most effectually, by removing all traces of the once important Abbaye, as well as those of the abodes of the " solitaires," who sought the society of the " sisters," and the means of mutual instruction, in these calm pleasing solitudes. Nothing remains but masses of loose masonry, and here and there a sort of crypt, with the garden-walls, of great thickness, buttressed by projecting spurs, out of which grow huge trunks of ivy, doubtless coeval with the period of Port Royal's prosperity. The colombier probably also dates from the same. The names of Arnauld, Pascal, Nicole, and, in its way, that of the Duchesse de Longueville,—who filled so distinguished a place in her country's domestic history,—rise to the memory as one wanders over the ground so often trodden by these contemplative recluses. No one who has learnt to value the efforts made by conscientious thinkers to advance the dignity of the human intellect, can visit this hallowed spot without reverence. The poor nuns, too, suffered their share of persecution for the sake of their mental independence, and must be numbered with the noble women who have deserved the crown of martyrdom

* Louis XIV. hunted the Jansenists out, and razed Port Royal to the ground, to please, it was said, Madame de Maintenon.

in behalf of something more precious than a visionary belief.

Reluctantly bending our steps outwards, we now once more rolled pleasantly along a macadamized road of the finest sort, through more corn country, and more beladen apple-trees, for about three-quarters of an hour; at the end of which a remarkably fine prospect opened out before us. From the summit of a high plateau we commanded a view of the whole magnificent valley of Dampierre, one of the most beautiful in France, of considerable extent, and presenting, what in this country has become a somewhat rare feature in its landscapes—I allude to the richly-timbered park and princely seat of a real "grand seigneur."

The high ground on the farther side of this valley is entirely clothed with fine timber trees, for a long distance; whilst the other slopes offer also a goodly spectacle of mixed forest scenery, with broken heath-covered banks. The eye rests delighted on such a landscape, the like of which in England it would be difficult to quote, unless perhaps it were some such spot as Helmsley Dale, (Lord Feversham's noble demesne in Yorkshire,) or Knowle Park and its neighbourhood, in Kent. The timber of the park at Dampierre is of a still finer growth; the climate favouring the formation of forests in France in a way to excite the envy of English visitors. Ash-trees, with a clean run of bole seventy feet in length and two or more in diameter—chestnut, oak, and abele of imposing size, with vigorous large foliage and undying crowns—here furnish out a sylvan picture of surpassing interest to the admirer of the vegetable kingdom.

Winding down by a skilfully made road, we gained
the lower ground, watered by the little river Yvette,
and entirely devoted to pasture, the herbage of which
was obviously rich and nutritive. The village of
Dampierre, seated on a rise, a little above the bed of
the stream, intersects, as it were, the grounds of the
Château de Dampierre: before the gates of which we
soon drew up, and were not a little astonished to
behold a mansion of imposing size, surrounded by
gardens and dressed grounds, and exhibiting every
mark of the most refined récherché taste and expensive keeping-up. The house was partially destroyed
during the Revolution, as were most of the residences
of the noblesse; but the proprietor of this, the Duc
de Chevreuse, not having emigrated, his estates were
restored to him in 1815, and his son, who now bears
the title of Duc de Luynes, (they alternate these
titles, it seems,) caused the building to be completely
repaired, so that no signs of damage are discernible.
The house is of the latter period of Louis Quatorze,
and was constructed after the designs of Mansard.
It stands in water, on three sides, and is seated in the
lowest part of the basin of the valley—looking up
wide alleys cut in the park, and surrounded by trim
gardens, decked with numerous orange-trees and other
choice plants, ranged in their boxes along the borders.
Green grass plats are carefully cherished here, being
almost the only place in which I have found them:
water, always at hand, enables the gardener to coun-
teract the effects of the sun, everywhere else fatal to
green-sward. South of the château, and amid wavy
woods, is a lake several acres in extent, with sailing
and row boats moored on its surface. The water is

not stagnant, being constantly fed by the stream running through this valley; and as we walked about the gardens we saw the water discharging itself by a gentle cascade, which I presume never ceases, since it is fully supplied at this driest of all seasons.

The interior of the château offers little to describe. We saw the state apartments alone, including the chapel; for, as is usual in all ancient noble establishments, the Duc de Luynes keeps his family priest, and has mass said daily. There are few pictures of mark, and none of any pretension to merit as works of art, in the rooms we passed through; though I am inclined to believe there *are* pictures in the Duke's possession worth looking at, as he is reputed to be not only fond of the arts, but given to encourage artists. The only object of interest in the way of modern art was a statue of Penelope fallen asleep over her spindle; very creditably executed, by a French sculptor. In a kind of crypt, enclosed within iron-bound doors, we were shown a silver statue of Louis the Thirteenth, in light armour, hat and feather; life size, taken at the age of fifteen or sixteen perhaps. This work, which is cleverly designed, was intended as a mark of grateful homage on the part of a Duc de Luynes towards the founder of his fortunes; the first Duc de Luynes having risen to greatness from the condition of a poor Italian gentleman, named Alberti, through the favour of that monarch. He married into the Montbazon family, refusing an alliance with the niece of the King, Mademoiselle de Vendôme; and his family may be considered as ranking among the most honourable of the nation. The present head of the family has the reputation of possessing all those qualities which grace high birth and station. Aiming at no great political importance, he employs his ample fortune in cultivating the arts, (he has the finest private collection of medals perhaps in the kingdom,) in promoting philanthropic undertakings, and in rendering useful services to those who need his generous assistance; a high-bred personal bearing conferring the last charm upon a character otherwise entitled to respect and love,—in short, a French Ellesmere.

I have no more room, so will close my sheet. Accept this sketch for what it is worth.

THE WAR FROM AN UNPOPULAR POINT OF VIEW.

LETTER I.

Beaconsfield, 26th November, 1855.

SIR,—In Sir Arthur Elton's letter which he addressed to you last week, he asks " Where do the advocates of war propose to stop?" It seems to me nowise difficult to answer this query. The " advocates" doubtless propose to " stop" nowhere short of their avowed end; which, as all English people know, or may know, consists in putting a check upon the power of the Czar in the South of Europe. Whether this be accomplished by driving Russia out of the Crimea, or by destroying her Baltic fortresses, or by gradually exhausting her resources, is not material. We shall assault and batter her in every way in which our armies and fleets can be employed to cripple and injure an enemy, with the view to compel her to accept such conditions of peace as the Western Powers deem available to the declared purpose,—namely, the prevention of aggressive acts towards Turkey, as well in Asia as on the Continent of Europe.

Thus much for the avowed aims and ends of this gigantic war. Now, then, I would beg to inquire who are the parties most interested in keeping Russia out of Turkey? Is it not the Turks themselves, who have in fact shown that they are able and willing to repel Russian invaders? They repulsed the Russians on the Danube, forcing them to retire, after a series of defeats, beyond the Pruth: and has not Omar Pasha beaten them at Ingour; and has not the army of General Mouravieff received a complete discomfiture by Turkish troops before Kars? If I am told that the repulse of the Russians may prove merely a temporary advantage, and that, without foreign assistance, Turkey will after no long interval succumb to renewed attacks, I rejoin, that it is not competent for a nation to go to war simply because she regards some other nation as likely to grow too formidable. If Russia has designs upon Constantinople, it would be easy for the Western Powers to watch her, and to furnish Turkey with means and appliances calculated to defeat such designs. That is, supposing it of vital importance that Turkey should be upheld in her integrity; a point which I will concede, if only for the sake of following out the views of the War party and canvassing their merits.

Now, having conceded this, I will pursue the inquiry as to what European peoples, apart from the Turkish, are interested in preserving the dominions of the Sultan intact. Is it the Jewish or Christian subjects of the Sultan? I doubt it. The majority of the subjects of Turkey in Europe feel no attachment to the Porte, by whose officials they are oppressed and insulted, and treated as inferior beings. Surely the example of Russian rule, as exhibited under the mild, just, and prosperous government of Prince Woronzow over South Russia, for the last nine years, up to 1854, must have had its effect in disposing those various races—over whom the Sultan reigns equally with Turks proper—to regard the advent of the Russians as anything but a misfortune. And, to say the truth, all impartial lookers-on must confess that the administration of which Odessa is the head-quarters offers a pleasing contrast to that of the Mahometan prince. Lord Stanley, with much frankness, recently exclaimed, "God forbid we should be fighting for Mahometanism!" Taken on its own merits, no humane Englishman ought to do so. But neither would I have him fight to *exterminate* Mussulmen, as such. The Mahometan creed is there, with all its attributes, and its civil disabilities as enforced against such of the subjects of the Porte as profess Christianity,—a dismal spectacle enough for an European, certainly, but one which is conveniently lost sight of when we talk of "fighting for the independence and civilization of nations," as is now commonly done at our public dinners and meetings in England.

In calling the attention of a warlike friend to these inconsistencies on our parts, he replied, "Yes, I allow that to uphold the actual régime in Turkey would not, properly speaking, appear to be promoting the civilization and independence we talk so much about: but, you see, we intend to press humane and equitable *changes* upon that Government; changes calculated to strengthen its hold upon the various fractions of its subjects, and to improve its internal position."

Now to the force of this plea I demur, on two grounds. Firstly, because I conceive that the real power of the Sultan would not be reinforced, but rather the contrary, by letting in the Christian element, thereby arousing violent jealousy in the minds of "the faithful;" secondly, because I would deprecate interference with the interior administration of another country, on principle. Furthermore, it is exceedingly probable that the interests of Russia would be promoted by placing members of the Greek Church in situations of influence and authority in Turkey. What more natural than that the religious affinity which subsists between the Russians and the inhabitants of some of the fairest provinces on the Danube should operate in favour of the protector and head of that particular section of Christian believers? I cannot, therefore, help concluding that the Porte would lose rather than gain, by relaxing their actual political disabilities, and admitting Greek Christians to official charges.

If, indeed, the national sentiment of England were sincerely bent upon enforcing humane and civilized government upon a neighbour for its own sake, we need not travel so far to find a fit occasion for displaying that sentiment. An ample field presents itself in the South of Europe, where two peoples, highly favoured by nature, inhabiting two countries, each capable of bearing all kind of fruitful produce, lie, people and land, beneath a withering, baleful despotism, which excites the pity and arouses the ire of all generous beholders. If we must go forth to redress the wrongs of suffering fellow men, by all means let us have a crusade to the shores of Parthenope and to the city seated on the seven hills!

But no: one of these odious despots is under the special protection of our supposed German ally; the other, under that of a power whose aid we are unable to dispense with in the prosecution of the present

war. Let us then drop the flimsy pretence of a
chivalrous purpose, and avow that the real motives
for attacking Russia lie in the alarm we feel lest she
should stretch her dominion, first towards Egypt,
and next towards the frontier of Caubul, and so,
doubly threaten the possessions—I might perhaps
say the ill-gotten possessions—of Great Britain in
Asia. Clearsighted Frenchmen are perfectly aware
that these fears constitute, with us, the impelling
causes of the war. " We understand them," said M.
de L. to me in May last; " and we accordingly do
not wonder at the extravagant homage which you
islanders lavish on our master,* since he lends you
powerful armies to fight your battles; for yours they
unquestionably are, and not ours." " Well," I
replied, " if he does so, he doubtless finds his account
in it." " True," rejoined M. de L., " he does so find
it; but France has not the slightest interest in this
conflict. She ought rather to wish for the maintenance than the destruction of a maritime power
capable of holding your domineering navy in check
in the Mediterranean: and then France has no
Oriental conquests to defend. But Louis Napoleon
was glad to enter into alliance with a first-rate European power, on any terms. Your Court alone, on the
occasion of the *coup d'état*, manifested a disposition to
recognise him and his dynasty; and in return, he has
expended freely, for English objects, the blood and
treasure of his helpless subjects. The French have,

---

* It is rare to hear Frenchmen of any class use the words Emperor,
Sovereign, or Monarch, in reference to their present ruler. They
habitually say " celui-ci," or " notre monsieur," and sometimes "notre
maître—seldom " Louis Napoleon" even.

it is true, always a certain relish for war; being, as we ourselves say, born *batailleurs;* and since, probably, this contest will, sooner or later, bring some territorial advantage with it to France, it may tend to popularize the present reign: and military enterprises being, as I have observed, the favourite vocation of the French, it suits the personal motives of Louis Napoleon to carry on some such; for, whilst the public is excited by prodigious external operations, plots and factions at home are, in a manner, hushed and shelved, and the national vanity overrides all other feelings." "All that you say may be well founded," I said, "but, somehow or another, it seems to me that you Frenchmen act as *if* you believed, along with my countrymen, in the generous aims we talk of?" "Not so," answered M. de L.; "we *fight,* as you have commonly done, equally well without a good cause as with one; we have, however, no voice in the matter. Our present ruler consults only his own will, and disposes of his subjects' life and property with quite as little concern for what they wish or feel, as does the ruler of that nation whom *he* proposes to advance in 'civilization' and 'independence,'—after the mode of the old saying, 'lucus à non lucendo,' I presume."

Having disposed of the false pretences on which the war was undertaken, I propose, in another letter, to consider the real objects; the importance of which, to England, I am far from denying, whilst I regret to think them uncertain of attainment.

LETTER II.

December, 1855.

SIR,—In my first letter, it was sought to prove that the "flourish" about upholding the independence and civilization of other nations was a mere pretence; that the sole purpose in view was, and is, the keeping Constantinople out of the hands of Russia, whilst at the same time the permanence of Turkish rule is obviously becoming less and less an object of solicitude. In fact, after the Turk has allowed foreign armies to come and occupy his capital and to fight his battles, it is pretty certain that the prestige of his authority must have undergone so great a diminution at home, that the disaffected portion of Turkey in Europe is likely to become troublesome, and will probably be disposed to throw off the Mussulman yoke at the earliest opportunity.

Then will commence a process, for anticipating the occasion of which much obloquy has been cast upon the late Emperor Nicholas. The dominions of the Sultan must be "rearranged;" we shall have helped "the sick man" to repel his danger so effectively that he himself will be destroyed in the struggle. For, supposing that a cessation of hostilities should be brought about by Russia's consenting to lessen her maritime force in the Black Sea, and by her covenanting to respect the "independence of Turkey"— politically speaking—I must take leave to doubt the Czar's disposition to observe the engagement any longer than he finds it enforced by the attitude of the

Western Powers. Therefore Turkey must either be left to be attacked and subdued at a later day, or the Western Powers must "occupy" the territory; and what, I beg to inquire, will this be, except taking possession of the "héritage du malade?"

Again, I hold it to be a serious difficulty in the way of such a proceeding, that the population of Turkey, whether Mussulman or Christian, feels averse to the religious creed professed by France and England. It is true that small account is ever taken of the feelings of a conquered and ignorant people, or of the preference they may entertain for this or that ruler by their invaders: but in the case of the Romaic races, and others, spread over that vast tract of country, any discontent which might exist would be fomented, and possibly fanned into active resistance, by the powerful neighbour who possesses a spiritual affinity and headship over these people. The whole body of Greek priesthood even now work heartily in favour of Russian ascendancy; and we all know how potent an engine sectarian influence is with half-educated minds, (and, indeed, over fully-educated ones, for that matter,) and how difficult it would be for us to cope with this advantage.

I regard the maintenance of the Turkish rule, in short, as out of the question, let this war end when it may. And it is not easy to speculate on the mode of replacing that rule, otherwise than by, as usual, clapping a foreign King upon the throne. We have heard it whispered that the Duke of Cambridge might, if inclined, play a bold stroke for a crown, and be enthroned as sovereign of the Danubian Principalities —which, indeed, might hereafter lead to his establish-

ment as king over Turkey also. Far be it from me
to entertain any repugnance to a contingency pro-
mising so much advantage to a fine country and to
well-disposed industrious peoples; but it would
scarcely find favour in the eyes of France. No doubt
Austria must be compelled to relinquish the " occupation," and to waive her pretensions to the exclusive
right of watching over the navigation of the Danube.
She has acted so equivocal a part all through the
dispute with Russia, that it would be no very harsh
measure on our side were we to refuse to let her
exercise any authority over the Principalities in time
to come. France will in all likelihood expect to
receive some advantage from the " settling" of the
affairs of Turkey; and nothing would suit the emperor better than to establish a military post on the
Bosphorus, such as might constitute the nucleus of a
future empire, and meantime enable him to push his
advantages in a thousand ways in the East: and for
an opening such as this, the French people would
have cause to feel really grateful to their sovereign.

Now, sir, if these vaticinations have any reasonable basis, you must perceive what a perplexing tissue
of consequences connects itself with their fulfilment.
It is not to be expected that Austria should quietly
look on and allow France and England to erect themselves into " executors and assigns" of the expiring
state. We must not pass over the hostility which
would animate the Court of King Otho, or the general
aversion with which French ascendancy would be
regarded; though that nation has contrived to earn a
reputation for abusing it wherever it has been planted.
But I look chiefly to the opposition of Austria, which

might, not unnaturally, end in her making common cause with Russia.

In any case, much embarrassment will attend the ultimate distribution of those countries. The inhabitants of Moldavia and Wallachia, I have reason to believe, would prefer to fall under Russian rule rather than under Austrian. Perhaps the simplest way out of this dilemma would be, to let those peoples choose a Government for themselves. Will the Allies accept so humiliating a solution? I fear not.

Conversing with a German friend lately (not an Austrian) on these thorny questions, he remarked, "Settle the Turkish succession as you will, we Germans can never approve your course. If you give advantages to Austria, we shall all condemn the decision of the Allies. If you augment the power and credit of France, the sentiment will be little less acrimonious. What renders Germany (and I always include kings and subjects in the word) so apathetic about this contest, is, first, the feeling of deep hatred towards the French, (for which, God knows, ample ground exists!) and secondly, a cold, jealous distrust of England. When any one of our numerous states has attempted to better its political condition by resistance to misrule, the Government of England has thrown cold water upon its efforts. In 1848, your then Foreign Minister went so far as to use menacing language towards the patriotic few who strove to kindle public spirit and effect needful reforms. England is, in truth, never found on the side of *peoples*, but always casts her weight into the opposite scale. And, I tell you plainly, *we* fear France quite as much or more than Russia, and wonder how you can fail to

apprehend danger from her stupendous military organization; connected as it is with anti-social passions,
an unscrupulous government, and an overweening
national vanity." "I agree with you," said I, "in
regarding France with uneasiness: but you must
observe that she can only send armies to the south of
Europe, or into Asia, on shipboard; which insures to
England a certain control over her movements by
reason of our naval superiority—whilst Russia can
pour down her hosts, landwards, into Bulgaria, or into
Syria and Egypt." "Well, but what do you say to
Cherbourg?" rejoined my Wirtemburgher friend;
"look at that splendid port, with its vast docks and
arsenal, and couple these with their propinquity to your
shores! Why, the money expended on Cherbourg,
during the last forty or fifty years, far exceeds in
amount the outlay upon Sebastopol!" "Yes," I
answered, "the rise and expansion of Cherbourg is,
beyond question, a formidable fact. But the English
seldom look far forward; they always adapt their
national policy and measures to circumstances as they
arise. We happen to be on friendly, nay, on loving
terms with the French emperor just now; so John
Bull takes little heed of what changes may by and by
supervene. Before this hot friendship sprang up
(from motives which were sketched out in my former
communication,) we really *were* alarmed lest Louis
Napoleon should come over and ravage our defenceless
cities and lands, if he did no more. But these fears
were dissipated by a sudden gust of mutual interest,
and we went off to the East together." "Your
interests," said my interlocutor, "are more commercial than anything else. You want to have 'the

run' of the Black Sea with all its immense supplies, and also to keep the Red Sea passage open for your Indian trade." "Exactly so," I retorted; "but why we should not be able to trade in the Black Sea, equally under Russian as under Turkish rule, I am at a loss to guess. Russia is more indebted to her commerce than to any other source for her increased importance, and the English are, perhaps, about her best customers." "Well, but you are not sure of Egypt continuing unmolested, if Russia should grasp the parent state," said the German. "Agreed," I replied; "but if we could defend Egypt successfully against France, what is to make us incapable of defending it against Russia?"

Englishmen really talk about the "designs of the Czar" as something which it would be vain to gain-say,—as though we, and every one else, would be easily beaten out of every possession which he might think fit to attack! No more talk of England's magnificent ships or floating batteries, of her gallant soldiers, of her admirable artillery, from the instant Russia is named as a possible assailant. Yet the *Times* is perpetually putting forward the superiority of the Western armies in open conflict, and adducing the victories over Russian troops by even Turkish arms, as evidence how little she is to be dreaded as an *attacking* foe. For my part, I see even less difficulty in barring out Russia from Egypt, should she make the essay, than in keeping her out of Turkey. And granting that she might get possession of Egypt,—which, however, is a monstrous hypothesis,—she would never find it her interest to isolate that country from European commerce; her principal object being to enrich her people.

I conclude my long disquisition by repeating, that the real objects of this ruinous war seem to me as disproportionate to the sacrifices it involves, and as little calculated to realize tangible benefits to Great Britain, as any war which could in these times be undertaken. The avowed purposes* are a sham; the real motives are the offspring of a timorous panic and delusion, reflecting small honour upon English dignity and self-reliance.

---

* *Id est*, the desire to uphold " civilization and the independence of nations."

AN ENGLISH RAMBLE.

FEW of the counties of England would seem to offer
less attraction to tourists than the agricultural
district of Buckinghamshire; nevertheless, a ramble
through its well-cultivated farms and truly primitive
villages is not without interest to those who can take
pleasure in rural scenery not unmixed with anti-
quarian features. Such an excursion the writer
lately made, starting from Chalfont St. Giles, im-
mortalized by having been for a time inhabited by
John Milton, during the plague of London in 1666.
Passing through the cheerful little town of Amersham,
you come to Shardeloes, the residence of Mr. Drake,
delightfully situate on rising ground, which is clothed
with noble timber for some distance, the valley below
being watered by the stream of the Misbourne, here
collected into a somewhat extensive lake. Great
Missenden is an ordinary country village nestled
between the hills: soon after quitting which, we
opened upon the Chiltern Hills, a chalk range running South-west and North-east, and forming the
lower boundary of the Vale of Aylesbury. The
little town of Wendover appeared the very abode of
dulness, as we quietly entered it between five and six
in the evening of a beautiful summer's day. Hardly
a human being was visible, harvest-time having
emptied the dwellings even to the children, who are
useful in the general work of "leasing," or gleaning,

s 2

in the wheat stubbles. This solitude and repose was, however, anything but unwelcome; for the weather was delightful, and the landscape truly English. The church, embosomed in trees; the fields around richly studded with sheaves of corn; the cattle at graze; and the hills tufted with shrubs, box, juniper, and the like,—altogether it was a scene at once cheerful, attractive, and picturesque. From this to Aylesbury nothing interesting, save to the farmer. From Aylesbury (a thriving country-town,) we took the Buckingham road for five miles, diverging to the left, intending to visit the village of Oving, where there is a fine old seat of the Aubreys: but the road being intricate we took a wrong turn, and found ourselves at another village, which on inquiry we learnt was North Marston.

Methought the church appeared worthy of a visit; accordingly we ascended the hill on which it stands. Some urchins, who ran after us offering to hold our horse, went and fetched the cottager woman who kept "the kay of the church." On entering, I was surprised to perceive a very handsome painted glass window, evidently of recent date: a substantial oaken ceiling, with pendants and roses, carved seats, communion-tablets, handsomely fitted; everything neat and well cared for. The exterior offered unusual architectural beauty, the nave being decorated with numerous Gothic pinnacles. I expressed to the good woman, our conductress, my wonder at all this, and asked who had embellished this church.

Woman—"The Queen, to be sure."

Traveller—"The Queen! what could she have to do with it?"

Woman—" Why, a precious good deal, I'se warrant. Did ye never hear of one John Camden Neild—a great miser—what left all his money and his lands to the Queen?"

Traveller—" Well, I think I do recollect, some few years back, hearing of a great legacy which had been left to the Queen. Was it about here that the lands lay?"

Woman—" Aye, sure! Mr. Neild owned ever so many farms round about this here place."

Traveller—" Had he any residence in the village?"

Woman—" No: he used to come and dra' his rents his own self, and then he stopped with one of his tenants, handy here: he lived very close, and had saved up millions of money."

Traveller—" Millions! that's not to be believed. I thought I heard that what he left to the Queen was about a hundred thousand pounds, or there-away."

Woman—" Lor blessy! 'twas ever so much more nor that."

Traveller—" I can't think it, somehow."

Woman — (looking embarrassed) — " Well, how much *is* a million?"

Traveller—"Why, a million is ten hundred thousand pounds."

Woman—(with a gesture of impatience, and proceeding to open an inner door)—" Ah! he'd more nor that round *here* away, let alone other places."

Over the communion-table, and under the handsome window I have mentioned, is an inscription in old English characters painted on a gold ground in memory of the testator, John Camden Neild; placed there by order of the Queen.

Proceeding about two miles farther, I reached the village of Granborough, with a little plain church, its cottages scattered in clusters, and offering indubitable indications of comfort and decent habits in the residents. The harvest had caused the cottages to be deserted by their owners; a few children (and those healthy and well fed) being the only living things to be seen. At Granborough I halted for refreshment; finding, by good luck, what has of late years become but too rare, a jug of genuine home-brewed beer. The landlord and his dame, full of civility, produced all that their humble house afforded; and both I and my horse left the spot with renewed energies. Our road to Steeple Claydon lay through pasturage enclosures, the gates of which were many and tedious to open. Passing through the grounds of Sir Harry Verney, Bart., M.P., we stopped to look at the Church of Middle Claydon, which adjoins his time-honoured mansion, formerly the seat of the ancient family of Chaloner: the park is enlivened by a sheet of water, and is well timbered. Mounting a neighbouring hill, I found myself at Steeple-Claydon, —a place interesting to me on account of my relationship with this family of Chaloner, many members of which lie buried within the precincts of its simple, unpretending church. The village is delightfully situate on high ground, with extensive views over the country on all sides. Nothing can be more agreeable to look upon than the cottages and farm-houses of Steeple Claydon. A few flaring flowers ornament most of them in front, while abundance of vegetable produce lies behind. Everything denotes the presiding influence of a considerate "squire" and a benevolent parson. On the western declivity of the hill I found a school-house of elegant design, rebuilt on the site of the old school, for the reception of the infant children of the neighbourhood, by Sir Harry Verney. With that reverence for bygone generous deeds which characterizes all cultivated minds, Sir Harry has caused the memory of the original founder to be preserved; the escutcheon of a Chaloner, carved in stone, being still in its place over the porch, the only part of the original building which remains. On the brow of the hill is a "vallum," of considerable depth and width, with a mound, where Oliver Cromwell, it is credibly affirmed, encamped during his campaign against the King's forces in this county. Sir Harry Verney has placed a brass inscription in a wall hard by, in order to keep alive the tradition concerning this interesting incident. In the chancel of the church at Steeple Claydon is a mural tablet to the memory of an Edward Chaloner, one of whose ancestors* the tablet records as having been knighted by the Protector of King Edward the Sixth, and by Queen Elizabeth sent ambassador to the Emperor Ferdinand and to Philip the Second King of Spain.

Quitting this pleasant spot, not without regret, I descended into the plain, and, by a sequestered track of a purely agricultural character, passed through the villages of Edgcott and Grendon-Underwood (the latter boasting a handsome and picturesque church), and, traversing for a short space the "Akeman way," one of the early Saxon highways, I came to Ludgershall, having a most primitive-looking parsonage-house, seated on an eminence; thence, through pas-

* Sir Thomas Chaloner.

ture-fields and enclosures, to Brill—a small town
somewhat singularly placed, on the summit of a lofty
ridge some 300 feet or more above the level of the
surrounding country.

This place was formerly the centre of a district
called Birnwode forest, resorted to by several of our
Plantagenet Kings for the purpose of hunting. King
John, Henry the Second, and Edward the Third,
spent much time here. From several points in the
immediate vicinity of the church, most delightful and
commanding views are obtained. The wooded residence and park of the Marquis of Chandos, Wotton
House, lies immediately under the ridge, to the
North; whilst beyond it stretch away for many miles,
the productive farms and comfortable shaded home-
steads of this rich and favoured county. But little
remains of the once extensive forest by which this
district was formerly covered. A grove of lofty trees,
close to the town, appears to be the sole remnant of
its departed glory.

Early on the morrow I descended from my
"monticule," on the South-west side, bent upon
finding the way to the site of an edifice of ancient
date, historically interesting by its having stood a
siege of a fortnight's duration, by the Parliament
forces under General Fairfax, in 1645; Boarstall
House, at that time belonging to Lady Dynham,
being successfully defended by Sir William Campion.
A pleasant drive of some three miles brought me to
the spot, now a rural solitude, once animated with
active and opulent feudal existence. The Gate
House, with its four massive towers, yet stands, and
in its pristine form, only shorn of its portcullis and

drawbridge; a striking picturesque monument of mediæval taste. It is confidently affirmed to have been erected in the reign of Edward the First, about the year 1324; John de Handlo, the lord of the domain, having obtained licence from the King to "fortify his mansion at Boarstall, and make a castle of it"—so ran the edict.* Three sides of the deep moat are yet open, and full of water; and one solitary secular tree (an elm) stands within its enclosure, sole survivor of many hundred oaks and elms which, no longer ago than the year 1810, surrounded this ancient feudal castle.

The woman who now resides in the Gate House recounted to me the following particulars. "My grandmother," said she, "lived and died here. She died about thirty years ago, when she was eighty-seven. I remember her very well, and have often heard her tell about the old house, and about the family of Aubrey. The 'great house,' she said, stood upon a deal of ground, and had prim gardens, and trees set in rows, with clipped hedges; and there were very noble rooms in the mansion. The late Sir Thomas Aubrey inherited a large part of Sir John Aubrey's estates. He died, like his uncle, at a great age. My grandmother remembered the forest being so thick all round Boarstall that you could not see the house until you came quite close upon it. Sir John Aubrey had, by his first wife, a son, who about the age of six or seven years came to an untimely death.

* [The property came, by inheritance, to the family of Aubrey, about one hundred and fifty years since; the last male descendant of which, Sir Thomas Aubrey, dying not more than a year ago, without children, the estates devolved upon a lady (married to Mr. Ricketts), the next in blood, residing at Dorton House.]

His nurse having giving the child a little medicine, wished that he should afterwards take some gruel. To make this gruel, she used some oatmeal which she found in one of the cupboards in the Gate House, where the kitchen was situate. It unfortunately turned out that this oatmeal had had arsenic mixed with it. The child at first refused to swallow the gruel, saying it was nasty; on which the nurse added some sugar, and thus the child was induced to eat it up. The poor boy died within three hours of this fatal mistake being committed. My grandmother saw the child when it was dying: it was a fine little boy, and the nurse had like to have gone out of her mind with grief. Lady Aubrey, the boy's mother, took on sadly, and after a few months died of a broken heart. The widower, anxious for an heir, married, after a while, another lady; but she bore him no child."

Sir John began to pull down the great house about eighty years ago, carting the stone and other materials away to enlarge Dorton House withal; originally a structure of the Tudor age, which it took him many years to complete. It is situate about a mile and a half East of Brill, nearly at the bottom of the slope, and in the immediate vicinity of a somewhat remarkable medicinal spring of a strong chalybeate quality. Sir Thomas Aubrey, on coming to the property, somewhere about thirty years ago, set about cutting down the fine forest which surrounded the site of Boarstall House. There were many trees of such bulk and value as to fetch the sum of 16l. per stick. The estimate made by the inhabitants was, that he had

cut down over 1500 timber-trees. As Sir Thomas
Aubrey did not inherit the Dorton estates, (which
were left to Mrs. Ricketts,) it was surmised that this
wholesale destruction of the Boarstall timber was
prompted by an unworthy feeling of jealousy; the
Boarstall estates being destined to pass to Mrs.
Ricketts and her heirs, in default of Sir Thomas
leaving a son.

After making a leisurely inspection of this interesting relic of the fourteenth century, I returned
to Brill; whence, passing by the spa or mineral
spring mentioned above, and close to Dorton House,
I reascended by a steep path to the pleasant village
of Chilton. It would be difficult to point out a more
charming drive. On each side of the ridge an extensive view is enjoyed; whilst on gently descending into
the village, the road is overarched by umbrageous
trees, and the ancient manor-house and handsome
church, in close proximity, are shaded by a grove of
magnificent elms.

After leaving Chilton, the road sinks down into
the valley of the Thames; and, passing through the
town of Thame, we followed a dull level line of
country to Prince's Risborough, a neat little town
nestled at the base of the Chiltern range. Ourselves
and horse standing in great need of sustentation, we
alighted at what was dignified by the title of the
"head inn" of the place; and, after seeing the good
horse cared for, opened the subject of *dinner* with the
landlady. *Traveller*—"What have you got in the
house, mistress?" *Landlady*—"Mighty little, I'm
afeard." *Traveller*—"Well, then, you'd better send
out and get us some mutton-chops, or something."

Landlady—" Oh! that won't be no use, for there ain't such a thing in the town." *Traveller*—" How do you know that?" *Landlady*—" 'Cos we've been and tried for some other travellers; and there's ne'er a butcher have got a scrap of meat. Ye see, to-morrow's our market-day; so they wont kill till the over-night." *Traveller*—" Well, then, bring out the bread and cheese; you've got *that*, I suppose ?" *Landlady*—" Ay, ay, we got that, sure enough!"*

Towards six o'clock, we jogged on; passing by the pretty little village of Bradenham, under the hill on which the church of West Wycombe, presenting a striking object, is perched. At its base stands the noble mansion and richly-timbered grounds of Sir Francis Dashwood King, called West Wycombe Park; than which, few more attractive and interesting seats can be cited. The road hence, to High or Chipping Wycombe, lay through a valley watered by a stream, and ornamented by the wood-crowned heights of Wycombe Abbey, forming a delightful landscape, gilded by the departing rays of a gorgeous sunset.

Here ends my humble "itinerary." May it interest some of your readers who still cherish a love of old English tradition, haunts, and dwellings; albeit my track led neither through romantic nor magnificent scenery.

---

* I repeat this prosaic dialogue, to show that frugal habits are still in fashion among the rural population of England.

POETICAL PIECES.

THERE appeared in the *Morning Chronicle* newspaper, about the month of August, 1828, an account of certain proceedings at Great Hampden, Bucks, in which the chief actors were, the late Lord Nugent, and the parson of the parish, named (I think) Lovett, or Lovel. The account purported to be furnished by Lord Nugent himself; but many years afterwards, his lordship, becoming in some sort ashamed of the part he had borne in the affair, thought fit (as I have been informed) to deny his participation therein. As an impartial witness, I think it right to prefix to the lines below a short narrative of what came under my knowledge in reference to this transaction, about two years after its occurrence.

Feeling a deep interest in the personal history and character of John Hampden, my husband and I made a journey to the place where he had lived as an opulent country gentleman, and where his remains were known to lie; I may not say *to repose*, since they had been disturbed by the irreverent curiosity of the parties already named.

Whilst halting at a retired alehouse, on a common about a mile distant from Great Hampden house, to refresh our horses, I entered into conversation with the woman who kept it. " Were you living here (I asked) when Lord Nugent and his friends had Mr. John Hampden digged up out of his grave?"

"Yes, sure; I were up at the church early next morning, and seed the poor gentleman in his coffin. He were stayed up with a shovel, set against his back, and he were left so all night."

"What colour was his hair? did you look well at it?"

"Yes; it were a kind of a reddy-brown colour. But there, I can show you some on it, if so be as you cares about him."

"Why, certainly; I should be very pleased to do so. But how came *you* to possess any?"

"Because I cut some off his head with my scithers, and I've got it now, up-stairs."

"Go and fetch it me, then."

The good woman went, and in a few minutes brought me a shabby piece of paper, containing a small quantity of brown hair. I asked her what induced *her* to cut it from Mr. Hampden's head? She replied that she had been told he was a very great man once upon a time, and so she thought it would be "a remembrance of a famous gentleman." What made him such, she knew not, she said.

I bore away the precious relic, giving the woman what I thought sufficient in exchange. Pursuing our way to the church, situate almost at the door of the ancient mansion within the walls of which the foremost members of the "party of resistance" were wont, in 1643, to hold their councils, we soon succeeded in meeting with the parish sexton, who was fetched from his cottage, a short mile from thence.

After spending some time in the church, looking at

the monuments of the Hampdens, I asked the sexton whether he had been concerned in the disinterment of Mr. John Hampden's body, in 1828.

"I was," answered he; "and I do not think I ever did anything in all my life of which I so much repented afterwards."

"Why did you take part in the business?" I inquired.

"Well, you see, our parson was my master, like, and he told me to take up the paving and go down into the vault, and so I did as I was ordered, without thinking; and me and another man fetched up two or three coffins for Lord Nugent and the t'other gentlemen to examine."

"And you found the coffin at last, wherein John Hampden lay, did you?"

"Yes."

They knew it to be him, the sexton said, by the fact of the right hand being severed from the arm, near the wrist. It lay by the side of the body, and was wrapped in cerecloth, apart from the arm. The body had also cerecloth round it, but the cloth had decayed a good deal. The face was still partly preserved by the embalming matter, and a small brown moustache could be perceived on the upper lip. The body was that of a well-built man of about five feet eight or nine inches in height; not that of a tall man.

When the curiosity of Lord Nugent had been so far gratified as that the actual remains of our distinguished patriot were exposed to his gaze, he proceeded to take still greater liberties with this illustrious man's bones. The sexton was directed to

T

take his knife and detach the arm at the shoulder-joint, in order that the party might carry it away to the mansion to examine into the character of the fracture, with a view to ascertain whether the mutilation had been caused by a pistol-bullet, or whether the hand had been amputated by the surgeon. It being well known that Hampden's death was occasioned by this wound, received on Chalgrave field, the question was, had he died of mortification consequent on the injury, or had the hand been removed, and some other mortal process such as fever, or perhaps lockjaw, supervened ?

I pass over the apologetic explanations which, as I perfectly recollect, accompanied Lord Nugent's recital of the transaction. The question which his Lordship appeared so anxious to clear up, seems to me at this date, as it seemed to me in 1828, wholly without historical interest in itself, and as affording not the slightest excuse for invading, after a lapse of near two centuries, the sanctity of the tomb. So thought, indeed, on reflection, the humble instrument of the sacrilege.

He proceeded to execute the order to separate the arm from the trunk (not without difficulty, he said), and it was then taken to the house, there to be more closely inspected. But as the day was closing in before these sad operations had been completed, there remained not light enough whereby to replace the hand in the coffin and restore this to its original position beneath.

Accordingly, the body (of which the frame still held together, sustained as it was by the cerecloth) was left in the coffin, on the floor of the chancel of the church, propped up in a sitting posture, by means of the sexton's shovel; the doors were locked, and all retired to their homes for the night.

As the sexton walked back over the fields to his cottage his feelings were painfully awakened to a consciousness that he had done disrespect to a great man of yore. "I was so grieved with myself," said this simple-hearted rustic, "that I took and heaved away the clasp-knife as done it among a lot of furze bushes, so as I might never set eyes on the knife more."

At early dawn on the morrow, the parish clerk and the sexton repaired to the church, into which, so soon as the doors were unfastened, there stole quietly a few of the poor working folk who lived near, chiefly women, the men being understood to go to work by six o'clock. They came to obtain a look at the unusual spectacle of an exhumed corpse, with a sort of vague curiosity, prompted by the instinct which even in ignorant minds invests antiquity with a reverent interest.

I inquired of the sexton whether he had observed any of the women cutting the hair off the head of the body on the morning in question. "Yes," he answered, "there were one or two whom I saw doing so." I told him I had obtained a small parcel of hair from the woman at the roadside alehouse. "Did he believe *her* to be one of those?" "Very likely," said the sexton; "she was here, I do remember. But do you set any store by the hair, madam? because if you do, I can let you have some which I myself cut off Mr. Hampden's head that same morning."

T 2

"I wish you would go and bring it me," I exclaimed. Accordingly, as we had ended our visit to
the church, the man returned to his dwelling, and, in
half-an-hour, brought me back a piece of paper containing a portion of hair. On comparing it with that
which the good woman had previously given me I
found it exactly similar in every point.

Persuaded of the identity of my relics, I afterwards caused locks of this hair to be inserted into
three or four gold rings, and pins, of which I gave
away several to persons who shared my interest in
the history of John Hampden, and whom I myself
esteemed and admired. Lady Theresa Lewis was of
this number, and the gift was accompanied by the
lines which follow. I need hardly remind the reader
that her ladyship had published a work entitled,
"*Lives of the Contemporaries of Lord Clarendon*,"
wherein the events of the civil war, and the conduct
of the leading men on both sides, are passed in review
with a feeling and conscientious style of treatment.

TO LADY THERESA LEWIS.

WITH A RING,

IN WHICH WAS ENCLOSED A PORTION OF JOHN HAMPDEN'S HAIR.

LADY! keep and wear this ring,
　Suggestive of a cherished name;
Resistance to a tyrant king,
　Its passport to enduring fame.

For relic of those stirring days
　No fitter shrine than thy fair hand,
Which late hath shed historic rays
　On heroes of our native land.

What though thy fondest eulogies
　Descend on loyal Falkland's head,
With no scant measure canst thou praise
　Th' opposing band, by Hampden led.

'Tis sweet to wander through the maze
　With guide deserving of our trust;
With thee to learn, from bygone days,
　That first of lessons—to be just.

For thou hast held the lamp before
　A page of England's chivalry;
Retouched the lines of fading lore,
　And brightened each sad memory.

Then speed the work—a task of love,
　To which thy heart inspired thy pen,
And wake the names of those who strove
　In holy cause, to live again!

FELIX MENDELSSOHN.

OBIT. NOV. 1847.

FELIX MENDELSSOHN BARTHOLDY paid us a visit at our residence adjoining " Burnham Beeches," in the summer of 1847. Some of his intimate friends were also our guests, and he appeared to enjoy this brief holiday with almost youthful relish. After wandering about, one day, in the old forest-like glades till he was well nigh tired with walking, he laid himself down on a green mossy bank, and listened to the sighing of the breeze overhead, blending itself with the many small sounds incident to woodland scenery, till he seemed absorbed in thought. After some little time passed in silence, he said, "I think I could set all this to music!"

In memory of this illustrious man's visit, I caused a stone to be placed on the spot, and planted flowers and shrubs around: even protecting the stone by an iron railing. In vain! the boys of the hamlet, with a horror of vacuity which seems to be common to both man and animal, amused themselves on Sundays, for want of better pastime, with defacing the lines on the stone,* and breaking off the willow and cypress twigs. I could not make head against such enemies, and after a year or two removed my humble memorial in despair.

---

* Consisting of the third, fourth, and fifth stanzas.

STANZAS ON FELIX MENDELSSOHN

WRITTEN IN BURNHAM BEECHES. JAN. 1848.

THESE ancient groves and solitudes among
Lately a bright celestial Being strayed ;
A brief retreat from out the admiring throng
He sought and found beneath their leafy shade.

With careless steps he ranged the forest's maze ;
Then, resting here a space, his raptured eye
He bent upon the scene with thoughtful gaze,
And bathed his spirit in its poetry.

To mark the cherished spot which once he pressed,
An humble mourner's hand hath raised a stone ;
For He hath sunk to an eternal rest,
Untimely parted from his young renown,

Ere his rich gifts and inspirations bore
Their perfect fruit in his creative mind ;
Ere swelled to flood, in life's meridian hour,
The Master's art to bless and charm mankind.

He stood confessed a genius—yet he scorned
An Idol's tempting privilege to claim ;
The virtues of the Man his course adorned,
And added lustre to his lyric fame.

Ah ! Mendelssohn, hadst thou but oftener sought
Calm Nature's presence—hadst thou oftener fled
The incense-offering crowd, and idly caught
The summer breeze to fan thy fevered head—

Haply, e'en now, within its earthly sphere
Had beamed the radiance of thy soul divine ;
And spared had been the unavailing tear,
Which from a thousand eyelids falls, with mine.

LINES TO JENNY LIND GOLDSCHMIDT.

WITH A MEDALLION PORTRAIT OF THORWALDSEN.

BEHOLD the impress of a noble mind!
Genius and native worth in thee combined,
Thorwaldsen! master of creative art,
A name embalmed in Scandinavia's heart.
I place thine image in a "sister's" hand,
For "art" makes brotherhood in every land.

Great powers both thou and she have wielded here;
And both have aimed, in their peculiar sphere,
To elevate the soul, and lift the eyes
Of mortals to a world beyond the skies.
Well may thy lineaments her home adorn,
Who, like thyself, to high distinction borne,
Now tastes the sweets of freedom and of rest,
By love, and by approving conscience blest!

May, 1859.

LINES SUGGESTED BY MORE THAN ONE RECENT DOMESTIC HISTORY.

(WRITTEN BEFORE THE DIVORCE COURT HAD BEEN ESTABLISHED.)

FULL many a sorrowful and tragic tale
Enfolded lies beneath the semblance frail
Of wedded harmony and calm content !
How oft a heart in aching bosom pent,
And careworn thoughts, are borne abroad unseen,
Veiled in the aspect of a cheerful mien,
By the sad mourner of a home unblest,
A faith unhonoured, and a life opprest !

Nor man nor woman may escape the pain
Which lurks in undiscerning Passion's train.
To short-lived joys, a long regret succeeds :
But whilst a lesson's taught, the learner bleeds.

Haply a pure and justly kindled flame
At Hymen's shrine a happier lot may claim,
For those who, blest with beauty, health, and grace,
Seek on those gifts a crowning charm to place,
And crave a sanction on their promised bliss.
E'en here will steal—in destiny like this,
That "bitter drop," which, mortal cup without
May never mixed be, and turn to nought
Their glorious inheritance—thence cursed
With inward canker—of all ills the worst.
No hand can minister to griefs like these,
Nor holy science bring the sufferer ease.
A lengthened martyrdom without rewards,
Is all that hope permits, or life affords.

Man marvels over—pitying as he goes—
Th' immense diversity of human woes ;
Yet, with short-sighted folly, fails to see
How large a share of this vast misery
Is due to man's own impious agency.

So taught the eloquent recluse, Rousseau,
In days not quite a century ago ;
Whilst in our own, there liveth not a few,
Whom woman's wrongs incline to think it true.

Ask—may the victim of a hasty vow
Ne'er seek release nor remedy ?   Ah no !
A maiden once enclosed in nuptial ties,
Must wear her fetters till she sins or dies ;
And suffer as she may, within these bounds,
No cure for sorrows and no balm for wounds.
No shield for her 'gainst contumely or harm ;
Law, that " deaf adder," hearkens to no " charm,"
If suppliant in a *female* form presume
To claim its aid against unequal doom.

Yet, surely, she may fly an unloved mate,
And find relief in undisturbed retreat ?
Not so—the law its powerless victim cites
To forced communion and unwilling rites,
Which sting with insult ; whilst the loathed caress
But desecrates the couch it may not bless.

Such finished torture England's code can boast ;
A formal framework, which, at woman's cost,
Flings a disguise o'er ruthless tyranny,
And drugs men's conscience with a special lie.

Not the Red Indian on Missouri's shore
His strength abuses by one fraction more
Than he who, aided by judicial might,
Counts as a feather in the balance, right,
And justice, sighs, tears, prayers,—nay, all beside
When weighed against his lusts, his will, or pride.

Whilst with a whine, the felon is set free,
And Justice shrinks from her own stern decree,
This, our belauded humanizing age,
Leaves woman prisoned in her "legal" cage :
Withholds her heritage, and ties her hand,
And bids her live a cypher in the land—
A serf in all but mind, yet mocked with show
Of gilded chains—poor solace to her woe.

Say not "Opinion's" force protection sheds
Around the weaker forms, and weaker heads
Of women—doth not "Law" itself proclaim
Their nullity?   Compelling them to frame
A fiction and contrivance, would they hold
A portion only of their rightful gold.
Nay, even this resource no more avails,
If, after marriage, Fortune's favouring gales
Should waft them riches ; for behold ! the man
Seizes the treasure, as "Law" says he can.
Nor may a woman's industry obtain
Its honourable guerdon—for again,
Her husband claims the product as his own :
And we look on, and ask "Can nought be done ?"

Thus, since the *State* directs that woman's fate
Should hang upon the "fiat" of her mate,
Slight hope that private feeling will assume
A juster tone or mitigate her doom.
Bereft of rights, she learns to wear her chain ;
And seeks, by art, the *mastery* to gain.
Unworthy study, which a juster code
Might turn aside, or prompt to nobler good.

The want of will in man—not want of power,
Defers redemption to a distant hour.
Far distant ! for what eye hath seen the strong
Relieve the weak *because* he did them wrong ?
And, sad to say, the sex itself ne'er yet,
Its degradation cared to terminate :

Else had they, long since, risen in the scale
Of social honour and domestic weal.
With urgent pleadings, couched in modest words,
Would wives besiege the conscience of their lords,
Nor " bate one jot" till these revised the laws,
A sure success might follow for their cause.
And, once on fairer ground, be theirs to prove
How well a generous confidence can move
Their souls to virtue, and their hearts to love !

November, 1855.

SINCE the above lines were composed, the Legislature have instituted a Court of Divorce. A woman whose husband treats her with cruelty, or can be proved to have committed adultery, is permitted to sue for either a legal separation or a divorce.

It is likewise competent to a woman to go before a magistrate and swear that her husband has deserted her for a given period, when the magistrate is empowered to grant the woman a warrant, to secure to her the undisturbed possession of her own earnings.

These two changes in the state of the law are regarded as valuable concessions to the interests of woman. But it requires no great discrimination to perceive that the amount of hardship inflicted by the law of marriage upon the weaker sex, is reduced but by a small amount under the change indicated.

In the first place, a woman who sues for a divorce must do so at her own expense. Now a married woman is never permitted to touch her own money, even if she has any—the man takes it all. If her fortune is in trust, the trustees always pay the annual interest to the husband. I would ask those best acquainted with such matters, whether a trustee is likely to supply monies to the wife for the purpose of suing for a divorce from her husband?

I need not expatiate on the repugnance which a well-conditioned woman entertains to going before a tribunal at all—especially in the character of an injured wife. We know that women put up with a large measure of harsh usage before they can bring themselves to appeal to the aid of law. Yet having, for cogent reasons, decided on doing so, where is the money to come from? and the least sum required is, I have been informed, one hundred pounds.

Whilst I admit the institution of a Court of Divorce to be a step towards a mitigation of the injustice under which women labour in this country, I am deeply persuaded of the necessity to superadd another boon, in order to render the first at all effectual. I mean that the woman should possess absolute control over her own property, married or single. Years of attentive observation and reflection have impressed me with the belief that this would afford to women the simplest as well as the most suitable resource against the ill-treatment of a husband. In spite of the extensively held dogma, that a woman ought not to be entrusted with the control over her own property, *because* she would of a surety allow her husband to get it from her, I venture to affirm that, having such control she would be better off than she now is, whether under the trustee system, or under the condition of a wife without trustees.

All that the "Trust" does is to prevent the husband

from wasting away his wife's *capital,* after wasting away his own; at least the portion "under trust," for any other portion he is free to waste away. But observe, he continues to receive the income of it, and to spend it as he thinks fit; the wife has no more control over her own than she had over *his* money whilst any remained. She has the satisfaction, if such it be, of maintaining him, but *he* has the arrangement of the expenditure, and we know what that comes to in such cases.

The trustee system is, in fact, a contrivance for keeping a woman in a species of tutelage, under the pretext of protecting her interests. But against whom? Why, against the individual to whom you confide the woman's happiness, honour, and person for life. He is conceived to be fit for such a trust, or you would not place your daughter in his hands; nevertheless, you put her fortune out of his reach, lest *he* should strip her of it! You will reply that circumstances may hereafter arise in which, "being tempted of the devil," the best of husbands will try to coax or coerce his wife into giving over to him her property, and she may be beggared thereby. To this I would rejoin that law takes no cognisance of folly and weakness. If it was not thought right to inter-dict Mr. Wyndham from exercising absolute control over *his* property, although for foolish, vicious, and discreditable purposes, neither ought the law to prevent a woman from committing the folly of bring-ing herself to want in order to please a spendthrift husband. But if women were brought up to deal with money matters, and to comprehend " business," they would acquire more solid habits of mind and firmness of character, and their property would not lightly be sacrificed to a misplaced sentiment. Furthermore, it is manifestly unjust to the woman to compel her both to maintain and to live with an unworthy husband, whether she will or no. She ought to be free to leave him, just as he is now free to leave her, when and for as long a time as it pleases him. As the law stands, the husband can compel her to return to him, to cohabit with him, and probably to undergo the bringing of more children into the world, to share and diminish the pittance which remains to the family.

In discussing the subject of the rights of property in the married state, people seem to me to contemplate exclusively the condition of the wealthy class. But to those who make it their study to observe the working of the law in the middle ranks of society, it is a familiar fact that, there, the trustee system is rarely resorted to. There are great difficulties in finding trustees at once willing and capable among the middle class. Then a settlement involves expense; besides, the wife's money commonly helps the pair to set up in some sort of business, by which a higher return is obtained; indeed the woman would hardly be upheld in refusing to let her property be merged in the common undertakings, and moreover, the husband is, in the majority of cases, a safer manager of it than any "trustee" of his own rank in life. Provincial tradesmen seldom have any dealings with funded property. Taking the dividends, too, is inconvenient to rural residents at a distance from London. The savings of maid-servants, indeed, are sometimes invested in the funds, but they usually find some one belonging to a higher class in life to manage their investment, and receive their dividends for them, by virtue of a power of attorney. When such persons marry, they never dream of a "settlement;" they know no suitable person likely to fulfil the obligation. They place full reliance on their future partner, and dislike trusting their concerns to men who have no particular relationship with them. I have known many examples of humble marriages, and in none was there ever a settlement or a trustee provided. I am bound to add that in more than one case the savings of the woman have melted away under the mismanagement of the husband; and, in some others, the husband has left the wife, to follow another woman, taking along with him all that the former had brought him, and over which he acquired, by his marriage, entire control. One case I have now in my mind, where the man, after his marriage with a maid-servant, went and sold out his wife's stock in the Three per Cents (the hard savings of twenty years) and decamped therewith, leaving her positively destitute. By the aid of a friend, who supplied the passage money, this poor woman, past sixty years of age, was enabled to embark for California, where a son by a former marriage, it was expected, would provide for her. But cases of married women being abandoned, after being robbed, are exceedingly common; and the law only protects them in the enjoyment of their own subsequent earnings, when a woman can swear that she has not seen her husband within a certain time. If he comes back to her, say once a fortnight, he may still seize upon all she has.

I might expand these observations to an infinite length, were I to permit myself to follow the ramifications of injustice which accompany the nullity of a married woman in the eye of the law. For example, cases frequently occur in which original trustees dying, no new ones are appointed, and the husband continues to receive the rents accruing on his wife's estate. I remember one, wherein wife having died many years prior to husband, and trustees having died before *her*, leaving no cognoscible heirs, the husband actually forgot all about the settlement, and bequeathed her property by his will as a portion of his own estate! It happened that his executors became aware of the existence of the settlement, but not until they had distributed the property as directed, and the family were only saved from the calamity of a Chancery suit by a fortunate harmony prevailing among the co-heirs. I could adduce numerous instances in which trustees have either acted negligently or fraudulently; but never have I heard of a trustee paying the wife's annual income to herself during her husband's lifetime. Her money is never at *her* disposal, whether she behave well or ill, is made happy or miserable.

As to expecting an alteration in the law, so as to assure equality of rights to both sexes in regard to property, this must depend on the spread of equitable sentiments in the public mind. " Women's rights" is nothing but a phrase. They have none, except such as men choose to invest them with; let women lay this well to heart. But if I were asked from what sources a beneficial change may be expected to proceed, I should specify two, and these are:—

1. The augmenting impatience of women under their disabilities; leading them to employ various methods of proclaiming it, and of appealing to what may be termed the conscience of society; setting forth the painful inequality in which the law places married women, in cases where property is in question, and also in those where unworthy treatment by husbands is endured without a chance of relief.

2. The sensible increase of the humane, benevolent tendencies in modern communities. Every attentive observer must have taken account of this fact; we are become more sensitive, more accessible to uneasy impressions when the sufferings or misfortunes, nay, even the discomfort of others, are brought under our notice. Most persons feel an impulse to buy off a disagreeable emotion, be it engendered by a mendicant, by a tale of woe, by a casual blow of misfortune befalling either individuals or classes, by sympathy with some victim of crime, or even by humane considerations as towards the brute creation. This is an age of subscriptions, of testimonials, of endowments, of institutions, of efforts, in short, for the mitigation of every variety of human ills.

Now, since we are grown so tender-hearted, it is nowise surprising to find that the swelling gale of sighs and complaints, proceeding from the weaker portion of the community, has found its way to the public ear. The "wrongs of women" have at last awakened a certain number of the stronger sex to a sense of their own want of generosity, and it may be regarded as a feature in the present stage of civilization in England, that the condition of women should lately have taken rank among the topics which engage the serious attention of thinking persons of both sexes. The debate which took place in the Senate of the London University, in May, 1862, as to the admission of women to the test of examination for certificates in some of the departments of learning and science, afforded a proof that the claim is not repudiated by that eminent body as unbecoming the sex. The Senate divided on the question, and ten members voted on each side. It was not so much because the women were likely to reach any distinction that they sought this privilege, but because it was calculated to pave the way for individual women of energy and talent to earn their living in the educational career. And ten members of the Senate were of opinion that women *ought* to be allowed to share in the advantages conferred by a certificate.

It is not unusual for men to object to the endeavours making by women to enlarge the area of their industry, " because," say they, " we do not wish to see them mingling in the race of competition with men. They are far more attractive and interesting when they confine themselves to occupations recognised as suitable to their sex, and do not invade the domain of intellectual labour."

In reply to such objections, I would simply observe, that we have reached a stage of society in which considerations of taste would seem to be overborne by the difficulty of finding the means of subsistence. Not to speak of the numerical excess of females over males, which is a well known element in the case, I would ask whether the so-called " feminine employments" are not filled to repletion by our women? and whether the fair candidates for emigra-

tion, with all its drawbacks, do not exceed the limit
of the funds available for sending them over the
seas? The objection made above must therefore
yield to the pressure of circumstances, for, even
at the heavy cost of losing their attraction in male
eyes, women cannot be expected to forego the means
of existence, nor, supposing some amongst us to be
sufficiently active and enterprising to attack science,
and to become professors or physicians, ought they to
be denied " a fair field and no favour." If they fail,
in consequence, to obtain husbands, that is their
affair. Men will, naturally, marry according to
their fancy. Leave to women the choice of adapting
themselves to the taste of men; it is not a matter for
society to regulate. But I have done with this (to
me) disheartening subject, for the present, after
adding the remark once made by a distinguished
foreign nobleman, to myself, in reference to the
leading idea of this essay. " There is no country in
Europe," said my friend, " in which women are
treated with so much injustice as in England, in what
regards property."

Volumes might be written—nay, are written—
about the difficulties and grievances of married life;
but I maintain, and shall maintain to the end, that
the first of all remedial measures to be sought for by
women, and for which they should clamour, beg, and
agitate, is " equality of rights over property with the
other sex." Although it is not likely that unhappiness will ever disappear from conjugal, any more
than from single life, yet, viewed as a measure dictated by justice, and sanctioned by the practice of
European nations, I believe that equal rights over

property would tend to raise and ameliorate the condition of a wife, and, by so much, augment the
morality and comfort of the household, to a greater
extent than any other change I could point out, likely
to find favour with English modes of thought and
feeling.

THE END.